ACT OF MURDER

Alan Wright

Alan Wright lives in Wigan, Lancashire, where he taught English for thirty-five years. He now works as a consultant for the Graduate Teacher Programme. He has had several plays and two volumes of secondary school assemblies published. He is fascinated by all things Victorian and is an avid reader of Golden Age detective fiction.

Act of Murder

A VICTORIAN MYSTERY

Alan Wright

Polygon

First published in Great Britain in 2010 by
Polygon, an imprint of Birlinn Ltd
West Newington House
10 Newington Road
Edinburgh EH9 1QS

www.birlinn.co.uk

10 9 8 7 6 5 4 3 2 1

ISBN: 978 1 84697 167 9

British Library Cataloguing-in-Publication data
A catalogue record for this book is available
on request from the British Library.

Typeset in Great Britain by SJC
Printed and bound by Bell & Bain Ltd, Glasgow

*To my mother and father, who gave me
the happiest childhood anyone could have.
To my wife Jenny, who is the best person I know.
And to my children Ian, Neil and Debbie,
who make me so proud.*

ROYAL COURT THEATRE

KING STREET   WIGAN

Under the Direction of Mr BENJAMIN MORGAN-DREW

For ONE WEEK ONLY

TUESDAY 20th FEBRUARY – FRIDAY 23rd FEBRUARY 1894

THE SILVER KING

A Drama in FIVE ACTS

By

HENRY ARTHUR JONES & Henry Herman

WILFRED DENVER..Mr James Shorton
NELLY DENVER – *his wife*................................Miss Susan Coupe
CISSY & NED – *their children*........................Misses H. Morton &
                                                                    F.Tookey
DANIEL JAIKES – *their servant*......................Mr Jonathan Keele
SAMUEL BAXTER – *a detective*........................Mr Morgan-Drew
CAPTAIN SKINNER - [*The Spider*]...................Mr Henry Parks
GEOFFREY WARE – *an engineer*...................Chas. Barrett
HENRY CORKETT – *Ware's clerk*....................Mr Herbert Koller
ELIAH COOMBE – *receiver of stolen goods*.... J. Ethers
CRIPPS – *a locksmith*...H. Montford
MR PARKYN – *parish clerk*.............................W. Merryman
BINKS & BERRYMAN – *tradesmen*.................H. Mann, V. Corns
BILCHER & TEDDY – *betting men*...................M. Sorby, A. Ellis
TUBBS – *landlord of The Wheatsheaf*............B. King
OLIVE SKINNER – *Skinner's wife*...................Miss Belle Greave
SUSY – *waitress at the Chequers*.....................Miss Lownett
SCHOOLGIRLS...Misses L. and G. Ball

Musical Director – Mr Ferdinand Balderstone

Doors Open at Seven – Performance to Commence at Seven Thirty

Performance on Friday February 23rd for the benefit of

MR JONATHAN KEELE

In grateful recognition of his MANY DISTINGUISHED YEARS on the stage

WIGAN PUBLIC HALL
KING STREET WIGAN
MONDAY 19TH FEBRUARY ~ FRIDAY 23RD FEBRUARY

WE ARE PROUD TO PRESENT:
MR RICHARD THROSTLE'S MAGIC LANTERN EXTRAVAGANZA:

A TERRIFYING

PHANTASMAGORIA

WHEREIN

A GHOULISH DISPLAY OF TERRORS NEVER BEFORE EXPERIENCED IN THIS OR ANY OTHER TOWN WILL BE PRESENTED TO A DISCERNING AUDIENCE.

SEE THE

SPIRITS OF THE DEAD
AS THEY RISE FROM THEIR GRAVES!

WITCHES OF THE BLACK ARTS
WEAVING THEIR WICKED SPELLS!

DREADFUL DEMONS OF DARKNESS
AS THEY SOAR ABOVE YOUR HEADS!

AVOID DISAPPOINTMENT!
ADVANCE TICKETS · 1 SHILLING · AVAILABLE ON REQUEST
DOOR PRICE ~ 1 SHILLING AND SIXPENCE

1

The man spoke in low, hushed tones, and everyone in the cavernous hall shivered, moving closer to their neighbour. The gas lighting, which had been slowly dimmed until darkness now prevailed, emitted a steady hiss that imbued his sombre words with the grimness of a cold graveyard vigil. His almost mesmeric voice now took on a whispered urgency, its tremulous note of terror becoming more and more pronounced as his account conveyed a lurid horror that seemed to spread through the entire hall like a midnight mist, rather as if each heavy syllable were drifting upwards into the darkness that now enveloped the audience like a winding-sheet.

'And on such a dark, moonless and dismal night, with the wind howling and the cypress trees shivering and swaying from the black force around them, there came a sound. The low, grief-stricken groans of a man ready to rise from the cloying damp depths of his own recently dug grave . . .'

Suddenly they saw a white face – the face of a rotting corpse! – rise with funereal slowness, its body seemingly swathed in a soil-stained shroud; rise, rise, rise, until it hovered high above them and gazed down, an eternity of sadness and loss etched for ever in its cold, dead features. Where its eyes should have been, thick worms, glistening in the filth of death and putrefaction, seemed to writhe and gorge their way through to the inner recess of the brain, while around the head, strands of loose cloth caked in filth fluttered wildly in the hellish breeze.

'Watch closely now. Watch and keep your breathing silent! Let no gasp of air reach the cold ether around us. Can you feel the chill of death close by? Now observe! The risen corpse is not alone!'

A woman near the back uttered a tiny scream as the gruesome shape of a skeleton slowly rose above the audience where earlier the corpse had appeared. But the skeleton was not alone. Several goblin-like creatures, their eyes blazing with anger and hatred, swirled around and around the skeleton as if paying tribute to their leader, some swooping as low as the ground and others soaring high to the very ceiling before plummeting downwards at a fantastical speed and forcing those nearby to cower and sway in terror. More women now began to whimper.

Suddenly, with a whooshing sound that took everyone unawares and generated a whole cacophony of screaming, the skeleton launched itself at the deathly pale corpse and there began the most frightful struggle for supremacy, a conflict rendered all the more ghastly by the unearthly banshee wail that now filled the entire room.

Women stood up, screamed and held their hands to their faces, as if trying in vain to keep their jaws from dropping senselessly to the floor. Now their menfolk, themselves sufficiently disturbed to stand and offer at least a semblance of manliness in the face of such terror, pulled their women close to them as the grisly scene playing out above their heads came to its deadly conclusion.

Then blackness. Total blackness.

*

'There's a one-eyed yellow idol to the north of Kathmandu,
There's a little marble cross below the town.
There's a broken-hearted woman tends the grave of Mad Carew,
And the Yellow God forever gazes down.'

Benjamin Morgan-Drew sighed, bemoaning the flattened vowels, and prepared to sit in his thirtieth seat of the day. As actor-manager he carried an enormous weight of responsibility, both towards each member of the company (away from London for eight long and arduous weeks) and towards the audience they had travelled so far to entertain. It was therefore his proud boast that he brought a meticulous eye and ear to every aspect of the performance, viewing the stage and its environs from every conceivable spot in the auditorium to check for visual impediments or acoustic inadequacies.

For this reason he insisted on one of the supernumeraries standing centre stage and reciting over and over again 'The Green Eye of the Little Yellow God'.

'No, no and again no!' he yelled. 'The words "with a passion of the strong" need to be imbued with the roar of a lion!'

This particular super (a local youth whose ambition to become an actor overcame the ignominy of treading the boards with the Morgan-Drew Touring Company as 'Railway Passenger No. 3') had been one of three offered as stock actors along with the hire of the theatre and the orchestra. It amused Benjamin to listen to his peculiar northern tongue twist its way around Milton Hayes's dramatic syllables, but he didn't allow his amusement to ignore shoddy projection, supernumerary or no.

'You want me t'roar like a lion?' the youth shouted into the dim light of the auditorium.

'No! I want you to project your voice with passion. Roar the words in the way a lion would. Just read the verses as loudly as you can.'

As the youth's voice boomed forth, Benjamin felt a hand touch his shoulder. He turned around and saw Herbert Koller sitting directly behind him.

'Herbert! How long have you been there?'

'Oh, a few minutes. I've been "standin' in t'dark", Benjamin!'

Herbert Koller wasn't much older than the youth who was manfully struggling through the verses on stage, and yet there was a world of difference between the two young men: where the local youth was hesitant, uncertain and still learning his craft, Herbert had about him a casual elegance, a confident manner that some interpreted as arrogance, with none of the awkwardness of movement that was being displayed on stage. When Herbert stood before the full glare of the footlights he seemed to transcend the banal confines of a theatre and take his audience wherever he wished. And of course, with his dark curls fringing a smooth forehead, and the finely chiselled, almost classical features, it was inevitable that his physical beauty would conspire to render even the most obdurate of females pliant and bewitched.

'How much longer are you going to torture that poor boy?' Herbert said, resuming his normal drawl and bringing his mouth close to Benjamin's ear. 'It isn't a performance, you know. It's an acoustics test. And it's quite evident the boy is no monologist. His vocal cords aren't suited to force.'

'His vocal cords will do what I demand!' Benjamin snapped back. He hadn't liked the tender way Herbert had referred to the 'poor boy'. 'Louder!' he called out to the stage.

Herbert gave a dramatic sigh and squeezed Benjamin's shoulder. 'Perhaps I should coach him? What do you think?'

'You will do nothing of the kind!'

'He returned before the dawn with his shirt and tunic torn!' roared the super with renewed gravitas, 'And a gash across his temple dripping red!'

'Better.'

'Bravo!' Herbert yelled through cupped hands, then gave a round of applause that brought a blush from the youth on the stage. 'All he needs is encouragement.'

Benjamin turned around once more and glared, his face reddening with a growing anger. 'You keep away from him, do you hear, Herbert?'

'Of course,' came the smooth response.

'And another thing. I need to speak to you about earlier.'

'Why?'

'Where were you?'

'Oh, I decided to take a stroll round this delightful town.'

'You missed the meeting.'

'Oh dear. Did I miss anything important?'

Benjamin stood up and turned fully and menacingly towards him.

The youth on stage peered out, his recitation slowly grinding to a halt. 'Have I done, Mr Morgan-Drew?'

He didn't get an answer. From where he stood it was difficult to see anything with any clarity. He had a vague impression of the great man bending low and saying something to Mr Koller, but the words were whispered and failed to carry beyond the footlights. Not that it mattered: as Mr Morgan-Drew had explained, an acoustics test helps assess the audibility of sound projecting from stage to audience, not the other way around. Yet from the darkness he did hear Mr Koller say something in return, followed by what he described to the other two supers later as a cackle.

'That was what it sounded like, swear on me mam's grave. That Mr Koller gave a cackle like a witch.'

*

'Well, it bloody well scared me!'

Constable Jimmy Bowery was sitting in the Wigan Borough Police Station canteen, holding court with several of the younger members of the force. It was that slack mid-afternoon period when they'd completed their patrols and were now enjoying a cup of hot tea before the pits and the foundries and the cotton mills disgorged their thirsty workforces and the drinking and the carousing began in earnest. At the far end of the room, two officers were earnestly engaged in a game of billiards, each resonant clack of the balls being met with a cheer or a curse from the few onlookers. One other, dressed not in regulation uniform but a dark grey suit that had seen better days, sat in the solitary armchair, evidently absorbed in the newspaper he was reading.

Outside, a horse whinnied at the crack of a cabbie's whip, and the sound of a heavy wagon trundling past the station temporarily distracted the raconteur.

'What did your missus say, Jimmy?'

'Reckoned I'd took her there for nefarious reasons.'

'What? The Public Hall?'

'She said I'd only taken her 'cos I wanted to give her the screamin' hab-dabs. I said don't be daft, woman, you've got them already!'

The others laughed. The youngest of them, Constable Turner, gave him a playful nudge. 'So did you get a cuddle late on, Jim? You know, "Ooh, Jimmy, put yer arms round me an' make me feel safe."'

Bowery frowned. 'Now then, Paintbrush,' he said. 'I reckon that's oversteppin' the mark.'

'Aye,' murmured one. 'He's right there, Paintbrush.'

'What goes on between man an' wife shouldn't be made a subject o' mirth, Paintbrush,' opined another, whose grave tones were accompanied by a sly wink to the others.

Constable Turner, whose rank and surname had rendered his soubriquet inevitable, gave a shrug and gazed into his mug of tea.

'So why did you take her, then?' another of the constables asked. 'I mean, if you knew it was that bad . . . These magic lanterns are not called magic for nowt.'

Bowery smiled. 'Well, tell the truth, lads, I did know it was goin' to be bad, on account of what I'd heard by the way. I'd had to move Clapper along t'other day, rantin' an' ravin' outside the hall, sayin' it was the work of the Devil and yellin' for all he was worth at the poor sods leavin' the hall. I was just about to drag him down here for a night in the cells when they all said how right he was. Said if I didn't believe 'im, why didn't I see for meself? So I let Clapper off with a crack round his thick skull and bought two tickets there and then.'

They all nodded sagaciously. They knew Clapper, alias Enoch Platt. Most people in Wigan knew him, and most people in Wigan avoided him as if he were contaminated with cholera.

'Besides, between us, like, she'd been havin' a go these last few weeks. Reckoned I never took her out any more. You know what they're like, women, eh?'

They all concurred, including Constable Turner, though he was as yet unfamiliar with the wiles and ways of the female of the species.

'So I thought if I took her there and scared her to kingdom come, well, then, Bob's your uncle!'

The man with the newspaper folded it slowly, placed it under his arm and strolled over to the table. He gazed down at Bowery and shook his head.

'Sergeant?' said the constable.

Detective Sergeant Samuel Slevin reached for the newspaper, a sudden movement that caused Constable Bowery to raise an arm for protection. But the newcomer smiled and carefully opened the newspaper, pointing at the main article.

'See that, Constable?'

Bowery leaned forward and squinted at the small print. 'Yes, Sergeant.'

'What does it say?'

For a few seconds the constable's lips moved soundlessly.

'Aloud,' said Slevin.

In a hesitant monotone, Bowery read: 'There is widespread speculation that the new Blackpool Tower, now nearing completion, may well become the victim of powerful winds and collapse into the town. However, the firm of Heenan and Froude, a highly respectable company responsible for the Tower's construction, say that its main supporting legs will be resolutely encased in concrete, ensuring complete safety, and that the project is on schedule for the coming Whitsuntide.' Bowery looked up. 'I don't get it.'

Slevin rolled the newspaper and tapped him on the head. 'Magic lantern nonsense? Phantoms and witches? If you want to impress Mrs Bowery, and render her terrified and speechless into the bargain, then I suggest you take her to the grand opening of the Tower in May – escort her to its very top, all five hundred feet of it, in one of its two hydraulic lifts and let her admire the view. That would at least be real, genuine fear, wouldn't it? And not this lurid display of tomfoolery. It would also give her the added advantage of seeing how small we really are. Show her the future, man. Then Bob would indeed be your uncle.'

With that, the detective left the room.

'What the 'ell does 'is lordship know?' grumbled Bowery when the door had closed. ''E wasn't there.'

There were sympathetic mutterings of 'Take no notice, Jem,' and 'Too big for his bloody boots, yon mon.'

Only Paintbrush kept quiet. It made a change, someone else getting it in the neck.

*

The Royal Court Theatre in King Street was a matter of yards from the Wigan Borough Police Station, and yet in aesthetic terms it was a thousand leagues distant. The deceptively small foyer entrance, with its staircase hidden behind musty drapes, gave an impression of stuntedness, inspiring a lowering of spirits and expectation that was not improved by the sight of the glass-fronted cubicle that served as the ticket office. It was barely a foot wide, and the person normally found inside serving tickets and programmes to an eager audience was appointed not for her sales acumen or approachable countenance, but simply because of the width of her shoulders: the narrower the better.

Yet once the paying customers stepped beyond the deep velvet drapes and mounted the grand sweep of staircase to the main body of the theatre, their world was instantly transformed. The first thing to enchant the eye was, of course, the stage itself

– or rather, the heavy curtains that suggested the marvel of what lay beyond – and the splendid curves of the proscenium arch, its tall golden columns edged with the most elaborate floral designs. But it was the splendid array of gilded boxes, richly decorated in gold and red, that confirmed the impression of opulence, and forced the more modest patrons in the stalls to glance upwards throughout the performance and marvel at the glamour that surrounded them.

From one such box – the one reserved for the mayor of Wigan and his especial guests later that day – Benjamin Morgan-Drew took little notice of the grandeur of the auditorium; he watched with studied impatience as the technical rehearsal was limping to its conclusion. That was the problem with touring. You were inevitably relying on the unreliable: where the script called for 'the sound of torrential rain', the effects on offer (a wooden box filled with dried peas and shaken slowly) produced something akin to a light summer drizzle or the snoring of gnats; the changes of scenery were taking far too long and were in danger of destroying the dramatic tension; and the theatre's gas lighting seemed to have a mind – and a voice – of its own. In his long and distinguished career, he had occasionally been subjected to the hiss of a dissatisfied audience, but for the footlights themselves to create such an audible sound of disapprobation might encourage some of the lower orders to take up the call and turn the stalls into a giant snake pit.

As he surveyed the painted scene at the rear of the stage, he sighed and thought of the Lyceum in London, where the *mise en scène* had no equal: the marvellous effects produced by a subtle blending of colours and lighting could create the misery and the danger of a winter storm in one moment and the dazzling possibilities of a lark-filled sky in another. But Mr Craven, Irving's genius of scenic artistry, was hundreds of miles away. Benjamin had to make do with coarse approximations of the play's dramatic backdrops.

He privately gave thanks that the abominable display of childishly projected phantoms in the Public Hall across the street would almost certainly draw an audience comprised in the main of miners, foundrymen, mill-girls and their kind. The so-called *Phantasmagoria* had been laughably described in the local newspaper, the *Wigan Observer*, as a 'powerful source of rivalry for the famous London touring company, and it is the opinion of this newspaper that such diversity of choice can only serve to enrich the cultural diet of the borough.'

Cultural diet! He had thought such fantastic demonstrations of hocus-pocus had long since died a natural death, and was surprised there was still a profit to be made from projecting ghostly figures onto a screen with the express intention of alarming an audience, albeit a gullible one.

'Tragedy or disaster?'

Benjamin wheeled around, startled by the disembodied voice behind him. 'Jonathan! What the blazes are you doing? I could have had an apoplectic fit.'

'Sorry. I saw you from below. Your frown was quite expressive.'

Jonathan Keele was the oldest member of the company. He had been an actor for more years than he would care either to remember or admit, and he had agreed to accompany the tour as a special favour to Benjamin, of whom he was rather paternally fond. Some members of the company relished his reflective moments, when he would regale them with tales of Macready, whom he first saw play Othello in Bath in '35 and who was responsible for infecting him with the curse of Thespis, or of working with the Bancrofts at the Prince of Wales Theatre in Tottenham Street.

It had been the kindest of gestures from his old friend that the final performance of *The Silver King* should be given over to his benefit, and Jonathan had been genuinely touched by this demonstration of affection.

Benjamin sighed and gazed back down towards the stage. Three or four of the footlights which had begun to flicker suddenly gave up the ghost. 'Is it any wonder?'

'Don't worry. These things have a delightful habit of coming together. Rather like a broken bone setting, eh?'

'Well, the simile is apt, at any rate. At least as far as the pain and the damage are concerned.' He gave his old mentor a rueful look. 'Worry is what I do. Worry is what pays our way, Jonathan. Do you know how long it took those imbeciles to change the flats?'

The veteran of the stage shook his head.

'Fourteen minutes! We had the curtain drop for fourteen unconscionable minutes! I mean, what is the audience going to do for nigh on a quarter-hour? Play I-Spy? They said it was an impediment in the grooves and they could solve it with a drop of oil. Oil? I ask you! And we've got the full dress rehearsal to follow. Our *tragedy*, as you say, will be just that. Thank the good Lord we're on King Street, Wigan, and not Charing Cross Road! I shudder to think what *The Era* would make of us.'

It was Benjamin's turn to shake his head. From the darkness behind him, Jonathan smiled, but placed a hand gently on the manager's shoulder.

'You take too much on yourself, Benjamin. All the weight of the world on your shoulders.'

'No. Not that bad.' He gave a smile that was hidden in the darkness.

'Benjamin . . .'

'Yes?'

He turned and saw the old actor bite his lip and stroke his narrow chin as if in contemplation of saying something that was perhaps quite difficult. But he merely stood there, his face half-covered by the shadows.

'What is it, Jonathan?'

But the moment had evidently passed, for Jonathan Keele

smiled and said, 'No matter. It will keep, I dare say,' before turning around and disappearing through the velvet curtains.

*

Georgina Throstle stood at the window of the Royal Hotel and felt the pain begin. It invariably began with a pricking sensation behind the eyes, as if a hypodermic syringe were piercing her eyeballs from the inside. The metaphorical needle would then slide its way down the side of her face, rendering her cheekbones raw and indescribably tender, the only analgesic for which was the external application of oil of peppermint and her own particular prescription from their local doctor. Yet they had forgotten to bring both the salve and the compound from Leeds, and although Richard had shown admirable concern and a brisk determination to seek out the nearest pharmacy, when she observed him leaving the hotel he was actually sauntering along the street with his hands in his pockets as if he were off to watch the races. It was insupportable! He had been gone an agonising half-hour and there was still no sign of his return.

Down in the street below, the fog, which had been a mere ground mist earlier in the day, had thickened alarmingly, and she watched an assortment of shoppers and street-hawkers, every one of whom was blithely unaware of her misery and going about their business with a vulgar nonchalance as they appeared and disappeared like wraiths. God, she despised this town!

These ghostly figures somehow put her in mind of her brother Edward. She gave an involuntary shudder and turned her mind to more pleasing thoughts. If Richard's plans bore fruit, why, they could soon become the foremost proponents of the magic lantern in the entire country, and he would be able to purchase the latest projection equipment, perhaps buy a small theatre of their own, somewhere in the West Riding, where they could establish a more permanent home for his presentations. After that, who knows? A grand tour of demonstrations in France, and Belgium, and perhaps even Venice. How she would love to visit Venice!

But she had to convince him first. He had to give up the *dark business*, as she tactfully described it. There could be no more of that if they were to achieve the sort of respectability and renown that she craved so much.

Suddenly, through the fog, she caught sight of Richard's casual, unhurried gait. He was strolling past the Legs of Man public house on the other side of the street, when a man, dressed quite respectably in dark coat and tall hat, emerged from the entrance and, evidently recognising her husband, approached him and extended his hand. Richard spoke at length to the stranger until finally, bowing low to whisper some confidence in the man's ear, he shook hands and they parted company.

By now her face was a raging torrent of spasm. The physician had told her the name of her condition – *tic douloureux* – and it was her sole consolation that she was the victim of an affliction elevated to Parisian grandeur by its exotic, romantic-sounding name.

She had to wait an age before she heard Richard's boots clacking along the wooden boards outside their second-floor room.

'I'm afraid they've sold out of peppermint oil,' were his first words as he ostentatiously extended his empty hands.

'What?' Georgina rushed from the window towards her tormentor.

'I've been to three chemists. Hence my apparent tardiness.'

'Tardiness?' The word was dripping with mockery. 'Do you wish to see me dead?'

'If you'll allow me to –'

'Do you wish to take a photograph of my pain-ravaged corpse and flicker it across the room in your next phantasmagoria? Is that what I am? A future source of horrid amusement for the lower orders?'

Richard Throstle reached into his pocket and pulled out a small brown bottle.

'What is that?'

'This, my dearest, is a highly recommended potion that has been prepared by a local chemist.'

'But what is it? If it isn't oil of peppermint –'

Richard shook his head with a smile. 'You don't apply this. You take it. It's Chlorodyne.'

She approached him cautiously, gazing down at the brown bottle and the clear liquid it contained as if it were a venomous snake.

'It's an analgesic. When I described your symptoms the chemist said this would do the trick.'

She reached out and held the bottle in her hand. Slowly she removed the stopper and lifted it to her nose. 'Ugh!' she grimaced, and held it at arm's length.

'Notwithstanding, dearest, it's the latest thing. Take it, and your faces will be history.'

She looked into his eyes. Was there another hint of mockery? Or was it something else? 'Who was that man you spoke to?' she asked, delaying the moment in spite of the throbbing in her face.

'Where?'

'I watched you. I was waiting in agony. As you knew I would be.'

Richard nodded. 'Oh, that? He is a board member of the Wigan and District Sunday School Union.'

She smiled involuntarily.

'He wanted to know if I would be willing to present *The Magic Wand* at their next gathering.'

'I see.'

She saw him hold her gaze for a second before continuing.

'I refused, of course.'

'Why?'

'Why? It's hardly a profitable venture, nor a likely prospect. Sunday afternoon with a gaggle of filthy little miners' spawn! Besides, it would mean staying here one more night.' He gave an impish smile. 'It might please Saint Edward if I did something virtuous for a change. But it would not please me!'

'Edward is beyond pleasing.'

Richard laughed. 'No doubt he'll be kneeling on some hard wooden board in a windswept old chapel on the moors as we speak.'

She smiled coquettishly. 'You make him sound like a . . . a sanctimonious dullard. The very idea!'

'No, really? How very unfraternal of me.'

'He would dearly love to provide some financial support.'

Richard laughed and threw his head back. 'And then insist we make nothing but Temperance slides and tales from the Bible! He'd finish with a whole barrage of chromatropes, dazzling the poor unwashed until they leave the room dizzy and blinded.'

'That's exactly how they leave his sermons!' she laughed, her pain temporarily forgotten in her desire to mock her brother. 'Dizzy with his bluster and blinded by his righteousness!'

Richard put his arms around her waist. 'Forget him, my dear. And amuse yourself with the thought of his outrage if he really knew what we had done.'

She detached herself and stared down at the threadbare carpet. 'You know how I feel about that.'

'You forget, my sweet, that you have played a most active part in establishing our . . . shall we say, repertoire of delight? Our very profitable repertoire of delight.'

Georgina blushed and placed a hand flat against her right cheek.

He reached out and took the medicine from her left hand, then went over to the basin and poured a small measure into a glass. 'Come, my dear, I can't bear to see you in pain any longer. Swallow this.'

She moved slowly towards him as if she were walking to a tumbril and took the proffered glass. Its pungent aroma seemed stronger, more volatile, now it was freed from its container, and she screwed her eyes closed as she raised it to her lips.

'That's my good girl,' he said as the liquid went down. 'And if it makes you feel any better, I will consider the offer from the gentleman representing the Sunday School Union.'

She gasped and clutched at her throat. 'It's bitter!' she croaked hoarsely. 'It's so very bitter!' She recoiled in disgust, not only at the vile taste of the analgesic, but also at the unpalatable fact that once again Richard had lied to her.

*

'Good of you to come.'

'The least I could do.'

'Considering how much we are paying for the privilege.'

Richard Throstle gave a knowing smile. There was, he acknowledged, something mischievously wicked about describing this fellow as a board member of a Sunday School Union. The lantern slides he had requested would have been most inappropriate for such a tender audience, not to mention the simple fact that, at twenty guineas, they would have been beyond the reach of the most philanthropic of charitable institutions.

'It will be money well spent.'

'That's to be judged. Still, you come highly recommended.'

Throstle gave a short nod, accepting the compliment. The small private room at the rear of the Victoria Hotel overlooked Wallgate Station. The air was already thick with cigar smoke, the two men of business sitting in leather armchairs with their backs to the window, while Throstle stood before them looking for all the world like a junior clerk about to be dismissed.

'When I watched that . . . what d'ye call it? That show last night?' said the spokesman, the one who had accosted him so recklessly on the steps of the Legs of Man. He thrust his cigar at Richard, who noticed specks of grey ash stuck on the man's whiskered chin.

'A phantasmagoria.'

'Aye. That's the fellow. Well, when I watched that, I noticed you had your wife assisting you.'

'Georgina is of some help on occasion, yes. Among other things, she is a most accomplished screamer.'

'I presume she won't be assisting you on Sunday, eh?' He gave a chesty laugh and looked at his companion, a thin-faced chap with sharp, piercing eyes and an intensity in the set of his jaw that caused even Throstle to flinch. He knew how wealthy and how powerful both men were.

The man licked his lips and gave a dry, ironic cough. 'Although,' he said, pausing to gain their attention, 'that all depends on what your definition of *assisting* is. Eh?'

'She could perhaps lend a hand?' suggested the other with mock innocence.

'Alas, my private showings are for a strictly male audience. They tend to be more appreciative of the artistic scenarios on display.'

Throstle smiled frostily and, after a few more minutes discussing the financial details of the venture, found himself on the steps of the Victoria Hotel, looking out at the fading lights of the murky afternoon.

He took a deep breath. The lewd innuendo about his wife had angered him, but he comforted himself with the excitement of what loomed on the horizon: if his plans came to fruition, then he would be entering an entirely different world, a world of infinite possibilities and untold wealth, where his art would become justly lauded among the discerning and he himself would be regarded as a pioneer of daring and enterprise, as courageous in his way as Sir Richard Burton in his pursuit of the Nile source.

Throstle allowed himself an impish smile as he developed the comparison: hadn't Burton, the rogue, made a fortune with his private translation of *The Kama Sutra*? Wasn't his own art simply a more graphic elaboration of Burton's daring prose? He must share these reflections with his dear Georgina!

The thought of her stirred his loins. He had left her asleep. The new medication had apparently proved rather more efficacious than that damnable oil of peppermint, and she had retired to bed with the curtains drawn and a desire for solitude. He had mumbled some excuse about going down to the Public Hall to inspect the lantern equipment for the evening's display, which had given him the ideal opportunity to pursue the business proposal further.

And yet . . .

He checked his watch. Four-fifteen. He thought of his *Phantasmagoria* that night, which was due to begin only at seven-thirty. Three and a quarter hours!

Time to kill.

Say, an hour or so to do the business. His beloved wife would undoubtedly sleep for a while yet. He turned to his left and walked quickly towards Standishgate, away from the Victoria Hotel and the foolish and sinful men inside. A hansom lurched suddenly through the fog.

'Springfield, cabbie! Mort Street!' he called through the trap-door above his head once he was settled inside. He could be in sweet Violet's arms in less than ten minutes if the idiot went at a brisk pace, though that seemed unlikely in this damned fog. Still, he would have ample time. And afterwards, well, with a modicum of luck and a compliant cabbie, he'd be back in the hotel room by six at the latest, standing over Georgina's still supine form and looking for all the world like the concerned and solicitous husband. The image made him smile.

He leaned back against the coarse fabric of the seat and wrinkled his nose. The stench of horseflesh mingled with the gritty dust of the swirling fog, and he held a handkerchief close to his mouth, savouring its slight fragrance.

He had never been one for prolonged and probing introspection; his philosophy was more pragmatic, forward-looking and unsullied by whatever he had done in the past, in much the same way as a huntsman spares no thought for the mud clinging to his boots in the thrill of the chase. Not that his destination this afternoon involved any sense of challenge, pursuit or hard-fought conquest. Violet was a sweet young girl and had her charms, to be sure, but they were the charms of the submissive, the already conquered prey. Yet there had been a time when things weren't so determined. He closed his eyes and permitted himself the luxury of reflection, viewing the memory more as an *hors d'oeuvre* to the main course, a pleasant way of passing the time in this rather uncomfortable carriage . . .

*

Bolton. November 1893. A waif-like creature standing on the steps of the town hall. Unlike those rushing to and fro, she was motionless, in spite of the fact that it was snowing quite heavily, and her shoulders were wrapped tightly in the flimsiest of shawls. There was something about the huge stone lion that rested with a lazy arrogance above the steps that had caught her eye, and she was gazing up at it with something akin to terror. Richard, on his way to arrange the hire of a hall, stopped just before the colonnaded entrance and watched her. He had always had an eye for that tantalising combination of prettiness, vulnerability and desperation; indeed, it was that self-same fusion that brought him such a tidy profit from his more adult presentations, some of his models at least being more willing to stretch their morality for the sake of his art than other, less impecunious females.

'Good morning!' he said, raising his hat and offering the girl an elaborate bow.

'Mornin',' she replied.

'It's hardly Leeds!'

'Wha'?'

He gave her one of his winning smiles. 'They built this town hall because they admired the one we have in Leeds so much. I personally think it's a pale imitation.'

He could see the tears beginning to well around the rims of her eyes. She couldn't have been older than eighteen. 'I've never been t'Leeds.'

'Look,' he said, holding his hands open to catch the occasional snowflake. 'It's very cold out here!'

She hunched her shoulders in response and looked at him with a growing suspicion. Several people rushed past, eager to reach the relative warmth and dryness of the town hall. One or two of them gave the girl a cursory glance, but showed no more interest in her than in the stone lion above her head.

'Are you waiting for someone?'

She shook her head.

'Then why are you here?' The vulnerability in her eyes gave him the confidence to ask such a direct question.

The girl dropped her head and mumbled something about her father.

'You're waiting for your father?' Richard felt strangely irked. The girl's face – what he could see of it through the snow and the embrace of the shawl – was quite fetching. She had the most amazingly wide brown eyes that would have appeared trusting if it weren't for the frown that accompanied them, and her lips were full and rich with sensuous promise.

'No, sir. Me dad's back home.'

'But you said something about him. What was it?'

'I said me dad'd kill me.'

'Kill you?' He gave a laugh that was meant to show he took her words as mere hyperbole.

'I . . . I'd best be off.'

'Wait.' He placed a hand on her arm. This was intriguing. The wretchedly pretty little thing had piqued his curiosity. What exactly was bothering the wench? 'Perhaps I can help?'

She shook her head and turned her face away from him, as if in shame. 'I'll get belted if I'm not back. Shouldn't have come in t'first place. Please let me go, sir.'

He pulled her gently up the steps. 'Well at least we can be dry. And then we can talk. What do you say? I'm a very good listener.'

After seating her in a secluded niche far away from inquisitive eyes, he listened to her sorry tale. Her name was Violet and she came from nearby Wigan, a town suffering more than most from the current coal strike that had apparently no end in sight. Her father was one of the striking miners, and she couldn't recall the last time they'd had a decent hot meal.

'What about your mother?' he had asked, feigning concern and interest, seeing that she had been conspicuous by her absence from the narrative.

'Dead,' came the flat reply. Then the curious addendum, 'to us, any road.'

'How do you mean?'

She looked him full in the face. God, she was fetching!

'I'm sorry. I didn't mean to pry.'

'I shouldn't be talkin' like this. To a stranger.'

A cue. To place his hand on hers, and offer the tenderest of squeezes. 'A friend.'

Could he detect the beginnings of a smile?

'Why have you come to Bolton?' he asked, although he now knew the answer. She wasn't known in Bolton.

She licked her lips, a simple gesture that did more to rouse his loins than any glimpse of flesh. He knew, at that moment, that he had to possess this girl. The negotiations would have to be handled with tact and a show of philanthropy, for it was clear that this young chick had never been plucked. And afterwards, well, who knows? Perhaps she would consent to pose privately, with another willing partner, and allow him to preserve her alluring beauty for all time? He smiled inwardly at the prospect. Then he spoke.

21

'Let me buy you a hot drink before we talk about how I can help you. You look starved in this bitter chill.'

She considered his offer for many seconds, glancing past the thick stone columns before her at the busy scene in the central sweep of the hall. Men were hurrying to and fro, some with sheafs of papers beneath their arms, and others with grave expressions on their faces. This was clearly not a place for her kind. She stood up, and gave him a warm and friendly smile as he stood beside her. Then she held out her hand to thank him. 'It's very good of you, sir. But I reckon as I've made me mind up. It were daft, comin' here, thinkin' I could . . . well, don't matter none. No harm done, eh? I'll make me way home now. And thanks for listenin'. You're a nice chap.' With that, she left him and walked quickly back through the stone columns and onto the snow-swept steps.

Richard smiled. The chase, as they say, was on.

He followed her to the station at a discreet distance, the heavy blizzard helping to conceal his presence. When she reached the station forecourt, she did indeed resemble a lost and forlorn figure. The snow had soaked through her inadequate clothing, her hair was matted close to her scalp, and her face was flushed with the unhealthiest of rosy hues. It was a simple matter to produce his 'I can't believe we've met again – it must be fate!' speech and take her by the arm (this time she came willingly) into the small tea bar across the way, where he displayed his most solicitous and paternal charms, listening to her woeful tale with benevolent concern.

Within an hour, the chick had been plucked.

*

The full dress rehearsal had done nothing to calm Benjamin's nerves. Susan Coupe, his leading actress and one on whom he had pinned the greatest hopes, was lethargic and lacked the melancholy spark that fired the selfless devotion so necessary in the role of Nelly Denver. She had moved around the stage like, as he put it, 'an elephant with child', and his words had brought forth not just a display of histrionics from Miss Coupe, but an outraged demonstration of chivalry from Mr James Shorton, who momentarily stopped being a drunken Will Denver – Nelly's husband – and strode to the edge of the apron, demanding an instant apology.

Ever since they had arrived in Wigan, she had been out of sorts. Why, the very first thing she did as they walked from the railway station was throw a faint, collapsing in a heap and only barely rescued from the hooves of a passing horse by Shorton's quick thinking.

That she was delicate in some ways, Benjamin had no doubt. But one of the reasons he had asked her to tour with them was the amazing transformation that usually took place once she stepped onto the stage. Gone was the vulnerable frailty of a young woman hesitant and nervous in the company of others, to be replaced by a consummate artiste capable of the most powerful and evocative tragic roles (her Desdemona had brought warm praise from Ellen Terry herself) and the lightest of romantic heroines. Yet her performances in rehearsals, including this most crucial one, had been frankly disappointing. He only hoped that, with the spur of an audience and an opening night in a new venture, the soaring spirit would once more take over and she would do justice to the role of the lovelorn Nelly.

'I feel I am to blame,' Benjamin lamented later, in the seclusion of his dressing-room. Herbert was standing behind him, massaging the very tense muscles in his neck. It felt so good. The boy had such a firm, tender touch.

Herbert gazed at his reflection through the looking-glass. 'How so?'

'The whole cast has been out of sorts. Perhaps I ought to have arranged some special dinner last night. A social gathering. As we did in Manchester. What do you think?'

Herbert slowly shook his head. 'They would have got drunk

again. And then all the petty resentments, all their little huffs, would have come pouring out.'

Benjamin closed his eyes. 'You're right. What a depressing scene that would have made!' He gave a sigh and reached up, holding the boy's hand and caressing its smooth contours. 'You have a wisdom beyond your years, Bertie.'

'Then it's as well I'm here, Benjie.'

Suddenly the actor-manager's eyes widened with alarm. 'Did you hear that?'

'What?'

Quickly, brushing away the hands around his neck, he rose from his chair and crossed the room. He unlocked the door and flung it open with a display of bravado.

The small, narrow corridor was empty.

He sensed Herbert standing behind him. Slowly he closed the door.

'Benjie,' said the boy, with an expression of concern on his face and in his voice, 'this is verging on madness, you understand? Every little noise. Besides, the door was locked.'

Benjamin nodded. But he had so much to lose if they were ever compromised.

'You are imagining these things.'

'I thought I heard someone breathing beyond this door.'

'The wind, perhaps?'

He gave a resigned sigh. A rational explanation, to be sure. But the longer this tour had gone on – and they were now into their ninth week away from London – the more he had become smitten with the young man. Of course, he felt sure none of the others knew of his true feelings – feelings which were not unheard of in their profession – but it would be disastrous for the success of the tour, and his subsequent reputation on returning to the capital, if he were to become the object of scandalous speculation. Hitherto, he and Herbert had skated on the outer fringes, so to speak. But gradually they were moving closer, with lingering touches of the hands and glances that lasted just that little too long, so that, soon – very soon, he hoped – they would venture more closely together towards the thinner, more dangerous ice in the centre. Wigan was the first venue where he had arranged lodgings for both himself and Herbert – traditionally, everyone on tour took responsibility for their own accommodation, but he had suggested casually one evening that he would make the arrangements if the young actor were amenable. The wry smile in response, and the tantalising uplift of the eyebrows, had gratified him beyond measure.

Nevertheless, they had to take the greatest care. It would be unbearable if something happened at this point to thwart his and Herbert's plans, albeit unspoken. He thought of the time when they would be fully and deliciously together as a moment of ecstasy, and when they finally returned to London perhaps Herbert would become a regular visitor to his home on Cheyne Walk. How blissful that would be!

But he would bitterly resent anyone doing anything to destroy the moment by turning it into the filthy slush of scandal. He could not allow that to happen. He *would* not.

*

Along the corridor, in the tiniest of dressing-rooms, Susan Coupe pulled herself away from a particularly extravagant embrace and tried to catch her breath.

'What is it?' her companion asked with a knowing smile.

The young actress swallowed nervously, and leaned back against a small dressing-table replete with all the paraphernalia of her trade: a range of small, round boxes containing her favourite pale peach theatrical powder; an array of greasepaint bases; several slender containers of various liner colours; and a faceless head draped with the wig she would be wearing for tonight's performance.

'I thought I heard Benjamin. We must be careful,' she whispered, with a furtive glance at the closed door.

'It's locked.'

'It's not that. You know what I mean.'

'No one suspects a thing, my dearest,' James Shorton whispered with a smile.

'But what if . . . Perhaps . . . perhaps this is as far as we can go.'

'Susan. Please look at me.'

He held her face in his hands. Those startling blue eyes of hers became watery, looking far younger than her twenty-one years. 'I have made you a solemn promise. I will not desert you now. I love you. And that means I will do what I have promised to do.'

Susan had the grace to blush. She hadn't intended her words to sound so self-indulgent. And yet, she herself had a great deal to lose. She had already trodden the boards at some of the greatest theatres in the world, most recently the Haymarket, and had accepted a tentative offer from Henry Irving at the Lyceum.

She had strong hopes, too, of sailing across the Atlantic with the great Irving on his next American venture, where she knew, given the chance, she would stun a Broadway audience, said to be the most critical but appreciative audience in the world. Many a night she curled herself around the comforting vision of an entire theatre standing in rapt applause as she stood on a stage bedecked with the most colourful of floral tributes, her fellow actors leading the tributes with smiles and envious glances.

It was a scene that grew darker on occasion. Gradually, as she drifted off to sleep and began to lose control of the gloriously satisfying *coup de théâtre*, the script would change. The cheering and acclaims of 'Bravo!' would be interspersed, infrequently at first, with yells of 'Dollymop!' and 'Judy!' from the darkness beyond the stage, until the catcalls gained momentum, row upon row of the audience now taking up the defamatory chant. Her nightmare self would turn to her fellow actors on stage only to see their eyes narrow with angry exultation.

She reached up and cupped his face with both hands. 'Why do you love me?'

He frowned. 'What a strange question!'

Slowly he placed his hands on hers and brought them down to her side. When he spoke, his voice was low and in deadly earnest. 'You are the most precious thing in my life. Whenever I close my eyes, your face – every delightful contour and feature – is before me. There are times when I feel such pain . . . there is a very fine dividing line between love and torment, and it hurts me so much to be apart from you.' He brought her lips close to his. 'I love you so very much.'

She felt the warmth of his breath, and the ardour it bore. She edged towards him, and as they kissed she felt herself almost floating with abandon that took her far beyond the dingy confines of this cramped room and away from the misgivings that would nevertheless be awaiting her when she returned.

*

When Georgina Throstle awoke, she felt a tremor of disorientation. For a second she thought she was back in Leeds, lying in a comfortable bed in their spacious home, where all was right and the sky forever blue. But the harsh call from a fish-hawker in the street below, urging passers-by to 'put some gradely jackbit on yer owd chap's plate!' in a sing-song lilt repeated over and over again, made her open her eyes with a heavy sigh. The pain from earlier had subsided into something more tolerable, a dull ache that was like the final rumblings of a distant storm, and the darkness outside the window told her that she had indeed slept for some considerable time.

She sat up, slowly and with exaggerated care in case the pain should come flooding back, and glanced over to the chair beside the wall opposite, where Richard would sometimes sit and read by the oil lamp on the table. But the chair was unoccupied. She had a sudden presentiment. Evidently he had gone out. But where? The Public Hall, to supervise tonight's presentation? Or to speak with the gentleman who accosted him earlier, the one he had lied to her about? Or simply to take an early-evening constitutional before his dramatic exertions for the *Phantasmagoria*?

There was, she knew with a heavy heart, a fourth possibility, one that swirled beneath her composure like sewage, and one which she had hitherto preferred to keep well hidden in case the stench should make her nauseous.

Such morbid thoughts! She scolded herself and walked over to light the lamp. The room was now merely in half-shadows, and she pulled her dressing-gown around her shoulders to ward off the chill before moving over to the window.

The fog had lifted a little, drifting around the flare of the gas lamps which illuminated the row of shops opposite and cast a dull, jaundiced yellow on their wares. She glanced to left and right, up and down the street, scouring the darkened features of each person, but seeing none that remotely resembled her husband. This was intolerable! He had effectively abandoned her to her own devices – why, she could have been murdered in her sleep!

Suddenly, she felt a cold breeze stroke the back of her neck, and saw the curtains before her sway in response. She heard something click, like the closing of a door she had never heard open, and then, before she dared turn around to investigate, there was a strange and brutish sound behind her, like the heavy panting of a wild animal, and she realised there was indeed someone – or something – in her room. She turned around quickly, saw the wild and frenzied look in the eyes, and the scream froze in her throat.

2

Billy Cowburn had flatly refused to go to the Pagefield for a drink after work. He could tell, in the resigned shrugs of the others, that they were not only getting used to his desire for solitude, they were also growing more than a little fed up. The time would soon come when they would stop asking. Sympathy went only so far. He wasn't the only miner who had suffered unexpectedly as a result of the recent dispute – some poor souls had given up the ghost altogether and hurled themselves into the Leeds-Liverpool Canal or the River Douglas – nor was he the only chap whose wife had made a fool of him and taken herself off with another.

Betty Cowburn had been duped by a silver tongue and the promise of plenty by one of the soldiers brought in to prevent any trouble from the strikers. The soldier had deserted, and they were both now on the run.

As he flung open his front door, his blackened face gave him an appearance more demonic than human. The coal dust that was almost ingrained into his face rendered his eye sockets an unearthly white, flecked with tiny specks of black. Narrow rims of redness ran along his lower lids. He walked through to the kitchen and laid his bag on the table, just suppressing his nightly call to his wife.

'Still can't get used,' he said to himself. 'I hope the bitch is lyin' face down. Some bloody farmer's field.' In his mind he coloured in the fantasy. 'Lyin' in some stinkin' bloody cowshit. An' some bloody bull's caved her skull in. Her an' that bastard.'

He savoured the image for a few seconds. Then he heard a

noise from upstairs. For a moment he thought it might be *her*, come back to beg for mercy, or more likely come to collect the rest of her clothes, which he had shredded into rags. But then he realised it would only be his daughter. And that was when he felt things weren't quite right.

Shouldn't she be downstairs getting his tea ready? He glanced over to the fire and the oven range beside it. He could smell nothing – no broth, or stew, or potatoes bubbling in a pan.

Bloody hell and damnation!

It was freezing outside – dark and foggy and freezing, and she'd let the fire die down. Just look at those ashes! He worked in that shithole all day and he had to come home to a bloody cold kitchen because she couldn't be bothered to stick a shovelful of coal on the sodding fire? Nothing cooking at all? What the blazes did his daughter think she was playing at?

He slammed both fists down hard on the table. With muttered curses he stood up and stormed to the foot of the stairs.

'Where's my soddin' bloody tea then, lady?'

Silence.

'Tha'd better get down 'ere an' explain thi bloody self, or I'll tan thi arse so bad tha'll be shittin' through thi mouth for a week! Dost hear me, Violet?'

But Violet, upstairs, had other worries. Her visitor had insisted on another gallop, in spite of frequent warnings of her father's imminent arrival.

'Don't worry,' he had said. 'I'll pay the extra if we go round the paddock just one more time. Fast trot, eh?'

They had pushed their luck too far this time, and the sound of the front door flying open had dampened Richard Throstle's ardour far more effectively than her warnings had achieved. So now, as he was moving with a sort of terrified speed to climb back into his trousers, she too hastened to make herself more respectable, frantically looking around her tiny bedroom for any means of either concealment or flight. It was hopeless. And then they both froze as they heard the heavy thud of Billy's clogs on the bare wood of the stairs, thuds that were getting closer and closer, accompanied by the most blasphemous of oaths and the direst of threats.

*

'Good Lord, Richard! Whatever is the matter?'

Georgina Throstle ran from the window where she had been standing and helped her husband to the bed. He was pale, his eyes were wide and wild, and he was panting with an exertion that denoted something akin to panic. She saw that his clothing was in disarray, his necktie missing and the shirt collarless.

'Allow me a few . . . minutes!' His voice was the hoarsest of whispers, as if his tonsils had been scraped with sandpaper.

He sat on the bed and closed his eyes. She noticed his hands were shaking. What on earth had caused him to tremble so much?

She went to the small dressing-table and brought forth a half-bottle of brandy, from which she poured a sizeable measure. 'Here,' she said, placing the glass in his still-shaking hand. 'Drink this.'

Like an obedient child, he placed the glass to his lips and drank it down in one gulp.

'Better?'

He nodded.

'Shall I call for a constable?'

This time he shook his head.

'Have you been attacked, Richard? Some footpad? This town is notorious for such things. The people are barely human.'

'I . . . have merely had a shock.'

She recognised, in the timbre of his voice, the early signs of falsehood and deception. Even in distress, he was saving his skin. Like a man drowning. 'There must have been a cause?'

He lay back with his head on the pillow. Small beads of

perspiration ran down his pale forehead. 'I'm afraid I have been rather foolish, my dearest.'

She blinked. If this was to be a confession of guilt, it would indeed be breaking new ground. 'In what way?' The concern in her voice was now diluted by reproach.

He sighed. When sufficiently recovered, he said, 'I went into a local hostelry. Just to give you some peace and to allow the compound to work.'

'I am most grateful.' She couldn't quite keep the sarcasm from her tone.

'And I fell in with what I thought was an innocent game of cards.' His voice became gradually calmer. 'At first I thought it was a game of Pope Joan, but then I couldn't see a board. So I thought, rummy then. They invited me to join them, and they seemed personable enough chaps, but imagine my surprise and consternation when I discovered the game in question was brag!'

'I can indeed imagine!'

'And you know my dear, they were rogues!'

'No!'

'Indeed they were! They managed to lighten my pocket by a couple of guineas until I refused to have any more to do with them. And I foolishly accused them of cheating, upon which the villains threatened to thrash me.'

'They stole your collar and necktie as compensation?'

'They were vile beasts! Manhandled me into an alleyway where I had the damnedest time.'

'What happened?'

'I gave a good account of myself, rest assured.'

'Until you fled?'

'Let's just say I withdrew quickly,' he corrected her with a smile.

*

It was the Cowburns' neighbour who sent her son to find a policeman. She had been busy stirring their tea – oxtail stew and boiled potatoes, her Nat's favourite – when she heard the shouting from next door. It wasn't anything unusual: Billy and their Violet often exchanged words at some time during the evening, either because of her frequent tendency to turn a piece of steak into shoe leather, or her failure to produce a well-starched collar when it was turning-out time. The rows over the last months had grown more and more bitter.

Ethel Grundy had some sympathy with Billy, whose wife had brought disgrace on the whole street by running off with yon soldier, but she didn't much care for that young lass of his. All uppity now, she was. Somewhere along the way she must have come into a bob or two, to be able to afford some of those clothes she'd been swanking around in, unless Billy Cowburn had suddenly become a lot more generous. And that, she told those who would listen in Rosbottom's shop at the end of the street, was about as likely as a pig winning the Derby. No, there was something about the way Violet sauntered down the street that said to Ethel: 'That lass is headin' for a bloody big fall. See if I'm wrong!' Nevertheless, she hadn't expected her dire prediction to come true so literally. The shouting had been followed by the heavy clomping of clogs and the bellowed imprecation that made even Ethel feel faint. Then she heard the front door fling open and saw a blurred shape move so quickly past her window that she couldn't tell if it were man, woman or beast. Then she heard Violet scream out, 'No you won't! You leave him be, you big bastard!', swiftly followed by Billy's snarling growl of 'Thee let go or I'll brekk thi filthy little neck!'

Evidently she hadn't obeyed, for immediately after the warning came the sound of crashing and screaming and the splintering of wood and a series of dull, heavy thuds. Then, as Ethel managed to sidle up beside the curtain to take a peek, she saw Billy Cowburn come hurtling out of the house with a heavy poker in his hand.

Once he had disappeared, she judged it safe to go outside. From next door she could hear a low whimpering, and a weak voice cry out, 'Help me . . . help.'

By this time others in the street had ventured forth. Several women, flanked by their children, now stood on their doorsteps, casting furtive glances in the direction of Billy's vanished form. Ethel saw her son, Zander, appear from the alleyway across the street where doubtless he had been playing pitch and toss.

'What's goin' on, mam?' he asked. He had both hands in his pockets and she could hear the rattle of loose change.

Ethel gave him a frown but said nothing. Instead, she leaned into the doorway of the Cowburn house and pushed the half-open door with her hand.

Then she stood back with a gasp. There, lying at the bottom of the stairs, lay poor Violet Cowburn, her body twisted out of shape, with one arm splayed out at an impossible angle and her legs stretched obscenely apart and resting on the lower steps. Her face was half-turned towards the doorway and blood was pouring from a head wound. People gathered round, not daring to venture beyond the lintel. Yet despite the fading light, they could all make out the smear of blood that ran in a wavy line all the way down the wall beside the stairs.

'Bloody swine's pushed her downstairs!' said one of them.

'Always did have a temper on him,' said another.

'Not fair, though, takin' it out on the lass.'

'Should've been that wife of his.'

A murmur of assent rippled through the group.

Ethel stepped carefully over the threshold and leaned over the poor girl, stroking her bruised head gently. 'I'll send for the doctor, lass.'

It wasn't clear if she'd heard. Violet's eyes were flickering, occasionally showing only a sickly pale white as her consciousness began to fade.

Ethel stood up and went quickly over to her son. 'Alexander!'

34

The boy, who was almost twelve, flinched at her public use of his given name.

'I want you to go to Dr Hallard's. Tell him Violet Cowburn's fell downstairs.'

He turned and set off on his errand, but he had only gone a few yards when she called him back, glancing around at the other women for their tacit compliance. 'And then go find a bobby.'

'Aw mam!'

'You can tell *him* summat different.'

'What?'

'You can tell the bobby Violet Cowburn was *pushed* downstairs.'

They all nodded in agreement. Some things couldn't be swept under the carpet. Zander Grundy ran down the street, bumping past a small group of miners who were on their way home after their nightly livener. They exchanged curious glances at the unusual sight of their womenfolk standing in a cluster at the very time they should be laying out their steaming hot plates, and their quickened pace implied a desire for an explanation.

*

The longer he spent applying the make-up, the calmer he became. A small, gilt-framed portrait of David Garrick took pride of place on his dressing-table, positioned strategically so that, as he prepared himself before the looking-glass, he could catch the reflected half-smile from the father of the theatre and a glimmer in the eyes that would signify approval, support, and – he liked to think on occasion – admiration. The portrait went everywhere with Benjamin: it gave him a sense of continuity, of his place in the scheme of things.

There was, as always, a professional tidiness about his dressing-room: to his right, within easy reach, lay the scissors and nail parers; to his left a compact side cabinet with three drawers, the top one of which was open to reveal a small row of diminutive gallipots filled with the colours he would be applying; beside that stood a squat tin containing crêpe hair for the various moustaches he would be sporting throughout the tour, and a tall wooden box that held the powder he always applied to his boots to indicate that he had travelled along dusty roads.

He looked at himself in the mirror and gave a wan smile. He had a sudden longing for London, for the familiar sights and sounds of Cheyne Walk. And that longing quickly became tinged with a sharp stab of loneliness. For it was true that, even in the capital, he had very few people he could call his true friends, his closest companions. Certainly the theatre was his world, his *raison d'être*, and his circle of acquaintances had the stage as its nucleus. But it was a terrible thought that, if this world of splendid fakery were ever forbidden him, why, he would be nothing more than a soul in Limbo. Jonathan of course was his oldest and dearest friend, but even that lacked the frisson that he desired. Perhaps Herbert, dear Herbert . . .

He smiled wanly once more, shook the thoughts away and resumed his preparations in the knowledge that others of the company, occupying the row of dressing-rooms down from his, were even now contemplating the approaching performance in different, highly personal ways.

Jonathan Keele, for instance, whom he had given the part of Jaikes and who was in the next room to his, had recently begun suffering the most agonising stomach cramps before every performance even though he had been treading the boards for over fifty years, while Susan Coupe, who had been allocated a room across the corridor, made every effort to conceal her highly-strung disposition by lying down on a small chaise-longue with a cold flannel pressed to her forehead prior to make-up. Belle Greave, who was sharing lodgings with Miss Coupe, would be taking her nightly glass of brandy to 'steady the ship'. James Shorton, next door to Jonathan, would stand before the looking-glass and recite the Tennyson poem 'Sir Galahad', extending the full range of his voice from whisper to thunderous indignation. Benjamin could hear the modulated tones of his nightly ritual shifting from tenderness to chivalrous defiance:

> *'How sweet are looks that ladies bend*
> *On whom their favours fall!*
> *For them I battle till the end,*
> *To save from shame and thrall.'*

And of course there would be Herbert, dear, confident Herbert, full of the swagger of youth and beauty, who despite his sang-froid in all matters temporal, habitually had an attack of the shakes that only completely vanished once he had spoken his opening lines.

Benjamin saw his eyes grow slightly moist as Herbert's image presented itself. He too was across the corridor, next to Miss Coupe. Was it possible he would, even at this nervous moment, be thinking of Benjamin? Sometimes it was difficult to gauge what the boy was thinking, and although he returned tendernesses with professed ardour, Herbert rarely initiated them. And that disturbed him somewhat. Or was that merely his own insecurity once again rearing its head, as it always did? Why shouldn't the boy be thinking of him at this very moment? It was a warm thought.

From a distance, he could make out the muted sounds of an auditorium slowly filling. The thrum of conversation was underscored by the strains of the orchestra making their final, seemingly tuneless, preparations.

Someone knocked at the door, breaking into Benjamin's thoughts.

'Yes?'

No answer.

He frowned in the looking-glass. 'Who's there?'

Again, only the usual sounds of bustle, of backstage shufflings and muttered comments. He glanced up at Garrick's portrait. Was the great man frowning also? Benjamin slowly pushed back

37

his chair and walked over to the door, which he always kept locked. 'Hello?' he shouted through the flimsy wooden panelling. Even though there was no reply, he could have sworn there was someone standing no more than a few inches away on the other side. He cursed himself for his sudden attack of nerves and reached down to unlock the door.

As he swung it open, he was more than a little surprised to see Jonathan Keele standing there, already fully made up and looking every inch the kindly old servant who sacrifices his peace of mind to stay with poor Nelly Denver and her children after her husband is falsely accused of murder.

'Jonathan? This is most unusual.' They were less than half an hour from curtain-up.

The ageing actor gave a slight bow, already bearing himself in a subservient manner. There was, however, a pained expression on his face. Something told Benjamin that the cause was not solely his stomach cramps. 'May I speak, Benjamin? It's a rather delicate matter. I'll be brief.'

Benjamin, both curious and alarmed at the use of the word 'delicate', stood to one side and allowed his older colleague to enter.

Keele still moved with some athleticism. Benjamin had often admired the lithe, casually confident way in which he glided through rehearsals, his ageing frame miraculously transforming itself into stooping and feeble old age when the part demanded. As Jaikes, he had to combine selfless devotion with the steely resolve of a faithful retainer, and he was indeed one of the great successes in the group, bestowing an avuncular gravitas upon the whole company that prompted the younger ones, perhaps missing the solace of home, to seek his advice and value his worldly wisdom. It was no more than his due that Benjamin had decided to grant his old colleague a benefit performance in the last-night show. But despite his long and distinguished career on the boards, an aura of melancholy hung around the fellow's shoulders like a cloak.

As he turned to face him, Benjamin wondered if Jonathan had been the recipient of some secret, some confession, which he now felt the need to share with the manager of the company. His first words therefore came as something of a shock.

'I have never judged you, Benjamin. In all these years.'

'Jonathan?'

'We both know that the theatre is a broad-minded and indulgent world.'

Indulgent. The adjective made him blink, a stone hurled into a tranquil pond. 'I speak as a friend now, Benjamin. As an *old* friend. And as such I may be bold enough to take a few liberties. You understand?'

'But of course.'

Keele nodded. 'You are . . . fond . . . of Herbert.'

It was a statement, not a question. The old man's eyes contained no censure, Benjamin was relieved to notice.

'I am. He is a fine young man. And one day he will be the finest of actors.'

A sad shake of the head. 'Oh I think he has already become that.'

From beyond the door, people were now rushing along the corridor from the communal dressing-rooms, the close swish of material quickly followed by muttered curses, nervous laughter, louder than usual greetings.

'How do you mean?'

Jonathan Keele gave a heavy sigh, the very facsimile of the sound he made on stage when the loyal servant Jaikes refuses point-blank to leave poor Nelly Denver to her poverty-stricken fate. 'You must be very careful with that young man.'

'Why?' He coughed to clear his throat. The question had slipped out like a hiccup, hoarse and involuntary.

'Let's just say he may not fully appreciate the meaning of the word "fidelity".'

The gentle way he spoke made Benjamin feel quite weak.

He was also more than a little disturbed to hear him articulate some of what had earlier been on his mind. 'Do you speak with knowledge, Jonathan, or through mere suspicion? I ask again. Do you speak with suspicion only?'

A reluctant and barely susceptible nod gave him the straw to cling to.

'Benjamin, I saw him in earnest conversation with an older man.'

'Where?'

'The Grill Rooms here in town.'

'Who was this . . . person?'

'I have no idea. But it was the way Herbert continually looked around . . . the way one does when the conversation is . . . sensitive.'

Benjamin responded with a forced smile. 'There could be any number of reasons why Herbert should be with this man.'

'Is there any reason why Herbert should give this man money?'

'What?'

'I saw him hand something over. Secretly. It looked like money.'

'But you're not sure?'

'No.'

Immediately Benjamin walked over to his table to complete his make-up. It was more a gesture of despair, in case the old actor should decide to speculate on the reasons for such a deed.

Jonathan stood behind him and patted him gently on the shoulder. 'Take care,' he said in a deep whisper. Then he turned and left the room.

Benjamin stared at his reflection, at the heaviness that lay behind the eyes, and with slow mechanical movements he completed the applications that would turn him into Samuel Baxter, Detective.

*

When Constable Jimmy Bowery, along with two of the larger members of the constabulary, arrived at Mort Street it was dark and still foggy. The gas lamps ranged along the street cast a dull yellow glow that just managed to penetrate the thick veil of fog and transformed the group of neighbours gathered outside the Cowburns' front door into something almost funeral. Even the miners, still blackened from their toils of the day, stood beside their womenfolk offering their own beery views of the violence that had visited their street. Some of them were reluctant to judge their workmate without first hearing what he had to say. Besides, Violet Cowburn might have been asking for it. This viewpoint was angrily rebuffed by the distaff side of the argument, which offered the opinion that no offence by young Violet warranted such a brutal and possibly deadly response.

The policemen had shunted their way through the crowd and Bowery had the onlookers pushed back, away from the front door. Some of the miners, still simmering with resentment at the role of the police in the recent coal strike, refused to be moved, staring defiantly into the faces of the constables. But the arrival of the doctor had brought a communal sense of concern for the young girl still lying at the foot of the stairs, and the men had retreated. Within minutes the girl was brought out, with Ethel Grundy holding her head steady as the doctor had instructed, and was placed in a waiting carriage for transportation to Wigan Infirmary.

As the carriage trundled slowly down the cobbled street to be swallowed up by the fog, and as the crowd was ready to disperse, with some of the men grumbling about being *clemmed to buggery wi' all this nonsense*, a murmur of excitement had rippled through them as someone spotted a forlorn figure, shoulders slumped and hands planted firmly in pockets, walk glumly past the vanishing carriage and make his way in a slouching gait towards the gathering of neighbours.

'Billy!' one of the men yelled out. 'Tha's getten company!'

Bowery, standing inside the doorway, wheeled around to glower at the one who had shouted, but all the coal-black faces returned the same blank, surly expressions. Farther down the street, the dim shape of Billy Cowburn froze beneath a gas lamp. Then he turned quickly and started to run back the way he came.

Before the three policemen could give chase, several of the miners moved with surprising rapidity to block their path.

'Let the lad be!' snarled one.

'It's his daughter, he can do what he wants!' rasped another.

One of them placed a clenched fist against Jimmy Bowery's face and said, 'Tha has t'get past me first!'

Constable James Bowery could never be described as quick on his feet. Indeed, his large frame, bulked out in almost every direction by a combination of flab and muscle, made rapid movement a mere memory of his youth. But the one thing he did pride himself on was his strength. It was this strength, as he reached up and gripped the offending fist, that caused his aggressor to wince in excruciating pain as he felt every bone in his hand splinter with a sickening crunch. He was on his knees, cursing and begging for release, within seconds.

Bowery nodded to the other two to give chase. A parting of Red Sea proportions opened up before them and they rushed down the pavement in pursuit of their quarry, who had disappeared up a narrow alleyway on the opposite side of the street. The rattle of his clog-irons on the unevenly cobbled surface echoed hollowly from the entrance which formed a narrow archway beneath two terraced houses. The two policemen, whose boots were only slightly better suited to running along the smoothly treacherous cobblestones, scampered through the entrance to be swallowed up by the fog and the sudden darkness of the alley. Bowery and the others could now only listen to the sounds of pursuit, then an almighty crash of splintering wood and muffled imprecations. Finally a silence, broken only by a strange rasping noise.

'They've getten 'im!' said one of the men through gritted teeth.

'Or he's getten them!' came the anonymous, more optimistic response.

All eyes were now turned on the arched entrance to the alley. A gas lamp hung above it, casting freak shadows. Suddenly, three shapes emerged like an unholy trinity and the source of the noise became clear – the two policemen were dragging what appeared to be the unconscious fugitive between them, his clogs scraping toe-first against the uneven flagging of the alley and his head dangling low and swinging from side to side as they pulled him roughly back to the street.

Bowery raised a hand. He didn't want the brute to be brought all the way back – no sense in parading their triumph before his neighbours – and so, with a glance of dire warning to the silent onlookers, he moved quickly off to join his colleagues and help them transport him as best they could to the even less welcoming environs of the Wigan Borough Police cells and a more intimate opportunity to question the man.

'Whoa!' came a voice from behind him as he made his way down the street.

He turned and saw one of the women – the Cowburns' neighbour – walking quickly towards him, flanked by two men.

'Don't interfere,' warned Constable Bowery, employing his most menacing tones. 'Or you'll be sharin' a cell with me laddo over yonder.' Which wasn't strictly true, of course, but the threat was clear.

The woman ignored him and strode on. Bowery was amazed to see her walk right past him with purposeful tread and make straight for his colleagues and their prey.

'Bloody women!' he muttered, joining the others. 'Be off!'

But Ethel Grundy would not be off. She stood her ground, gazing down at the slumped form of the fugitive with a grim expression on her face. For a moment, Bowery thought she was about to launch into the prisoner and pummel him into the cobblestones in a paroxysm of neighbourly outrage. But then he saw the other women gather around her and heard one of them say, 'Tha were right, Ethel. Tha's getten eyes like a bloody hawk an' no mistake! Fog or no bloody fog!'

Bowery felt it was time to reassert his authority. This wasn't a sideshow. 'Right then, you've had your eyeful, now get back to your husbands.'

Ethel switched her gaze from the unconscious figure, whose head was lolling at a most uncomfortable angle, to the large red-faced constable towering over her. She thrust her jaw forward in a pugilistic gesture of defiance. 'That's exactly what I'm doin', you big daft sod.'

Bowery looked at the other constables. 'What?' was all he could think to say.

Ethel Grundy pointed a finger at the man they had arrested. 'That poor bugger yonder, who you've knocked seven bells out of, isn't Billy Cowburn.'

'Who the hell is he then?'

'Well, he's my husband, mister policeman. That's Nat Grundy. Looks like Billy bloody Cowburn's buggered off.'

*

'Let me see if I understand this correctly,' said the chief constable, Captain Alexander Bell, who was standing behind his escritoire with both hands behind his back and gazing up at the plasterwork swirl of the ceiling.

Before him, Constable Jimmy Bowery clutched his helmet to his chest as if it could offer some sort of protection from what was about to be fired his way.

'You were in charge of two men.'

'Yes, sir.'

'And you were to arrest one William Cowburn for violent assault on his daughter.'

'Yes, sir.'

'The suspect duly appearing out of the fog, like a genie from a bottle, as it were.'

'Dunno 'bout a genie, sir. Looked more like . . .'

'The simile is immaterial!' Bell snapped at the unfortunate object of his wrath. He paused, then said, 'And under your orders, the two constables gave chase when Mr Cowburn appeared?'

'Yes, sir.'

'And the two constables were still under your orders when they reappeared with someone they had arrested in the alleyway?'

Bowery, who felt it unnecessary to offer a verbal response, opted for silence.

'Yet this someone was a completely innocent man who just happened to be walking home through the alleyway?'

A nod. He held back the excuse offered by the other two constables – that all these bloody miners looked the same when covered in coal dust.

'An innocent man whom your men knocked into the middle of next week? So, Constable Bowery, tell me this.' He walked over and put his face inches from the perspiring constable. 'Where in God's name is William Cowburn? Hum?'

'Don't know, sir. But we've got a notice out to all the lads. Keep a sharp eye out for the bugger.'

Captain Bell smiled, but there was no warmth in it. 'Sharp eye, eh?'

'Yes, sir. He'll turn up. Where can he go?'

His tormentor treated the question as rhetorical. 'Any idea why he threw his daughter downstairs?'

'His neighbour said she'd heard a racket earlier when Cowburn got home. Seen a man running past her window. Hell for leather.'

'What man?'

'Dunno, sir. She only caught a glimpse. Then Cowburn licks out after 'im. I don't reckon he was offerin' him a cup of tea.'

'How's the girl?'

'Paintbrush – I mean, Constable Turner – is up at the infirmary now. I sent him to sit with her till she come round.' Bowery lowered his helmet as he spoke, quite proud of this show of initiative on his part.

'Well, get Constable Turner back and take his place. It's called clearing up your own mess. It's what makes us different from animals, constable. Don't you think?'

Captain Bell watched Bowery turn and leave the room. Damn the fellow! Time was that such slackness would have brought forth a charge and a spell in an incarceration cell with extra duties and loss of privileges. Even that was comparatively lenient. There had been a time in the army when incompetence like that shown by Bowery would be punishable by flogging. He even remembered ordering one feckless individual to be branded, the letters BC on his forehead denoting Bad Character. Only in Constable Bowery's case it would stand for Bovine Clown.

He glanced up at the clock hanging on the wall of his office. Six-twenty. He was cutting it fine. Of all the nights to be called upon to issue a reprimand! If he moved quickly he just had time to dress for the theatre. Briskly he lifted his topcoat from the peg by the door and left the room. As he did so, he almost collided with his detective sergeant, Samuel Slevin.

'Ah, sergeant!'

'Sir.'

'You finished for the day?'

'Yes, sir, unless . . .'

'Oh no. There's nothing that can't wait.' The chief constable was halfway down the corridor when he called over his shoulder, 'Only our constables making a pig's ear of something that should be a simple arrest.' He turned as he reached the far door.

Slevin saw the unusual glint in his superior's eye, a flicker of anticipation that animated his normally cadaverous features. It wasn't his place to ask the obvious question, though. It would smack almost of insubordination.

'Well, I must dash, sergeant. *The Silver King* awaits, eh?' With that cryptic pronouncement he breezed through the door and disappeared from view.

Slevin gave a shrug and followed at a similarly rapid pace. If he hurried, he could be home in ten minutes – and then he might get half an hour with his son Peter before Sarah took him upstairs.

As he passed the entrance to the Royal Court Theatre, he saw a crowd was already forming along the pavement for the evening performance, and some of the more elegantly dressed were already inside, talking animatedly. He caught sight of the huge playbill advertising the production, *The Silver King*, and smiled to himself. Some detective he was. This notice had stared him in the eye for the past week as he made his way home to Wallgate, and yet he had appeared confused when Captain Bell mentioned it.

He raised his hat to the bored young lady who sat in the tiny booth in the foyer, and the response he got – a sort of puzzled frown and a scowl for his impertinence – only served to heighten his good humour.

*

Enoch Platt stood outside the Public Hall, clapping his hands together as fast as he could. He was of average height and sturdily built, his shoulders curved downwards from a thick, sinewy neck. He was somewhere in his late forties, and his grey-black hair hung in matted strands like dead snakes. He wore a dark brown overcoat, open to the waist to reveal a filthy collarless shirt that must have once been white. His thick black moustache hung over his mouth, obscuring his upper lip completely.

Those queueing to go in, most of whom knew him at least by sight, gave him glances ranging from sympathy, amusement and annoyance to barely concealed antipathy. Enoch, in return, gave each one of them a glowering scowl and scrutinised their faces with especial and disconcerting closeness. Or rather, not so much their faces as their eyes. Once he had fixed someone with his eyes, that person had only two options – to look away or to challenge and confront. For most people, the former was infinitely preferable.

Some did take verbal exception to his penetrating glare. But once it reached the point of physical contact, Enoch generally came out on top, straddling the one who had suddenly become his enemy and drooling saliva onto his face as he thumped and cursed in rapid succession.

Now he was clapping his hands with such ferocity that he suddenly reached a crescendo of manic applause; then he stopped and stared intently at one of the people queueing, a man standing with one foot on the stone steps of the building. He was a man of similar age to Enoch, but smaller in stature, the faint traces of black etched around his eyes betraying the slightly haunted look of the miner. Beside him his wife held onto his arm and pulled it closer to her.

'I see you!' cried Enoch in that curiously hoarse rasp of a voice. He had raised an arm and was pointing a thick finger in the man's direction. 'Another waitin' at t'doors of hell!'

Unlike most of his selected victims, this man turned his gaze fully upon Enoch.

'Sod off, Enoch,' he said with a snarl.

Enoch stepped forward until he was a matter of inches from the man's face. Their eyes locked together.

'I been there!' Enoch rasped. 'I seen hell!'

Those behind were rather startled to see the man lean forward, so that his nose was almost touching Enoch's. Only the ones standing closest to the tableau heard what the man said next.

'Aye. An' I've seen it too. An' I'm not likely to forget it. Now piss off!'

There was what appeared to be a flicker of recognition in

Enoch's eyes. Whatever the cause, it was sufficient for him to pull his head back and divert his glare elsewhere. He stepped back to survey the queue and once more began to clap, slowly this time, as he scanned the faces for another victim.

*

All eyes were on the splendidly ornate box where the mayor of Wigan and his lady wife were about to take their seats. The first sight the audience got was the brightly glittering chain of office made of sterling silver, the gilt shoulder-pieces with the seal inscription '*Sigilum Comune Villae et Burgide Wigan*' resting proudly on his broad shoulders. His worship beamed down on the audience with a paternal pride and gave them all a hearty wave. The Royal Court Theatre was packed to the rafters, and surely this gave the lie to those who had mocked the idea of such a prestigious touring company spending time in the borough for the entertainment and edification of not just the middle classes but, hopefully, the labouring classes too.

Suddenly there was a hush in the theatre as the orchestra struck the opening chords and the various lamps around the upper boxes and down below began to dim slowly. Then the curtain opened, and the audience applauded – and some of them ventured an appreciative whistle – at the bright and startling colours that depicted the skittle alley at the Wheatsheaf, Clerkenwell.

*

Meanwhile, as the audience at the Royal Court Theatre were watching that faithful old servant Jaikes wander into the Wheatsheaf in search of his dear master Will Denver, another audience, composed mainly of those from the labouring classes, was being entertained in a far more dramatic and macabre fashion not fifty yards away.

Having weathered the storm of righteous outrage Enoch Platt

49

had unleashed upon them, they were given a foretaste of what to expect as they entered the hall through an elaborately constructed passageway covered in black cloth. All along the winding route to their seats, they saw lurid figures of hooded monks with faces hidden deep in the shadows cast by heavy cowls. There were drawings of gravestones shifted from the perpendicular with gaping black holes beneath, and wizened bodies hanging from gibbets, ravens pecking at their bloodied eyes.

The Public Hall, where Richard Throstle's *Phantasmagoria* was about to begin, was abuzz with anticipation. Word had spread around the town that this was no ordinary magic lantern show. Some who had already witnessed the performance had sworn vehemently that darker forces were at work here, that the sudden and ghoulish appearance of spirits and goblins was not solely the product of Mr Throstle's legerdemain and expertise, and that the things they had seen (and, according to some, the things they had *felt*) owed some of their existence to the forces of the Devil, for surely it was only Lucifer himself who could create such devilish and gruesome scenes. They were unwilling to discount Enoch's warnings out of hand, whatever they might say to the poor fool.

'Another full house,' Georgina whispered as Richard stood behind the makeshift curtain prior to his dramatic appearance.

'Yes,' her husband replied, although the way he scanned row after row of excited customers betrayed a less than enthusiastic appreciation of another rewarding night's work.

'Whatever is the matter?' she snapped.

'Nothing.'

Georgina frowned and placed a hand on his arm. Now was not the time for him to perform below par. Audiences were notoriously fickle, and the platitudinous saying still held true: you were only as good as your last performance.

'You surely don't think those ruffians will be in the audience, do you?'

'Of course not.'

'If they were, as you say, card sharps, well it would do them no good to pursue you simply because you accused them. It would draw unwarranted attention to themselves. Besides, look at the number of witnesses we can call upon.'

'I know,' replied Richard, whose eyes were looking for someone else entirely. If that brute of a father, who didn't seem to be the sort of chap who would baulk at the presence of a thousand witnesses, should barge his way into the auditorium and launch his accusations before launching his fists . . . He could still hear the clang of heavy iron against the metal frame of the tram window as the vile beast had hurled his poker in a final, frustrated attempt to injure him.

But he could see no such person. Perhaps hiding behind the bedroom door as the cretin burst into Violet's bedroom hadn't been such a bad idea. He couldn't have had a very good look at him. Might only have seen his retreating back, for he had certainly kept his head down. And he felt sure young Violet would have kept his name firmly from her lips. Oh, if only he had shown some restraint and spurned his baser instincts! It was only another romp, and she had warned him of the imminence of her father's return. But he knew what his baser instincts were like: impossible to refuse, impossible to satisfy. They would get him into serious trouble one day, he had no doubt.

Georgina watched as the assistants made the final checks on the lanterns. The biunial projector, a masterpiece of mahogany and brass, was their most expensive and effective piece. It was already lit, but she went over to ensure the supply of oxygen and hydrogen, controlled by two small valves within the frame, was correct. Once the combined force of the gases became lit, it produced a powerful jet that illuminated the block of limelight, which in turn gave off the brightest of lights, the equivalent of a thousand candles, more than enough illumination to enable both the photographic slides and the hand-painted images to fill the screen with a crystal clarity.

'It's time!' urged his wife. 'No more delay!'

'How do I look?'

'Suitably ghoulish, Richard. Just the right amount of white powder to bring out the evil in your cheekbones.'

Richard Throstle took a deep breath and walked slowly, with his usual funereal gait, to the raised dais at the front of the hall to face his audience. Behind him, a chromatrope display of kaleidoscopic images in sombre reds and blacks was slowly rotating, creating an almost mesmeric backdrop to what he was about to say.

The applause had barely died down when he raised his hands and pointed to the large screened area behind him. 'Ladies and gentlemen,' he began in sonorous, heavy tones, 'there are forces at work in this world of ours that we have no control over. Death is with us always, and the shadows that pursue us beyond the grave are the very stuff of our nightmares. Tonight, we are going to see a display of evil, a display of such terrifying vividness that I urge – nay, I beg – each and every one of you to remain firmly seated in your places and grasp the hands of your loved ones. For it is only by the love we feel for each other, that strength of Christian fellowship that burns so strongly inside us all, that we can defeat the wild and savage spirits that we will see displayed all around us this night.'

He paused, as he always did. Now he had them. He looked into their eyes, wide and sparkling, saw the clandestine way even the largest of fellows held on to his wife's hand in a show of manly support. He held the silence for a further minute before walking slowly to the rear of the hall, where the first of his machines – the praxinoscope – would lull the audience into a false sense of well-being, with its early slides of dancing dervishes rapidly flashing through the drum to give the appearance of movement. Then, the rising skeleton would be next, after which he would move to the centrepiece of his show, the *Phantasmagoria* and the unearthly visions it cast all around the room, rendered even more sinister by his ghoulishly compelling narrative. He patted the triunial lantern resting nearby, with its stack of three lenses and its brass and mahogany outlines displaying something far more polished, far more powerful than anything these people had ever seen before. Soon it would be used to its full potential, dissolving and mixing those special effects that would align themselves with the other wheeled lanterns to create a spine-tingling spectacle they would talk about for years.

*

'I shall reach Bristol tonight. Wilfred Denver is dead! Tomorrow I begin a new life!'

James Shorton's voice resonated throughout the theatre with its seductive blend of hope and despair, and the audience, who had listened with great interest and rising emotion as poor Will Denver found himself innocently accused of murder, stood as one as the curtains drew to a temporary close and the house lights slowly came up. They had seen the destruction of his family harmony and the shame he had brought upon his beloved Nelly by his reckless gambling and surrender to drink; they had seethed with anger at the wiles of the wicked Coombe and Cripps and Corkett, and had actually hissed with fierce venom when the evil Captain Skinner (also known as The Spider) had shot Geoffrey Ware and planted the revolver near the insensible Denver. They had subsequently shared his despair as he awoke to discover the corpse, mistakenly thinking he was guilty of vile murder, and was pursued by Detective Samuel Baxter; they had gasped with astonishment at the hand of the Divine when the train he was travelling on crashed and he was believed killed. And finally, by the close of act two, they all shared his desperate hopes for the future, and they wandered off to the refreshment area talking with great animation as to what that future might be and if he would ever see his darling wife and children again.

Meanwhile, things were not quite so harmonious behind

the curtain. No sooner had the curtain fallen than Benjamin stormed off stage, refusing to say a single word of congratulation or encouragement to anyone, and locking himself inside his dressing-room with a dire warning not to be disturbed for any reason whatsoever.

The cause of his dissatisfaction wasn't immediately clear.

'I thought we carried the audience well,' was James Shorton's opinion.

'You were magnificent!' was Susan Coupe's slightly less impartial view as they walked down the narrow corridor with Belle Greave between them. The latter had yet to appear on stage and had been watching from the wings.

'Why is Benjamin so angry?' asked Belle in a whisper as they passed his locked door.

'He seemed a little wooden to me,' Shorton replied, refusing to follow her example and lower his voice. 'Especially when . . .'

Herbert Koller came bounding down the small flight of steps and gave the three of them a cheery wave. 'Quite a benign gathering out there, eh?'

'Indeed they are, Herbert. The best is yet to come, isn't that so, Miss Coupe?'

'One would hope so, Mr Shorton.' She gave a curtsey and the two women retired to their dressing-rooms, leaving the two men facing each other.

Herbert seemed anxious for the leading man to leave. 'I need to speak to Benjamin. Do you mind, old chap?'

Shorton shrugged and moved farther down the corridor. Something had obviously occurred between the two of them. As Detective Baxter, Benjamin was supposed to warn the impetuous Corkett (played by Herbert) to put away the pound notes he had been displaying to all and sundry in the Wheatsheaf. There had been nothing either in the script or at rehearsal about the detective physically grabbing hold of Corkett's hand and twisting it so violently that he winced, rendering the young cove's response of 'Shan't! Who are you?' somewhat feeble and incongruous. The look that was exchanged between them in full view of the audience was far more poisonous than anything the dramatist Henry Jones had imagined. Perhaps Herbert Koller had come to remonstrate with his close friend for the unscripted encounter? If so, it was hardly the time. The interval lasted a mere fifteen minutes, and Herbert was on stage almost immediately afterwards.

Just before he entered his own dressing-room, Shorton could hear a series of impatient raps echoing down the corridor, immediately followed by Herbert's angry voice.

'Benjamin! Benjamin, open the door! Open the bloody door!'

Shorton shook his head and smiled to himself, although the smile faded when he stepped into his own dressing-room and saw what was propped against his looking-glass.

It was a telegram from his wife.

3

There were many in Richard Throstle's audience who felt that they would never smile again. The vast majority of those seated in that dark and forbidding place were a far cry from those enjoying the trials and torments of *The Silver King*. Here were men from the coalfields and the foundries, accustomed to the grit and earthy stench of dust and heat, men who prided themselves on their toughness, who scorned the metaphysical and shied away from any display that could be construed as sentimental. Many of them – the miners certainly – spent most of their days deep underground experiencing at first hand the dangers, the close proximity of death.

Yet every one of them sat in rigid silence, heads erect and eyes narrowed, as high above them the projected images of three witches glared down, appearing to shower them with the vilest curses. All around, the sound of thunder and the startling flashes of lightning filled the hall, swiftly followed by the horrid sight of a graveyard, where mounds of earth slowly grew and grew until the white skeletal hands came forth and corpses rose from the earth.

And through it all, the deep, sonorous tones of Richard Throstle.

'Imagine that final day, my friends, that Day of Judgement, when we shall all be judged by what we have done, for isn't it written that death and hell were cast into the lake of fire . . .'

Suddenly the whole scene around and above them was transformed into a mighty flame-filled lake with the roar of an all-devouring conflagration that burned until all the corpses and the skeletons, and the evil-cursing witches, shrivelled and screamed for the last time and darkness returned to the land.

Behind the screen, Richard held his hand above his head, an instruction to one of his assistants to refrain from raising the lighting for a few more tremulous seconds. Beside him, the other helpers slowly put down their instruments – the trumpets and the drums that had created all the cacophony of horror – while Georgina herself depressed the main valves linking the oxygen and hydrogen cylinders to the lanterns, their low hiss immediately silenced. He smiled as he could hear the gasps and the whimperings from the audience. Then, finally, he turned to his assistant and whispered, 'Let there be light!'

As the lights slowly came up there was an audible gasp and a scattering of nervous laughter that could be heard over the sound of rapturous applause. Some of the men coughed and nodded to each other, and raised their eyes to the heavens in a signal of manly understanding and amused compassion towards their skittish wives.

Later, when the hall was empty and Richard's assistants were securing the lanterns for the next performance, Georgina beckoned her husband to sit beside her in the front row.

'What's this?' he asked, taking his place beside her. 'A tryst?'

But the expression on her face precluded any thought of dalliance. 'I want you to be honest with me,' she said.

'My dearest, I am invariably honest.'

With a wry smile, she gazed down at his hand, which had intertwined itself with hers. She spoke quietly, as if conscious of the assistants scurrying around at the rear of the hall.

'I must confess I am a little . . . confused. Wouldn't it be better to speak at the hotel? Less public?'

She lifted her head and he was surprised to see tears welling in her eyes.

'My dearest – have I offended you?'

'Offended?' She uttered the word with a heavy emphasis, and

appeared to be on the verge of elaborating when she stopped and took a deep breath. 'Have I been a disappointment to you, Richard?'

He held her hand tightly. 'Of course not. But why should you think . . .'

'Haven't I done everything – and more, much more – that a wife can reasonably be expected to do?'

'You have been my rock, my darling wife.'

She looked him fully in the face. 'Yes, I believe I have. I have even done things of which I am now deeply ashamed.'

Richard sighed and looked around. There was no one within earshot. 'You have done nothing whatsoever to be ashamed of. I know the thing to which you refer. To which you always refer. And it is of no consequence, I assure you.'

'No consequence!' Georgina gave a hollow laugh.

Richard looked blank. 'I think you're tired. Tonight's performance must have been more fatiguing than we expected.'

'I am not fatigued, you stupid man!'

Two of the assistants stopped what they were doing and looked down the row of seats at their employers.

'Get on with your work!' Richard snapped, twisting his head around quickly. 'Or there'll be no work tomorrow, I assure you all of that!'

Chastened, they resumed their tasks.

'So please tell me, Georgina, what this is all about.' His voice now was tinged with a growing exasperation.

'This afternoon,' she said. 'You lied to me.'

He gave a nervous smile. 'I did not lie, dearest. Those card sharps were the very stuff of nightmares, I can assure you.'

'If by that you mean they were not real, then I accept what you say.'

Before he could respond, she went on. 'But I am not referring to these mythical card sharps, nor to the alleycat you must have been tomming. No. I refer to something else entirely.'

Richard, his face a picture of relief and confusion, begged her to continue.

'The man you spoke to, the one you say asked you to present a show of touching morality to his Sunday School children.'

Richard averted his gaze.

'I knew it!' she said with a note of triumph in her voice. 'You promised me that sort of thing was done with. If Edward were to find out –'

Richard laughed. 'So what if he were to find out?'

'Well, I should like to remind you of his promise to provide his backing. His considerable *financial* backing.'

'Georgina, my dearest. Have you ever considered the possibility that I might be able to secure other, shall we say, more worldly backers? Backers who would be a little less squeamish than your sainted brother?'

'But you promised that things would change.'

'Oh, change is very much what I have in mind, my sweet. It simply may be necessary to effect it without the involvement of dear anointed Edward.'

*

Violet Cowburn sat up in her hospital bed and placed her hands gingerly on her chest. 'Three broken ribs!' she said. 'How can I do anythin' wi' three broken ribs?'

Constable Bowery, who was sitting beside the bed, slowly shook his head. It was a conundrum, he seemed to be saying.

'It hurts me when I breathe.'

'It would.' Jimmy Bowery glanced down the long stretch of beds in the female ward.

Why wouldn't she answer his question? Didn't take much breath to give a simple bloody nod. So he tried again. 'It was your dad did this, wasn't it, Violet?' I mean, did your dad throw you down the stairs?'

'Me dad? Did 'e 'eck as like!' She turned away and began to

cough, which caused her to wince in agony and clutch at her chest once more.

It was no more than he expected. If Ding Dong Bell had thought he would come away from the Royal Albert Edward Infirmary with a statement confirming Billy Cowburn's guilt, then he couldn't have been more wrong. This lot stick together like feathers to a duck's arse, he reflected ruefully as he stepped out of the building and contemplated the prospect, at last, of a strong, thick-headed pint of stout. And if she refused to squeal on her brute of a father, that left them with bugger all to charge him with.

He walked quickly through the gates and turned right, lifting the collar of his greatcoat around his face to ward off the freezing fog. Although he could barely see a yard in front of him, he trod purposefully forward. If he got a move on, he could be in the Royal Oak in ten minutes, and the brisk trek down Wigan Lane would give him a thirst that would need some quenching.

*

Detective Samuel Baxter grabbed hold of the swaggering young Cockney Henry Corkett by the collar and hustled him off stage. Or so the stage directions instructed. There was nothing to suggest anything more forceful than that, certainly no mention of ramming the young ex-convict's arm halfway up his back and almost snapping his neck back as they made their final exits.

Fortunately, audiences never get to see stage directions, and the viciousness of the arrest only served to satisfy the desire for retribution against all those involved in the framing of poor Will Denver for murder.

When James Shorton stepped forward as a Will Denver newly restored to the bosom of his family, he spoke the play's closing lines with great passion and an extravagant display of arm-waving and heart-clutching:

'Come! Let us kneel and give thanks on our own hearth in the dear old home where I wooed you, and won you in the happy, happy days of long ago! Come Jaikes, Cissy, Ned, Nell – come in. Home at last!'

It drew a standing ovation. The company stood before their opening-night audience in a hand-holding display of solidarity, and the audience cheered and booed as the heroes and villains took their final bows. But the most rapturous reception of all came when Will Denver and his wife Nelly stepped forward. There was a particularly vocal display of appreciation for Susan Coupe – the entire company applauded along with the audience, for her performance that night had truly been masterful, combining the pathos of a wife bereft of her dearest love with the resilience of a mother determined to survive and protect her children in spite of everything Fate could throw at her.

At the final curtain call, Benjamin Morgan-Drew stepped forward and delivered a small speech of gratitude that contained words of admiration for the people of 'this wonderful town, who have taken our whole company into its bosom and shown us such unprecedented warmth and hospitality.'

'It was unprecedented in Manchester, too!' James Shorton whispered to Miss Coupe, who raised a hand to her lips to conceal the smile.

Yet the beneficent smile that the actor-manager had bestowed upon his beloved audience froze into a hellish scowl the moment the curtain closed for the fifth and final time. The rest of the company stood around in small groups, congratulating each other on a job well done. Benjamin and Herbert Koller, however, were last seen moving purposefully into the wings and down the steps to their dressing-rooms.

'What the hell were you thinking of?' stormed Herbert as Benjamin locked the door behind them. 'You all but broke my arm!'

'And you all but broke my heart!' sobbed Benjamin, who had slumped into the chair facing the looking-glass and, having removed his wig, held his head in his hands, all pretence gone now.

'Benjamin. What the hell are you talking about? What do you mean? Why wouldn't you let me speak with you at the interval?'

'You have been *seen*.'

At that, the young man blinked and steadied himself. This was obviously not what he expected.

'What do you mean, *seen*? Seen doing what?'

A pained guffaw burst from Benjamin's lungs. 'That is hardly a denial designed to reassure me.'

'But even a man on trial for his life at the Old Bailey is granted a glimpse of the evidence against him.' He had adopted his usual tone of flippancy, a mask behind which he often hid when the topic became overly sensitive.

'You speak of "evidence". That in itself is interesting.'

'Look,' said Herbert, a note of exasperation creeping into his voice, 'just tell me what this is about.'

'Who is the *gentleman* whose company you have been keeping?'

'What gentleman? I can assure you there is no such person.'

'I have been told – by a reliable source – that you have been seen dining with a man and, shall we say, ensconced with him most intimately.'

'Ensconced!' Herbert repeated the word with a heavy intonation. 'Oh my! Ensconced! And intimately! What does that mean, exactly, Benjamin? Were we rogering each other on the table between the first and second courses?'

'Please do not be vulgar.'

Herbert moved towards him and placed a hand at the back of his neck, stroking him lightly. 'Benjie. This is ludicrous. I may have spoken with a man during an idle moment – in fact now that I come to think about it, there was such a man who engaged me in conversation only the other day. He too is a stranger here, one of these travelling buffoons still demonstrating those ridiculous displays of magic lantern slides that terrorise the unwashed of these grubby little northern towns. I thought they had died a death years ago. We swapped stories of our respective experiences. That is all. And of course we had to lower our voices, and thus give every appearance of intimacy. It would do us no good whatsoever to be overheard denigrating the very people who pay to see us!' He paused, allowing his words to twine themselves into a rope that would bring Benjamin back from the abyss.

'You gave him some money.'

Herbert caught his breath and turned away for a second before swinging around with fire in his eyes. 'Your spy is, on this occasion, mistaken.'

'Really?'

'The *money* that was exchanged between us was, in fact, several of our playbills.'

'Playbills? But what –?'

'Where do we perform next on this grand tour of ours?'

'Liverpool.'

'Which is precisely where this fellow is headed after *his* show concludes here. He said he would distribute our notices.'

'That is most . . . philanthropic of him.'

Herbert laughed. 'Yes, I rather think he is one of nature's philanthropists.'

Benjamin gave a heavy, shoulder-sagging sigh. It was a gesture compounded of defeat and self-delusion. Finally, after a few seconds' contemplation, he lifted his hand to clasp Herbert's. 'I'm sorry,' he said hoarsely. 'Perhaps I jumped to conclusions.'

'Jumped? I'd say you hurled yourself with all the frenzy of a suicide from Waterloo Bridge!'

'Can you forgive me?'

'Of course. Besides, it does show me how strong your feelings for me are, does it not?'

'It does, my darling boy. It does.'

He stood up, and they embraced. Herbert looked at his own reflection in the looking-glass, and thought how there was something rather touching about the top of Benjamin's head, where the signs of incipient baldness were hidden by a strategic combing of the hair.

*

'This is splendid! Splendid!'

Captain Alexander Bell was not the sort of man to utter superlatives. He took his position seriously, and the grim zeal with which he pursued his duties was firmly etched in his angular, almost cadaverous features. Detective Sergeant Slevin, in his more satirical moments, had characterised the fellow as a living *memento mori*, and had more than once fallen foul of his unyielding views on criminality.

Tonight, however, there was a rare smile on his face. The reception at the town hall, hosted with great aplomb and no stinting of provisions by the mayor, looked to be a grand success. To be invited here tonight to meet this great troupe of thespians after witnessing such a powerful and moral tale as *The Silver King*, with its vital message of the benefits of temperance and marital devotion, was a very great moment indeed.

For, if the truth be known, Captain Bell was stage-struck.

During his military service in India, he had been a member of the *Punjabbers*, a dramatic club for the entertainment of the officers and their ladies. There had been something about adopting the persona of another that seemed like a liberation, a release from the burden of duty for the two hours he spent on the boards.

'It is a red-letter day, Captain Bell! Such a gathering in the Wigan town hall, eh?' The mayor beamed at the company. 'Just think! An hour ago we were giving that fellow over yonder a torrid time!'

He indicated a suave-looking actor, tall and good-looking,

who had played the part of the Spider, Captain Skinner, and who was talking idly to Susan Coupe and James Shorton. To Captain Bell, the latter seemed somewhat distracted, looking around the room and barely listening to what the Spider was saying. But his attention then focused on the delectable Miss Coupe. If anything, she was even more beautiful off-stage, divested of the make-up that highlighted her worry lines and the sad droop of her eyes. There seemed to be an innocence about her, more child than woman, as she occasionally placed a light hand on Shorton's arm in response to some amusing comment from her fellow actor. The chief constable and the mayor watched in admiration for some time, until they were joined by Benjamin Morgan-Drew.

'She lights up the room, does she not, gentlemen?'

The mayor readily agreed. 'She does that.'

'She is destined for great things, our Miss Coupe.'

'Really? Is she that well thought of?' asked the mayor, whose reading matter did not extend to *The Era* or *The Theatre*.

'She has been mentioned by Irving himself as a rising star. There is talk of her accompanying him when he next sails to America.'

While the mayor looked perplexed, his chief constable explained. 'Henry Irving is the foremost actor of our time.'

'I saw his Hamlet in seventy-four,' Benjamin added. 'It was breathtaking.'

'For such a great figure to bestow such compliments on a relatively young girl is an honour indeed,' Captain Bell averred with a quick glance at the erstwhile Nelly Denver.

'Ah!' said Benjamin with upraised arms, 'you must meet Mr Herbert Koller, another of our young lions of the stage!'

Both men turned to greet the young man who had just entered the room. He seemed distracted, his hair somewhat moistened by the fog, and he smoothed his errant locks in a rather self-conscious way before accepting a drink from one of the waiters. Captain Bell was immediately – and disturbingly

– struck by the handsome features of the young man. He had seen many such men in India, their smooth sculptured looks enhanced by their tanned skin, and he had had occasion more than once to reprimand them for their over-familiarity with the ladies. Herbert sauntered over, gave the two men a friendly smile and shook their hands.

'Herbert will himself be a prominent national figure in years to come,' Benjamin declared.

He's like a proud father, thought Captain Bell.

'Well, if you'll excuse us, gentlemen, we are like blood.'

'Really?' said the mayor.

'We must circulate or die!' With that, Benjamin escorted Herbert to the refreshment table, where he poured himself a small glass of sherry.

'Clever chap, that,' the mayor said with a nod. 'Wish I could write plays like him.'

It took another five minutes for the chief constable to explain the difference between an actor-manager and a playwright.

*

As they walked the short distance back to the Royal Hotel, Georgina had felt the pain return to her face and refused Richard's offer of a drink in the hotel bar. Granted, it wasn't the most salubrious of venues, but it was far better than the many other hostelries in town.

'Then I'll escort you to our room and come back down for a nightcap,' he said as they stepped into the hotel foyer. 'I see my friend Mr Jenkins is already in place.'

A man dressed in a shabby, dust-stained suit that had seen too many train compartments gave Richard a wave that ended with a speculative curl of the hand, the way a Roman emperor might have summoned his senate for a flagon of wine.

Around the reception desk, several people sat on the few chairs available, reading the day's newspapers or simply engaging in idle conversation, sharing the day's experiences of shopkeepers too stingy even to consider the wares they were peddling, one of them describing in muted tones the benefits of the latest lithographic developments he was anxious to share with the town's printers.

Georgina pressed her hand to her face as they crossed to the stairway and muttered, 'God defend me from travelling men!'

Once they were in their room, she removed her hat and coat and sat at the small table by the mirror. She knew perfectly well why the pain had returned: her assumption had been correct, as she knew it would be. Richard was once more indulging in those vile practices. Surely it was only a matter of time before he was caught, and then what lay in store for her? He would go to prison, of course, and she would be left alone and destitute.

'Here you are, my darling,' he said, returning from the bathroom with a small glass containing her compound.

What was it called? Chlorodyne, that was it. She recalled the bitter taste and was about to reject it when she remembered how swiftly it had worked, and the oblivion it had rapidly brought.

He stood over her and watched her swallow the analgesic. 'There's a good girl!'

'Good? No, Richard. I think not.'

He helped her undress and then gently settled her beneath the sheets, gazing down at her pale and troubled face. 'I will be only a short while. A warming brandy, perhaps, and a perusal of the day's papers.' He reached down to kiss her, but her eyes were already closed.

*

The pain had forced Jonathan Keele to make his excuses and leave the reception early. As he stepped out into the chill of the corridor, he caught sight of Benjamin and Herbert standing by the stairwell, having an animated discussion. He felt a pang of sympathy for his old friend, but realised with a heavy heart that he had done all he could do. And he had other things to worry about, hadn't he?

He placed his right hand inside his coat and pressed it gently against his stomach. The bloated sensation was becoming worse, and it had been weeks since he had felt anything like a genuine hunger for food. Strange, how the disease was even now at work a matter of inches from the flat of his hand, and he could do nothing at all about it.

Once he left the town hall, he held his muffler close to his mouth to ward off the thickening fog. Then, as he clambered into the hackney carriage waiting at the foot of the steps, he smiled at the futility of such a gesture. What could fog, filthy fog, do to him now? He could do as the witches in *Macbeth* and 'hover through the fog and filthy air' with impunity. Such irony! Disease had made him fearless of death because it had already claimed him for its own.

And the prospect of his own mortality did bring with it the warm consolation that wrapped itself around him far more effectively than any muffler: he would soon see his dearest Catherine once more. The child would no longer be floating in some dark and dreadful ether, condemned by those who see suicide as an act against God. No. He would take death as an opportunity to seek her out, to rescue her lost and lingering soul from its Limbo of misery, and give her eternal comfort in his arms.

As the carriage rattled through the dimly lit streets to his destination, he wondered if, when he found her, his granddaughter would still be thirteen, would still retain the flush of youth on her cheeks, the sparkling smile and the infectious giggle. Or would her face be pale and bloated, the eyes dull and sightless, as they had been five years ago when they fished her from the river?

*

Georgina Throstle, groggy and disorientated from the effects of the Chlorodyne, had found herself in a foul mood when her husband finally deigned to come to bed. He had fumbled with his key outside the door and, as on many such occasions in the past, he found the simple matter of unlocking a hotel door quite beyond him. She had struggled out of bed and let the drunken fool in, and immediately her head began to swim. She had the urgent need to lie down and allow the dizziness to take her back to the oblivion of sleep.

Richard, swaying on the edge of the bed, watched her hold a hand over her eyes, and with a leer he reached out to grab her.

'Please, Richard, no . . . no . . .' Her words were slurred, and he felt his loins stirring. She was shaking her head now, slowly from side to side, and he saw her eyes turn white with approaching unconsciousness.

Damn the woman! It would be just the thing to send him off to sleep. He decided to stroke her for a while. That usually did the trick.

So he lay beside her and caressed her smooth alabaster skin, and as he did so he thought of Violet, and that brute of a father. Was he even now scouring the cobbled streets of Wigan to seek vengeance for his deflowered daughter? More likely he was lying insensible in his filthy pit of a bed.

He tentatively placed a hand on Georgina's breast and caressed the cold nipple. No response. Perhaps the compound was stronger than he thought. By the pale moonlight filtering through the flimsy drapes, he could just make out the shape of her slightly parted lips, but after a few more seconds of attempted arousal he gave up, and as he turned away from her he saw the whites of her eyes finally disappear beneath her closing lids.

He would never again see those eyes open.

4

The first to notice something was amiss was the young lad who occasionally helped out at the hotel. He ran errands, did odd jobs such as shoe cleaning, or running to the entrance to Central Station to purchase a newspaper or a periodical. This morning he was carrying out the less than pleasurable duty of conducting any of the chamberpots left outside the rooms to the rear of the hotel, where he would pour the noisome contents down the privy. As he passed number twelve, he heard someone shout out, 'My God! My God!' He paused. Then the voice called out, 'There's no pulse. All this blood! It's murder! Murder!' upon which he dropped the chamberpot he was carrying, ignoring the yellow liquid soaking into the threadbare carpet, and ran downstairs for help.

*

The door to Captain Bell's office at Wigan Borough Police Station swung open, and the duty sergeant stood there with a disturbed expression on his face.

'What is it?' Captain Bell snapped.

'Sorry to disturb you, sir. But there's a bit of a commotion at the desk.'

'What sort of commotion?'

'It's a chap sent from the Royal. Says they've found one of their guests. Dead, sir.'

Bell sighed. 'Then it's a case for the doctor and the coroner.'

The sergeant lowered his voice. 'From what he says, sir, it's a case for us.'

His superior stood up and followed the duty sergeant back along the corridor.

At the desk, he found a nervous-looking young man who presented himself as the assistant manager of the Royal Hotel. He spoke for only a few minutes, but the chief constable's brow darkened visibly as he listened to the young man's hesitant and almost terrified voice. He then dismissed him with instructions for the room to be kept locked and for no guest to be allowed to leave. Then he turned to the duty sergeant with a glance at the clock high above the front desk.

'Where the blazes is Detective Sergeant Slevin? He is five minutes past his time. This is unconscionable!'

As if on cue, Samuel Slevin walked up the steps outside the station, whistling a lively tune. The duty sergeant tried to forewarn him, but the chief constable moved quickly.

'When you have finished warbling like a cockatoo, sergeant . . .' Captain Bell planted himself firmly in front of his senior detective. 'You need not bother entering the station.'

'What?' said Slevin, misunderstanding the man's words. 'But I'm barely five minutes late, if that!'

Captain Bell leaned forward. 'I mean you are to go up to the Royal Hotel, where some body is waiting for you.'

'Somebody? Who?'

'I said, some *body*, sergeant. There has been a murder. Of the vilest kind.'

*

Number 147 Darlington Street had provided lodgings for theatricals for many years. The walls of the front room were richly decorated with playbills advertising productions from Wigan all the way down to Penzance. Some of the posters, gifts from grateful guests, had far more exotic names, announcing productions in such far-flung places as the Theatre Royal, Melbourne, the Kroll Opera House, Berlin, and the Corinthian Theatre in Calcutta.

The proprietress of the lodging-house was a large-framed woman with a hearty sense of humour and a fearsome reputation as a strict upholder of moral conduct. Mary O'Halloran had come from Charlestown, County Mayo over forty years before, a young girl of ten who had seen many of her family die in the great potato famine and whose da had vowed to put some food in their bellies if it was the last thing he did. After some years working in the mines he had eventually died from the black spit, his lungs rotten with disease, and her ma had had to throw open their doors and take in lodgers to make ends meet. Later, when her ma passed away, Mary had become so steeped in the colourful world she heard so much about at every mealtime that it had been an easy decision to continue with the business.

She had a particular fondness for Mr Morgan-Drew. He had stayed on previous tours, but this was the first time he had brought his own touring company. She had seen him on stage in earlier productions and had marvelled at his ability to become another person, apparently with ease, but when she spoke to him in the intimate confines of her own home, she saw something else there – a deep sense of loneliness in his eyes.

She had romantic ideas of his meeting some middle-aged actress, perhaps widowed and eminently respectable, who would cause the sadness to fade from his eyes.

Certainly, since he had been back in the town, she had seen a lifting of his spirits and a sparkle in his eye, though she wasn't quite sure of the origin and would most certainly not offend the man by making enquiries.

This morning it had been difficult to waken Mr Morgan-Drew. Although she was quite a flexible woman, and accepted that actors lived by rules others would consider bohemian, she had always made it clear that there were to be no late-night shenanigans of either an immoral or an alcoholic nature. Furthermore, although she often gave her more favoured guests a late-night key on the understanding that anyone arriving home after hours would comport himself with a silent dignity, last night when he returned, Mr Morgan-Drew had been neither silent nor dignified.

She had heard him and the young man who occupied the room next to his – Mr Koller – speaking in an urgent and often vulgar manner below her window on the street and later in the front parlour. Here their tones became even more strident, compelling her to hammer on the bedroom floor with her da's walking stick. Thankfully, silence had ensued, and she heard them both whispering on the landing before retiring to their respective rooms. But she was determined to broach the subject this morning, unpalatable though it might be, which was why she was now waiting outside Mr Morgan-Drew's room, having knocked on the door for the umpteenth time.

Finally she heard a grunt from beyond the bedroom door.

'What?'

'Mr Morgan-Drew?'

'Who else would it be, you silly woman? Henry Irving?'

'Well I think not. From what I hear he is a sober and respectable kind.'

'What is it you require?'

'I require a word or two with you and Mr Koller.'

There was a pause from beyond the door that lasted so long that Mrs O'Halloran knocked once more.

'I am indisposed at the moment, Mrs O'Halloran. Allow me the courtesy of a few moments' ablutions.'

She gave a snort and declared that she would be awaiting his pleasure in the parlour, and if he would be so kind as to arouse Mr Koller next door and ensure his attendance also.

'I promise to arouse him, Mrs O'Halloran!'

'Good.' Her mission partly accomplished, she returned downstairs, where she would prepare for her two guests the heartiest of breakfasts.

*

When Detective Sergeant Samuel Slevin arrived at the Royal Hotel, there was already a sizeable gathering in the small foyer. He was immediately met by Mr Jameson, the hotel manager, who explained that these people were travelling businessmen who were anxious to be on their way and were more than a little unhappy at being unable to check out of the hotel.

'This unpleasantness is not very good for business,' said a perspiring Mr Jameson. 'Word spreads, you know.'

Slevin couldn't tell whether he was referring to their enforced delay or the fact that there was a dead body upstairs. 'Well, the sooner I see the remains of the victim, the quicker they can be on their way.'

'Excellent.'

The manager stood back to allow the detective access to the stairs to the left of the doorway. 'It's number twelve.'

'How long have the Throstles been resident?'

'A few days. They have hired the Public Hall for their magic lantern show. Highly respectable people, you understand, sergeant.'

'Of course.' He stopped halfway up the stairs. 'Your reception area. Is there someone on duty throughout the night?'

'Of course.'

'But your main entrance is open for residents arriving late?'

'As at most hotels, sergeant.'

'I see.'

Once Slevin had reached the door of number twelve he gave a silent nod to the young boy standing there and looking on the verge of collapse at any moment. Why on earth had Jameson placed a lad barely in his teens outside the scene of a murder? He turned around, held up his hand to forestall any further assistance from the manager, and took a deep breath before pushing the door open.

Death was never a pleasant sight. As he slowly opened the door he saw the lifeless shape on the bed, the eyes blank and glassy, and the lips pulled back over the teeth in a parody of a smile. But it wasn't the expression of horror on the pale features that caused him to gasp.

The sheets were thrown back to expose the lower half of the torso, and the area surrounding the thighs and groin was a soaking mass of blood that glistened even as it congealed. He turned away and surveyed the state of the room. Every drawer of the dresser had been ripped out, its contents strewn haphazardly across the floor. What was obviously the Throstles' valise lay open, revealing clothes and personal effects. As Slevin fought back the bile rising in his throat, he took a step closer to the bed and his foot accidentally caught the rim of the chamberpot. Now he noticed something else about the unfortunate victim: he had not only been stabbed but vilely mutilated, disfigured beyond belief, unmanned in the most grisly, inhuman way. Horror piled upon horror, for as he turned away, he caught sight of the chamberpot, and what it contained.

*

Ethel Grundy sat across from Violet Cowburn and felt a wave of sympathy for the lass. She didn't usually have much time for the girl, the way she swanked down the street with her head held a little too high for Ethel's liking. It was as if the girl couldn't wait to leave the place she was born and had grown up in. Her mother had run off, cocking a snook at the world and his missus. Perhaps that sort of thing ran in the blood?

Yet such thoughts were far from Ethel's mind now. Violet had come home that morning. Ethel heard movement next door, somebody rattling a saucepan and raking the grate. She gave a tentative knock on the front door and was shocked to see the pale, pain-wracked face of young Violet, who was standing there and swaying most unsteadily.

'Ee, lass, what the heck are ye doin'?' she had said, and caught the girl just before she swooned.

Half an hour later, after Ethel had made the fire and the coals were already beginning to glow, they were sitting at the table with hot cups of tea in their hands, and Violet had explained why she had made her way home from the hospital.

'Me father'd starve if it were left to 'im. He's got nobody to do for him, has he?'

'No more than he deserves, after what he did.'

Violet shook her head. 'He'd every right, Ethel.'

'No man has a right to throw his only daughter downstairs.'

Violet took a long sip that seemed to burn her lips. 'You saw, didn't you?'

'Saw what, lass?'

'The man. The one who ran away.'

'Oh him.' Ethel looked into the flames of the coal fire.

'I thought . . . I mean, the way he hid, like a frightened rabbit. And then he just pushed me into me dad, and flew downstairs and out of the door before you could spit.'

'There's plenty like that, lass.'

'Aye. I know, Ethel. But . . . I can't blame me dad. That'd just be addin' one sin onto another. It were my fault, all this. But I've no one I can talk to, see?'

'About what?'

'About what I've done.'

'And what have you done?' Ethel asked, though she thought she knew.

Violet looked away. 'I . . . I'm sorry, Ethel. I'd best keep some things to meself, eh?'

'If you have to. But I'm only next door, love. You ever need anythin' . . .'

Violet reached out and grasped her neighbour's hand. 'I know. Thanks.' Now it was Violet's turn to gaze at the burning coals. 'You don't happen to know where me dad is, do you, Ethel?'

*

Voices were raised angrily in the residents' bar of the Royal Hotel. The front doors had been firmly closed to all but the most necessary callers – a local doctor had come and gone, and he was followed by a succession of constables who escorted the hotel residents into the bar area, where they placated them as best they could. Then came the grand entrance of Horatio Bentham, M.B. and C.M. (Edin.), who had been house surgeon at the Royal Albert Edward Infirmary for over twenty-five years and who would be carrying out the post-mortem examination. Finally the angry protestations grew muted, the interviews suspended for the moment, while the bearers from the infirmary morgue brought down their melancholy burden beneath a swathe of calico sheets.

Slevin spoke a few words with Dr Bentham before returning to the manager's office that lay beyond the small reception desk. Here the victim's wife had been installed, sedated and in a state of shock.

Georgina Throstle was lying on a chaise-longue with a damp cloth over her eyes and one hand resting on her head. One of the hotel maids was seated beside her, patting her hands and looking most uncomfortable in the process. She gave Slevin a look of relief as he silently indicated that she should leave the two of them alone.

She was indubitably a handsome woman, he thought, as he took his place beside her and introduced himself. Her jet-black hair was swept back in a tight bun, and her face was well-formed, with prominent cheekbones and a sharpness to the tight curve of her mouth. With great care, she lifted the cloth from her forehead and turned to look at the policeman. Her eyes were heavy, and it seemed to be a desperate effort to keep them from closing.

'I'm sorry, ma'am. But if I could ask you a few questions?'

She let her hand curl in the air by way of reply but remained silent.

'Tell me about last night. What time did you both retire?'

A deep sigh. 'Eleven-thirty or thereabouts. Richard went back down to the bar. I was asleep when he returned, but he woke me fumbling for his key. I vaguely recall staggering to the door to let him in.'

'Was he intoxicated?'

'I have no idea. I was asleep again almost immediately.'

'The hotel manager tells me you have been quite busy this last week. You have a show.'

'Yes. A magic lantern show.'

'Can you tell me what happened when you awoke this morning?'

'I heard nothing! Nothing at all!' Suddenly her eyes were wide open, blazing at him with a fearsome intensity, and she sat up, gripping his arm tightly. 'How is that possible, when he was . . .' She slumped back, exhausted. 'The medicine.'

'Medicine?'

She slowly shook her head from side to side and gave a sharp laugh. 'It was meant to nullify my pain. My goodness! It did that all right. Nullified every one of my senses, too, by the looks of it.'

Gradually, with infinite patience, Slevin discovered that she had taken an analgesic – Chlorodyne – to help her to sleep, and the compound had been brought by her husband the evening before.

'It would have rendered you quite impervious to any disturbance, ma'am.'

'So while I was sleeping, some . . . some demon . . . entered our room and . . . and . . .' The scenario was too much for her, and she broke down into a flood of tears that only subsided when, once again, a heavy tiredness seemed to overwhelm her.

He took a deep breath and reached to hold her hand. She looked up at him through eyes that were raw with weeping.

'This will be most difficult, ma'am, but if we are to find the foul fiend who did this to your husband, I need to know more.'

She sniffed and nodded.

'When you awoke, did you see anyone in the room?'

'No one. I just felt . . . I was cold, and damp. And when I reached down I could feel a wetness . . . oh Richard! Dear Richard!'

'Do you know of anyone who could do such a thing to your husband, ma'am?'

'No one! He was the most solicitous of husbands. Of men.'

'Your room was in disarray. Someone was evidently looking for something. I just wondered if anything had been taken. Robbery could well be the motive. Perhaps your husband awoke and discovered the villain.'

She looked about to give a response when suddenly she stopped, as if she had remembered something. 'I thought he was lying.' she said finally.

'Ma'am?'

Now she was alert, her tiredness in abeyance as something struck her. 'Yesterday afternoon. I had taken to my bed, for my face was most painful, and Richard went out. He told me he'd fallen in with some card sharps who tried to cheat him. He returned here breathless and . . . and said they'd pursued him. I simply thought it was a lie.'

'Why would you think that?'

Again she hesitated. It would be indiscreet for her to say anything further in explanation. 'An intuition, sergeant.'

'Did he say where he had met these card sharps?'

'He did not.'

'But he seemed . . . perturbed by them?'

'Yes. He told me they had manhandled him in an alleyway.'

'I see. Did you have valuables in your possession?'

'No. Apart from a few jewels, my necklace, a brooch . . . but they were not taken.'

'Were they well hidden?'

'I keep them in a small case beneath the bed. Richard has often mocked me for using such a hiding-place. "It's the first place a thief will look," he used to say. But I was surprised to find they were still there.'

Slevin took out a notepad and wrote something down. He would get Constable Bowery to follow this particular line of enquiry. It wouldn't be difficult to confirm, if, as her husband had said, he had been chased through the streets of Wigan by a group of ne'er-do-wells. It wasn't something people would have missed, fog or no fog.

'Can you think of anyone else, now or in the past, who would wish to inflict such harm on your husband?'

'None, sergeant. Richard was a very popular figure. Ask his audiences.' She placed a hand against her right cheek. 'It has begun,' she said in a whisper.

'What?'

'It has begun. I knew it would be only a matter of time. Will you pass me my reticule, sergeant?' She indicated a small tortoiseshell purse on a nearby table, its gold pique-work sparkling as a rare shaft of sunlight penetrated the lace curtains.

Slevin dutifully brought it to her and watched as she withdrew a small brown bottle. 'Ma'am?'

'Yes?'

'Is that the compound your husband had prepared for you?'

'It is,' she said as she pulled off the stopper. 'It brings blessed relief.'

'Then I think you must refrain – at least for a while.'

She looked at him as if he'd said something improper. 'What is the matter?'

'You have already been given quite a strong sedative by the doctor sent for by the manager.'

'So? That was a sedative. This,' she held it up and he could see it was still over half full, 'is an analgesic.'

'And as such rather dangerous to take so soon after your previous medication.'

'What nonsense!'

But before she could react he had swiftly removed the bottle from her grasp and placed it out of her reach.

'Really, sergeant! That is brutal and insensitive.'

'And necessary.'

'But what about my face? What do I do about my face?'

The phrase 'grin and bear it' stuck in his throat. 'I'm afraid you must allow the sedative to do its job,' he said finally. Then he stood up as she closed her eyes in a mute display of indignation. The latter part of the interview, he reflected as he left the room, had witnessed a subtle shift from horror at her husband's brutal death to concern about herself. He wondered if that was a reflection of the way their relationship had been. He certainly had the impression that Mrs Richard Throstle had been rather niggardly with the truth. Still, he would speak with her again, he had no doubt.

*

Constable Bowery was standing in the porticoed entrance of the Royal Hotel, keeping the idle and the curious away. When he saw Sergeant Slevin in the foyer speaking to the manager, he snapped his fingers at one of the younger constables just inside the door and told him to take his place.

'Excuse me, sergeant,' Bowery said when the sergeant was about to go into the residents' bar.

Slevin turned and gave him an impatient glance.

'Only, is it right what they say?'

'And what's that?'

'Poor bugger had had his old chap sliced off? Balls an' all?'

'That was one of his wounds, yes.'

'An' they'd been dropped in a pisspot?'

'Yes.'

'Bloody 'ell! Just think of it, eh?'

'I'd rather not. Now I have to speak to several very irate travellers, constable, so . . .'

'I saw 'im.'

'Who?'

'The victim. I took the missus to see 'im t'other night.'

'Really?'

'Course, I knowed it weren't real, all done with them lanterns an' all, but the missus . . . you shoulda heard her scream.'

'Quite. Now the manager tells me they had nine guests staying here last night – that's seven plus the Throstles. There are six of them in the bar and we need to take down their names and addresses, and ask them if they noticed anything strange or unusual last night, or any previous night.'

'They'll have seen summat bloody unusual if that bugger were up to his tricks. Him an' his lanterns. You know what I reckon, sergeant?'

Slevin was about to push open the door to the bar, where he could hear raised voices and protestations of outrage. 'What?'

'We could be lookin' at the spirit world.'

In spite of his desire to press on, Slevin stopped and looked at the constable, whose expression showed a deadly earnestness.

'I mean, that bugger conjured up all sorts durin' his show. There were sights yonder I'd never seen before. Can't all have been fakery now. Stands to reason. He might've called up demons what didn't want callin' up, eh? They say you should let the dead stay dead, an' if you disturb 'em, well, the spirits can turn very nasty indeed. My cousin went to a sittin' once an' she . . .'

Slevin raised a finger and pointed it at Bowery. 'You utter one word of that superstitious drivel again an' you'll be on mortuary duties for a fortnight. That should curb your enthusiasm for the dead. Understand?'

Bowery nodded and the admonitory finger was lowered.

'Now,' Slevin said. 'Let's get busy.'

'Hang on, sergeant,' said Bowery, anxious to show he still had a grip on the real world.

'What now?'

'You said there was seven guests apart from Throstle an' his missus?'

'Yes?'

'Well, if there's only six of 'em in yon bar, then where's t'other bugger?'

'He isn't here, constable. Early riser, apparently. And I'm glad to see you retain a grasp of basic arithmetic.'

Constable Bowery, on whom irony was wasted, smiled and followed his sergeant into the small bar.

The results of the interviews, once Slevin and Bowery had shared their findings, were less than encouraging. No one had seen or heard anything unusual the previous night, although one of them – Mr Golding, the Inspector of Mines – had spent half an hour in the bar late the previous night and seen the victim, who had been enjoying a convivial drink and more than a few sniggered confidences with the hosiery salesman, Mr Jenkins. Golding had shared the conversation briefly, explicating the range and compass of accidental deaths in the coalmines.

'And how did Mr Throstle seem?' Slevin had asked.

'Interested, sergeant. That's how he seemed.'

'In what?'

'Why, in my experiences.'

'And Mr Jenkins?'

'Oh he's an affable sort of chap, if a little boring. Told us about his two daughters, immensely proud of them, he was.'

'Did he appear to be . . . worried about anything?'

'Who?'

'Throstle.'

'Not at all. Confident is the word I would choose.'

'Didn't mention card sharps, by any chance?'

Golding shook his head. 'He seemed in high spirits. The future is beckoning, he kept saying. Expansion is the word.'

'Is there anything you can tell me that might shed some light on the dreadful fate that lay in store for him?'

The Inspector of Mines looked to the ceiling for inspiration.

'He did happen to ask me if I had any opportunities for female company in my line of work.'

'That was a strange question to ask.'

'Yes, it was. I told him of course that the very nature of my work with the mines precluded much contact with the gentler sex. '

'Did he elaborate?'

'On the subject of women? Not really. But he did say – now this was when he had taken more than his fair share of drink, and he began to slur his words most alarmingly – he did say that I was quite right. I should keep away from them, because they are demons. That was it. Demons. "And they have fathers that are worse than demons." I quote him verbatim, sergeant. It just seemed a curious thing to say.'

'Thank you.'

Mr Golding had nothing more useful to add, and so he retired to his room to consult his papers.

'What's all that about fathers?' Bowery asked in the solitude of the empty bar.

'Perplexing, constable. That's what it is. But perhaps also revealing.'

Bowery blinked. How could something be perplexing and revealing at one and the same time?

'I should like to speak to the missing Mr Jenkins.'

'You reckon he's our killer, sergeant?'

'No, constable. But I should like him to corroborate something Mr Golding, our esteemed Inspector of Mines, said. It appears that Mr Richard Throstle had an eye for the ladies. Ladies with fathers. What does that suggest to you?'

Bowery thought. 'Well, it suggests *young* ladies, sergeant. Dads don't tend to turn into demons when their daughters get past a certain age. They don't get angry any more if someone tips their cap at 'em – they get grateful.'

Slevin gave him a pat on the back. 'Excellent, constable! Reason founded on the rock of experience. The best kind.'

Bowery, who had no idea what the sergeant was on about, nevertheless smiled. It wasn't often he got a pat on the back from Sergeant Slevin.

Then a very rare thing happened. Constable Jimmy Bowery had a flash of inspiration.

'That's a bugger,' was how he articulated the sensation.

'What is?'

'Well, it might be owt an' it might be nowt.'

Slevin sighed heavily.

'Yesterday we were called out to Springfield. Billy Cowburn. Know 'im?'

Slevin shook his head.

'Well, neighbours reckon he heaved his daughter downstairs.'

'Why?'

'Neighbour said she saw a chap runnin' from the house, an' Cowburn after him cursin' an' threatenin' to rip him apart. Looks like he'd caught 'em at it.'

'Where's Cowburn now?'

'Ah,' said Bowery, letting his gaze fall to the floor. 'Well, we had him an' then we didn't.'

'Thus giving our esteemed chief constable occasion to harangue you in his office last night.'

'You heard.'

'I did.'

'But what I'm sayin', sergeant, is that it could've been Throstle what run, and Cowburn what did for him, eh?'

Slevin pondered this scenario for a while. 'I think we'll have a word with Miss Cowburn,' he said finally.

*

Georgina Throstle had of course given instructions for the evening's *Phantasmagoria* to be cancelled. The manager of the Public Hall, Mr James Worswick, whom she had summoned to her new room at the Royal (thoughtfully provided by the hotel management and situated on the ground floor), had been the embodiment of sympathy and understanding. Unaware of the exact details of her husband's unfortunate demise, he was therefore at a loss to explain to anyone who would listen to him later how his words could have reduced the poor woman to a state almost of delirium.

'I shall ensure your late husband's equipment will remain safe and unmolested,' he had assured her.

Now, in the dark seclusion of her room, she sat at the small writing-table by the window and pored over Richard's papers. Among the items he had carefully kept in his briefcase were the detailed records of his more 'exclusive' material. This was normally kept under lock and key back in Leeds. Some of the slides, she knew, were kept with him at all times, and she cast an eye over the small notebook he used to record these.

The entries he had inscribed were couched in the most innocent of terms: 'Rose Blossoms'; 'The Flower Girls'; 'The Organ Grinder'; 'Picking Cherries'.

Yet she knew what those slides contained. The fact that the first set – 'Rose Blossoms' – had been underscored in the notebook told her that these had been brought with him and were even now stored in the safe in the Public Hall office. She would have to retrieve them and decide what to do with them. She had no doubt now that the man she saw Richard talking to in the street, whom he had described as a pillar of the community, had entered into some financial arrangement for a private showing of the slides. Now, with Richard dead, it would be prudent to destroy any evidence of such wickedness, for she herself could be considered guilty by association.

And yet . . . these slides had made him considerably more money than anything else, and in destroying them she would in effect be destroying the means to financial independence. It pained her to admit it, but Richard had been right.

Did she really desire a future with her sainted brother, who rose every morning at five and chanted the *Te Deum* in a voice so grave and forbidding you'd think he was offering a lament for the dead rather than a hymn of praise? A brother who, because of her earlier life as a governess, would now, after her period of mourning, expect her to earn her keep by teaching his parishioners' children in Sunday School, after having sat through yet another of his interminably long sermons?

'I mustn't be hasty!' she thought, closing the notebook gently. 'Above all things, I must consider my future.'

*

Enoch Platt lay in his bed, covered with his greatcoat and gazing at the small curtained window. Slivers of morning sunlight managed to creep through the grubbed holes in the fabric. Not that he took any notice of the light, or the sun, or the myriad of street noises coming from beyond his bedroom window. No. He was seeing a blackness so total it felt like the onset of Death itself, and hearing the cries that came from all around him . . .

Cries that had been laughter only a few minutes earlier, laughter mingled with the sound of picks striking the coal face, and the dull gritty trundle of the corves being pushed along the tracks, and the frequent bursts of coughing and curses. Then they heard the distant rumble, like thunder in the next county, swiftly followed by a huge blast that sent Enoch and the others flying through the suffocating dust clouds until they came to near the shaft. Coal tubs and huge wedges of timber lay scattered in all directions, and from afar came a dim red glow that illuminated everything, rendering it akin to a scene from hell itself. He coughed, and fought to gain control of his breathing, but the dust was swirling and clogging up his nostrils and stinging his eyes. He could just make out the shattered remains of countless bodies, limbs ripped from their sockets and bodies twisted at impossible angles. Then he dropped down to his knees, where he felt his hands touch someone's face, and stooped low to see who it was. Despite the storm raging all around, and the cries of those still trapped beneath the tons of rubble from the collapsed walls, he took great care to wipe his eyes clean of the dust for a few seconds to examine the one he had found. His heart raced as the dim glow of flames from afar revealed his brother, Joseph, his eyes open and gazing back at him. Gazing but not seeing.

It was then that he noticed the dust speckling his eyes, tiny dots of grit colouring the blue eyes grey, then black, with no reflex flutter from his lids. He tried to close those eyes, clogged thick now with dust, but as he held his brother's head in his hands he realised with a sickening sensation of horror that it moved too easily, and when he gazed fearfully down he saw the neck had been severed just above the breastbone and there was no sign anywhere of the rest of his broken body. With a low, keening groan he raised the head in both hands, and the groan became a high, piercing scream that was deadened only by the next explosion which slammed into his ears, bringing both welcome darkness and a permanent dislodgement of the brain.

*

'Now that we're here,' said Detective Sergeant Slevin with a look of venom towards the hapless Bowery, 'we might as well make use of it. But I can tell you, constable, I am less than pleased by this wild goose chase.'

Where Violet Cowburn had lain in some distress the night before, now a female of indeterminate age was sitting up and singing at the top of her voice.

'Transferred from the Idiot Ward,' said a tight-lipped matron. 'She has tubercolosis, though you wouldn't think so, listening to that caterwauling.'

'You must have a great deal to put up with,' said Slevin, giving her a smile. 'Now, would it be possible for you to tell me where I might find Dr Bentham?'

'In the operating theatre and under no circumstances to be disturbed.'

'I wouldn't dream of doing such a thing,' Slevin replied. 'But the great doctor knows me well, and he has promised to do something for me.'

'Oh?'

'Both he and I would owe you a debt of gratitude if you were to pass this on to him.' He produced the small brown bottle containing the potion Georgina had been taking for her neuralgia.

'What is it?'

'Ah,' he said with another of his winning smiles, 'you have my question all ready. That's precisely what I want you to ask him. On my behalf. What exactly is this potion?'

She took it uncertainly.

'Tell him I'll look forward to his opinion on the potion. Good day.'

Before she could say anything further, he and Constable Bowery were already leaving the ward and its unruly patient behind.

'What do you reckon's in the bottle, sergeant?'

'I don't know. Probably what Mrs Throstle says is in it. But it will do no harm to check.'

As they travelled towards the Cowburn house at Springfield, suffering the uneven rattle of the hackney as it bounced along on the cobbled surface, Slevin pondered the gruesome circumstances of Richard Throstle's death. Why, for instance, had he been mutilated in such a manner? If you want to kill someone, then you take the quickest and most economical route, surely? Yet somehow the murderer had gained access to the victim's room – the door was undamaged and the lock untampered with – and rendered him pliant in some way. There had been no visible signs of a blow to the head, so it was possible he was suffocated before the murderer set about his vile task. But what if Mrs Throstle had awakened at any time? True, she had taken her analgesic, but surely the murderer wasn't to know that? And what if she had awakened at the moment of execution? Perhaps then she too would be lying in the infirmary mortuary beside her husband. The more he thought about it, the more he felt that there was something deeply personal about this crime, and that robbery was far from the crazed mind of the creature who perpetrated the act.

'Presence of mind,' Slevin said aloud as the hackney trundled its uncomfortable way past Mesnes Park.

'Beg pardon, sergeant?'

'Would you have the presence of mind to do what she did?'

'What who did?'

Slevin tightened his lips in exasperation. 'Mrs Georgina Throstle.'

'Why? What'd she do then?' Perhaps, he thought, if the sergeant occasionally let him share whatever he was thinking about then he wouldn't have to ask such questions. Bowery was no mentalist.

'When she awoke and discovered her husband so abominably defiled in death, she had the presence of mind to look under the bed to see if her jewellery had been stolen.'

'Perhaps she was fond of 'em.'

'Her husband is lying there drenched in blood with his member swimming in a pisspot and she thinks of her baubles? A remarkable woman, constable, don't you think?'

'Could've been the shock?'

'Yes. Yes, it could have been. Let's keep an open mind, eh? When we return, I want you to take a couple of men and do the rounds of the public houses and drinking dens.'

'Bloody 'ell, sergeant! Do you know how many of them there are?'

'A fair number, I should say. But if Throstle was threatened by card sharps, then surely he would have had enough sense to restrict his wanderings to the town centre? He's hardly likely to take an afternoon constitutional up Scholes or Beech Hill, now is he? Specially in all that fog. No, restrict your enquiries to the town centre.' He gave a smile of mock compassion. 'There. See how logic and deduction are a boon to detection, constable?'

Bowery sighed. He had a vision of blistered feet, and sullen and hostile responses. There were still a good number of such places in the town itself. 'What are we lookin' for?'

'Card games. Gambling of any description. Throstle told his wife he was chased by card sharps.'

'But we know that was a lie, sergeant. It was Cowburn who did the chasin' after skimmin' his young wench downstairs.'

'That's as may be. But we cannot ignore the possibility that he was referring to an earlier encounter.'

'It's a wild goose chase, sergeant.'

'Is it?' Slevin asked innocently.

Constable Bowery folded his arms, stared glumly through the window and silently swore. He would have cursed out loud if he had known what was waiting for them in Mort Street.

*

The morning after an opening night is always thought of as a dead time, when the euphoria of the night before, especially when the audience is as rapturous and generous in its applause as it was at the Royal Court, has long since faded like echoes in an empty hall. In her small room at the lodging-house, with Belle Greave still snoring loudly in the adjoining room, Susan Coupe had spent a few hours preparing her next role – that of Portia in *Julius Caesar*.

Later, as she left her lodgings in Greenhough Street, having politely but firmly declined Belle's offer to accompany her, she walked quickly down the incline towards the town centre. The warnings from her landlady were still fresh in her mind: 'Whatever you do, love, don't go *up* Greenhough Street. That'd take you to Scholes, an' that's the last place a fine-lookin' lass like you wants to end up in.' Scholes, she went on with gruesome relish, was a 'lively place', where policemen never ventured alone and whose

Saturday nights were often a veritable bloodbath outside several of the seventy or so public houses.

Susan had shuddered, the advice reinforcing her dislike of the town. The notorious district might well be set apart from the more respectable part of town where she was lodged, but the very existence of such brutish creatures disgusted her. She had seen many of them over the last few days, slouching past in the late afternoon, their faces smeared and blackened by coal dust and their eyes somehow seeming to select her, of all those in the street and outside the many shops, for prurient attention. Must the male sex always regard women with such a leering desire?

Yet James, dear, sweet James, was so very different. When he held her in his arms she felt so safe, so impervious to whatever the world might hurl at her.

The young actress walked along the pavement, her thoughts well hidden by the demure smile set permanently on her lips. But passing a butcher's shop she felt a revulsion upon seeing thick bloody slabs of meat and slender rabbits hanging from rusted hooks.

'Stick to yer ribs, them, love!' Standing in the butcher's doorway stood a huge bear of a man. His thick whiskers covered bright red lips and he gave her a proud smile as he swung one of the dead rabbits to and fro.

'No, thank you,' she replied, making an effort not to offend.

As she walked to the edge of the pavement, squirming her way past a small group of women jabbering away in their unintelligible accents, she caught sight of James standing on the opposite side of the street, waving to her and raising his hat to catch her attention.

'You look worried,' he said as she reached him, immediately linking her arm in his.

'But not any more,' she said. She fought back an impulse to rest her head on his broad shoulders.

'Well,' he beamed, and took a deep breath of air. 'The fog has lifted, the afternoon is crisp and fine, and we mustn't waste a second.'

'You seem in a better mood today. What have you done about the telegram?'

'Sent a reply, of course.'

Susan Coupe lowered her eyes. 'I see.'

He turned to face her fully and held both her arms that were hanging listlessly at her side. 'Not that sort of reply. I've told you, she merely wants to make sure she'll be adequately provided for. The alimony she is receiving is already one-fifth of what I earn, and she is keen for that to increase once the suit is concluded.'

'Such a mercenary woman!' She paused. 'It's just that any form of communication with *her* . . .'

He leaned forward and touched her nose with his forefinger. To Susan, it was a deeply romantic gesture. 'Now, let's forget about her, and everything else for a while, shall we?'

'Quite right,' she said with a sudden laugh. 'Where shall we go?'

'Aha! I thought a bracing winter's walk. Just allow me to lead the way, my dearest. A special treat.'

She loved treats. She loved James. And at that moment, as they strolled arm in arm along the crowded pavements, Susan allowed herself to hope that there might be a time in the near future when the two of them could stroll as freely and as leisurely through Hyde Park or along the Mall with no fear of what the past once held, no fear of being observed by the woman who was still his wife. Portia's words came to her just then:

'O Constancy, be strong upon my side!'

*

They were both surprised when Ethel Grundy opened the door to the Cowburn house and gave a snort of disgust. 'Well, if it isn't one of the three blind mice!' was the way she addressed a red-faced Constable Bowery. 'My Nat's had to miss a day's work 'cos o' you an' your bully boys. Come to pay yer respects an' stand him a round, have yer? We're only next door.'

'We did consider bringing him in and charging him with impeding the pursuit of a fugitive,' said Slevin, coining a new offence and watching her anger turn to concern.

She gave a nod to the Cowburns' front room behind her. 'Well, I can't stand here wi' you lot. Young Vi's inside. I've been lookin' after her. There's no bugger else'll do it, is there?' She moved quickly from the doorstep and entered her own house, slamming the front door with pointed force.

The Cowburn door being left conveniently open, they gave another cursory tap on the knocker and went inside.

Violet Cowburn was seated in an armchair facing a roaring fire. She didn't turn around, even though it was obvious she was aware of their presence.

'Afternoon, Violet,' said Slevin, who introduced himself. 'You've already met Constable Bowery.'

'Oh aye. Fair made me heart stop when I woke up in yon hospital bed and saw that ugly face starin' down at me. Thought I'd died an' gone to hell.'

'I can sympathise,' Slevin said, with a sly wink at his colleague, and took a seat in the chair opposite the girl.

He saw the pain etched deep in her face, a face which, under other circumstances, would have been quite fetching. Her light brown hair was tightly parted down the middle, although wisps of hair hung limply above her eyes, which had a dull, glazed cast. Both her cheeks were flushed red from the intensity of heat from the coals, and as she sat there he noticed how she placed her right hand from time to time against her ribcage, and how at such times her eyes narrowed into slits expressive of an intense agony.

'We need to ask you a few questions, Violet.'

'He's not here.'

'Who?'

'Me dad. Not been back. I was thinkin' of sendin' for you,

matter of fact.' She gave a weak laugh, then clutched her side as the pain seared through her body.

'My constable tells me that your fall yesterday was an accident.'

''S'right.'

'And the row between you and your father was just a coincidence.'

'Me dad did nothin'.'

'I'm glad to hear it.' He paused and gave Bowery a glance.

'So you lot can stop houndin' him. He's done nowt wrong.'

'It's actually about someone else that we've come to see you, Violet.'

'Oh?'

'According to our information, there was a man here when your father came home from work.'

'Ethel bloody Grundy.'

'Pardon?'

'That one should keep her ear from our bloody wall. Funny it's not got mildewed. She's just been in now, fussin'.'

'It's what neighbours do. She must be worried about you.'

'She wants to know what's what.' But from the subdued tone of her voice, it was apparent that she had welcomed her neighbour's concern.

'But the man who fled . . . shall we say your father's wrath? This man. Who was he?'

Violet shrugged. 'Don't know what you're on about.'

'A man was seen running away from here, Violet. A man who was being chased by your father. We have an idea who he was, by the way.'

'Well then, why ask me? You can't arrest a man for just . . . bein' here. Can you?'

'No, indeed not.' Slevin looked up at Bowery, who was standing near the front door and watching the girl intently.

'But if you could tell us his name, it would help us in a completely different . . . situation.'

'Why? What's he done then?'

'Nothing,' said Slevin truthfully. 'Nothing that we know of. Nothing unlawful, that is.'

'I don't understand.'

'Violet, last night a man was brutally murdered in the Royal Hotel.'

She caught her breath, clutched once more at her ribs. 'What?'

'Please can you tell us the name of the man who ran from your house last evening?'

He saw her eyes dash frantically around the room, focusing on nothing in particular but searching for something to hang on to. She reminded Slevin of a cornered animal. He knew what desperate thoughts were racing around her mind, and most of them concerned not Mr Richard Throstle but her father.

'Who got murdered?'

'I'm afraid it was Richard Throstle.'

Her eyes grew wide with shock. He could see tiny images of flames reflected in her pupils.

'He was the man your father went after, wasn't he?'

Violet merely sat there, unable for a few seconds to comprehend the horror of what she had just been told.

'We just need to speak to your father, Violet. It would help if we knew where he was likely to be.'

'I don't know!' she screamed. 'Leave me alone.'

She tried to get up, but the pain was too much and she slumped back in the armchair. At that moment, the front door flew open and Constable Bowery was struck with tremendous violence by a flailing fist. Before he could respond, Slevin was pinned to the chair by several men who tore through the back door with the force of a hurricane. Within a few seconds he was staring at the sharpened blade of a hunting knife as it moved ever closer to his throat.

5

Benjamin waited for Herbert to arrive from Mrs O'Halloran's.

Herbert had complained of a headache and severe tiredness, and so their good landlady had allowed him to return to his room once he had breakfasted. During the night, he and Benjamin had slept together for the first time, and they had giggled and joked about having first-night nerves. Then the warmth, the proximity of their bodies and the heated embraces that seemed to go on for ever, had combined with the still-lingering sense of elation at their first-night success to give both of them a feeling of not just liberation but wild abandon. Herbert had been drunk, of course, but that made him no less attentive, and the night had passed so quickly that it had come as quite a shock when Mrs O'Halloran had knocked on Benjamin's door with her veiled admonition.

They had giggled almost like schoolchildren as her heavy tread receded, and, after Benjamin had carefully checked that the landing was clear, Herbert had stolen back to his own room.

The night had made Benjamin feel much younger, given him a sensation of well-being that was almost intoxicating. He had not demurred when, with a conspiratorial wink, Herbert had told Mrs O'Halloran of his mythical headache.

'I just need some bloody sleep,' he had whispered in Benjamin's ear when she left the small front room. 'I'll be along later.'

So instead of catching the omnibus into town, Benjamin had felt a good brisk walk would be in order, his mood still one of such contentment that it was all he could do to refrain from smiling inanely at anyone who passed him.

He should have known it wouldn't last.

As he sat in the front row of the empty theatre, gazing up at the stage and the painted scene depicting the garden at the Grange where Will Denver is finally and happily restored to his family and all wrongs have been righted, he felt his earlier elation transform itself into a dark presentiment of sadness.

Herbert had lied to him.

'And how's Mr Koller this morning, sir?' the stage-doorman had asked as he entered the theatre by the side entrance.

'He is very well, Norman,' Benjamin had replied jovially.

'Must have the constitution of a lion, then.'

Benjamin frowned. 'What do you mean?'

'Well, he seemed quite partial to the stout. Quite partial.'

'Stout? What on earth are you talking about, man?'

So the stage-doorman told him.

It was always the way, wasn't it? Was it for ever his life's curse that any joy should be merely ephemeral, like the flash of lightning that inevitably heralds the storm? Back in London there had been a succession of young men – stage-hands, aspiring actors, even a dramatist for one delicious summer – yet they all flared brilliantly like a thousand lucifers until the inevitable darkness came. Convention, fear of discovery, leading to the inevitable shame of exposure and incarceration, combined to turn burning passion into cold feet.

Until Herbert. They had been together now for two months – secretly, of course. Yet until last night they had never fully consummated their feelings. Wasn't it the cruellest of ironies that such glorious abandon should be followed by suspicion and betrayal?

Questions buzzed around his brain like persistent and angry wasps. He recalled their heated words of the previous night, as Herbert, accusing him of dallying with one of the supers, had suddenly stormed out of the reception. And before he could give chase, that poltroon of a mayor had insisted on introducing him to a succession of colliery owners, bankers and 'eminent merchants'. The mayor had then insisted on arranging for a hackney to be brought 'at the town's expense', and he had been beside himself with worry as he clattered through the thick fog with Jonathan Keele's words of warning ringing in his ears, only to find Herbert looming out of the fog like an apparition, walking hurriedly along Darlington Street, a few doors away from Mrs O'Halloran's.

'Where the hell have you been?' he had roared.

'I've been wandering round this Hades like a lost soul,' Herbert had snapped. 'I wanted to be alone.'

'Alone!' He had almost fallen out of the cab in his haste and his anger. As the carriage rattled off into the oblivion of mist, he had felt the strongest of urges to throttle the young swine.

But then Herbert had smiled. Such a disarming smile!

'Alone, Benjie, because I wanted to be sure.'

'Sure? Sure about what?'

'About what I want us to do when you invite me into your bed.'

He would remember those words, uttered with such gentleness, such passion, for the rest of his life. They had entered the house then, making sure to sound the closing of both their doors, before Herbert came silently into his room, into his bed, and into his arms.

He heard footsteps backstage, and braced himself for what he must do. From the wings came Herbert's tall, familiar figure, and he strolled on stage with that casual, lithesome confidence that just stopped short of a swagger.

'Benjie! What on earth are you doing down there? We did the acoustic test yesterday, remember?'

'Yes. No, Herbert, please don't come down. Not yet.' He raised an imperious hand, and Herbert, who was about to descend, stopped centre-stage.

'What's this? An audition? I thought you said last night I fitted the part perfectly.' There was a lascivious leer on his face, and a mocking tone in his voice that Benjamin hadn't heard before. Or had it been there all the time and he simply hadn't detected it?

'No. I just want to talk. Don't worry, there is no one here at the moment. The stage-hands aren't due for another hour.'

'You want to talk? Is that all, Benjie?'

Again, did his words contain parody, a trace of mockery? In the absence of the gas lighting in the auditorium, Herbert's face was shrouded in shadow, the only illumination coming from the wings.

'Last night,' Benjamin began.

'Oh, by all means let's discuss last night.' His voice – seductive and alluring, or teasing and derisive?

'I mean after the mayor's reception.'

'You had better explain, Benjie.'

'I have discovered that you weren't exactly honest with me.'

'*Discovered*? Good Lord, this sounds like the work of an informer. Or a tattle-tale. Yet again!'

'You told me you wished to be alone.'

'Correct.'

'But now I find out you went to a hotel.'

Herbert laughed loudly, raising his head and holding out his arms. When he spoke, it was in the words and the sharp Cockney tones of Henry Corkett. 'I say, you know – I'll just tell you how this happened – now it ain't my fault, it's my misfortune.'

Benjamin recognised the lines from *The Silver King*, at the climax of the play, where young Corkett is caught red-handed with Lady Blanche Wynter's jewels and taken into custody by Detective Baxter. 'It would become you better, Herbert, if you refrained from frivolity and simply told me the truth.'

In spite of the exhortation to remain where he was, Herbert took a sudden run towards the orchestra pit and overleaped it with amazing agility. Benjamin gasped at the physical audacity of the move.

'Now then,' Herbert moved along the row of seats until he came to the one beside Benjamin. 'May I?'

Benjamin nodded, thrown somewhat by the display of gymnastics he had just witnessed.

'First of all, who let the cat out of the bag, shall we say?'

'I was told in confidence.'

'Confidence? Ah. Wonderful word, that.'

'I simply want to know why you went to the Royal Hotel, which lies, incidentally, in the opposite direction to Darlington Street and the bed we shared in the early hours . . .'

'I wished to be anonymous. Alone. Where I could allow myself to become one of the audience. Before assuming a role I have wanted for so long now.' He grinned salaciously. 'A part I have longed for.'

'But you didn't tell me.'

'Why on earth should I?' He leaned closer so that his voice became a whisper. 'Do you want me to admit that I was nervous? That I really did have first-night nerves? And I needed a drink to steady myself. Is that what you want? Because it's true. I did need a drink. As I told you last night, I have never done what we did.'

Benjamin looked down into the darkness.

'Well, then. Allow me sometimes to breathe, Benjie. Besides, you know there are times when I need to be away from those I am working alongside so closely. It's a form of release. Please don't be angry.' He placed a hand on Benjamin's clenched fist and stroked it slowly, curling his finger along each knuckle, opening out and caressing his palm in tiny, sensuous circles.

'I am not angry,' said Benjamin. It was barely a whisper. He glanced up at the stage, dark and soulless now, and felt his heart beat at a lighter pace. They would be alone for some time yet.

*

Despite the chill in the air, it felt good to be near the water. They passed several people along the canal bank, and were greeted with the occasional cheery wave from those piloting boats laden with coal or machinery. The sun was shining, and there was a crisp layer of frost on the ground. In the far distance, the sky adopted a different, darker hue, carrying with it the threat of snow. When they spoke, tiny billows of breath cloud bore testament to the cold, but it didn't seem to matter to the two members of the Morgan-Drew Theatre Company.

'Do you feel guilty, my darling?' Susan Coupe asked as he removed the telegram from his pocket, wrapped it tightly around the heavy weight he had brought for the purpose, and hurled it into the canal. They both watched it sink slowly into the dark waters.

'Of course not,' James Shorton replied.

'And when we get back, do you think our lives will change?'

'In some ways.'

'If she leaves you alone.'

'She will have no choice.'

'And then truly we'll be free?'

'Truly.'

She turned her gaze to her left, and saw the dark waters of the canal lap against the high stone bank. Mrs James Shorton. And there was the tantalising prospect of joining Henry Irving at the Royal Lyceum, where he had promised her the finest opportunities, perhaps Desdemona, or Ophelia, if Miss Ellen Terry were ever indisposed. And to sail the Atlantic with Irving's company, perhaps with James at her side and similarly favoured by the great man! She breathed a deep sigh of contentment, and placed her head on James's shoulder once more.

James felt the light pressure, and then he too took a deep breath, but it wasn't one of contentment. He was adept at concealing what was really on his mind, and he did so now, even though it was quite a simple matter to fool someone so filled with optimism. In a way, he was desperate to leave this place and return to London, but they had further engagements to be fulfilled before that. There were things he couldn't really talk to Susan about. Whenever he broached the painful subject she reverted to the clam-like creature she had once been before they met and fell in love. But there would come a time when they would have to discuss the matter with a frankness that hitherto they had avoided.

That he wanted her, he had no doubt. He loved her so much it burned him deep inside, a feeling so very different from what he had felt with Elizabeth.

Yes, there were things that had to be faced, and only when they confronted the obstacles to their union would they be truly free.

Susan, misconstruing his deep exhalation of breath, snuggled so close to him he could smell the sweet fragrance of her hair.

*

'Nah then!' the man snarled, thrusting the point of the knife against Slevin's throat. 'I'm just about bloody sick o' comin' 'ome an' seein' toerags in my house.'

Two men, one of whom had dealt Constable Bowery a powerful blow to the head, were standing with their backs to the front door, arms folded and faces stern. One of them had a long scar down his right cheek. These men would batter a man senseless and worse, Slevin reflected. The knife began to cut into his flesh and he winced in pain.

It was Violet Cowburn who literally saved his neck.

During the violent intrusion, she had sat there almost mesmerised by the rapid turn of events. But now she was suddenly alert, her voice filled with fear and loathing.

'I don't want to see any father o' mine swingin' on the end of a rope! He's a copper, for Christ's sake!'

'Aye,' said Billy Cowburn. 'I gathered that from yon mon's uniform.' He gave a sarcastic nod to the still recumbent and apparently unconscious Bowery.

'I told him it was an accident.'

'What was?'

'Me fallin' downstairs.'

'Oh aye. Accident!' He spat the word in Slevin's face. Slevin could smell the stale stench of beer on his breath. 'That why ye're here?'

Slevin blinked and swallowed hard as the knife-point was withdrawn a half-inch. 'Partly.'

'What the bloody hell does that mean? *Partly?*'

One of the men standing by the door walked over. 'No soldier boys now to protect yer arse, have ye?'

The mention of the military brought the knife back against Slevin's neck.

'We've come to ask just a few questions. But not about the . . . accident yesterday.'

'Well I reckon we should gut the swine an' throw him in the Duggy.'

The River Douglas, flowing down from Rivington Moor a few miles away, ran through the town until it joined the River Ribble at Preston. It could carry a corpse for miles at a forceful pace before it was detected, and even then it could for ever be swallowed up by the stronger currents of the Ribble.

'Dad. We don't want blood on that armchair, do we?'

'Why not? It was that bitch's any road. Doesn't matter to me.'

'All he wants is to have a quick chat wi' me. Not you. That so, mister?'

Slevin nodded. He could lie if she could.

'Let me an' Rodge take him out back,' said the one with the scar. 'That'll keep thi armchair clean, eh? Be like guttin' a rabbit.'

But before Cowburn could consider the proposition, there was an almighty roar and Slevin barely caught sight of Bowery's huge frame launching itself at the fellow left by the door. There was a sickening grunt and the loud splintering of both wood and bone as Bowery's fist slammed hard into the man's face, knocking him backwards with such force that he smashed through the closed door and landed with a shriek on the pavement outside. Within seconds Slevin hoisted his foot deep into his assailant's groin and Cowburn slumped to the floor, gripping his genitals and dropping the knife at the detective's feet. The scarred thug was slow to react, but when he saw Cowburn collapse in agony he too dropped to his knees and reached for the heavy iron poker that rested on the grate. He then swung around wildly, lashing out and catching Slevin hard on the back. Galvanised into a raging fury now, Slevin lowered his head and hurled himself at the man's midriff, landing just below his waist and causing him to stagger backwards, his large frame smashing against the mantelpiece and scattering the various ornaments and daguerrotypes. As the man straddled the coal fire now, Slevin dived between his outspread legs and scooped out the ash pan, filled with glowing lumps of coal, from beneath the grate. Gripping the hair at the back of the man's head, he raised the pan and slowly tipped its contents towards the man's face.

'One more move and I'll burn your eyes to kingdom come!'

The man froze, the scream in his throat withheld in terror.

'Now get me some bedsheets,' he snapped at Violet, who didn't stop to question the command. Mutely she left the room, casting a glance at the supine body on the pavement outside, where several women were already gathering.

Constable Bowery now grabbed Cowburn by the throat and raised him to his feet. The miner was still clinging to his genitals and groaning in agony.

'Best count 'em, pal,' said Bowery. 'At least you've still got yours though, eh?'

Cowburn was too dazed to comprehend anything that was said to him, and he just stood there, swaying.

Violet came downstairs clutching several sheets, which Slevin ordered her to tear into strips. Once she had completed the task, he gave Bowery the ash pan with instructions to 'ram the contents down his gullet' if the man so much as thought about moving. But Scarface too had lost the will to fight, and both he and Cowburn submitted meekly to the process of being tied around the arms and linked together with their groggy ally outside in a makeshift chain gang.

'Now then, Violet. If you want us to go easy on your beloved father here, you'll tell me what I want to know.'

'What?'

'The name of the man who was here with you yesterday afternoon.'

She looked at her father, bent double and muttering vile curses not unconnected with his genitalia. He was evidently in too much pain to take notice of anything his daughter had to say.

'It was him you said. Richard Throstle.'

'We'll need to talk at greater length, Violet. I'll come back later. You're in no condition to come to the station.'

'No!' she almost shouted the word. 'I'll come there. We've given the neighbours enough to gawk an' gossip at. I'll come with you.'

Before he could forestall her, she moved with agonising slowness to the small cupboard beneath the stairs where she obviously kept her outdoor coat.

'I'll be able to keep an eye on him,' she said, nodding at her father. 'Make sure you don't give him another good hidin' to pass the time on the way back to town.'

They stepped outside and walked in a straggled line to the end of Mort Street, where Slevin had ordered the carriage to wait. They were watched by a curious audience. There were muttered curses of 'Bloody Cowburns again, eh?' but she brushed them away with disdain, her head held high despite the spectacle she and her father were once again affording them all.

*

Dark shapes floated around in his head. He could see them, and every so often, when the shapes were brilliantly illuminated by the blast of an explosion, he wanted to warn the others, tell them that the blast was on its way and that a roaring fireball was rapidly searing its way down the long dark tunnels like a raging monster. If only he could warn the others working the seams farther down, past the fire doors and the thick wooden sprags holding the millions of tons of earth steady above them.

So he clapped. Once. Twice. Again. And again. And again. Clapped as loud as he could because that was the only sound he could make. Something had happened to his voice down there. A scorching, thick, cloying, bitter taste of dust was blocking his throat. So he clapped. That was how the Mines Rescue Team found him alive after three full days of darkness, total and utter blackness during which he cradled his brother's head and sang lullaby after lullaby, only placing it gently on the ground to clap, and clap, and clap. It was the sound of the clapping that drew them.

Now, Enoch Platt shuffled down the row of terraced houses, mumbling to himself and clapping his hands together whenever he passed a group of people. He wasn't mad. He knew that, even though they often looked at him with pity, or disgust, or even fear. No. Granted, he had seen things that would drive anyone mad. These were the dark shapes that he still saw. They were inside his head. If he passed a row of shops, with women standing outside clutching shopping baskets and sharing stories, he only had to turn his head to look at them, perhaps to begin to say 'Good morning' or 'How's your Tommy doin'?' and then the black clouds of dust would begin to swirl in front of him and make their faces grainy and unrecognisable, and he would be back down there with the blast about to return, holding Joseph's severed head in his arms.

A sharp clap, to tell them it was on its way.

They would turn away from him and he would shuffle on past

them, but not before he moved as close to their faces as he could, to get a good glimpse of their eyes through all this blackening, blinding dust. It was the eyes, he knew, that told him. How many eyes had he seen after the blast? With his lamp held high, and the black dust settling like dry rain all around, he had peered down at all their eyes, and some were open and some were closed, and he could tell straight away if some that were open would never close, and some that were closed would never open. And always, always, he saw his brother Joseph. The eyes, and the dust that settled on them. Tiny black spots on white.

Now, as Enoch came to the corner of Darlington Street and Warrington Lane he stopped beneath the railway bridge and leaned back against the dank walls. He liked it here. When he clapped, the sound echoed so loudly everyone in Wigan must hear it. But he didn't like it when the trains came and he was standing under the bridge. Then he was forced to cover his ears.

As he stood there, he could hear the sounds of a man and a woman, talking and laughing. He couldn't see them, not yet, and at first he thought they were the sounds in his head, from the time when the blast changed everything. But then he told himself, 'Don't be so daft, Enoch. No bloody women down t'pit. Not any more. Pit brow, now. Just t'pit brow. It was dad as worked wi' women. It was dad as told him an' their Joe 'bout the tricks the sluts got up to.'

Just as the thought came to him, two figures appeared from the dust-stained brickwork to his left.

A man and a woman. No. A man and a young lass. Nice young lass, too. Not a slut, any road.

They didn't see him at first, and he watched them with interest as they strolled past, heading towards Warrington Lane. But then, as they got closer, he could see the black dustclouds swirling around them, and he had to warn them, even the young lass who shouldn't really be down here in the pit. So he jumped in front of them and clapped as loudly as he could.

The lass screamed. It echoed off the walls of the bridge and Enoch rushed towards them both to check their eyes, to see if they had been caught by the blast and were to live, or if they were caught by the blast and were to die. The lass cowered behind the young man and continued to scream, while her defender stood erect and raised his hands to ward off the attack from Enoch Platt. But Enoch was strong, and he grabbed both hands, forcing them downwards while at the same time thrusting his face so close to the man that he could smell the soap on his skin. Then, as the man struggled in vain to free his hands, and as the young lass whimpered behind him, Enoch stared long and hard into his eyes. Then, slowly, he let go of the hands and stepped back, clapping his hands together once more as the coal dust began slowly to disperse.

Thank God the man wasn't dead, thought Enoch. You could tell by the eyes.

*

Georgina Throstle had had a busy afternoon. First, she had gone across Standishgate and down King Street to the Public Hall, where she made certain checks on the cameras and the slides that Richard had kept locked away in the sturdy safe the proprietor had thoughtfully provided. As she suspected, one of the boxes containing a series of slides was labelled 'Rose Blossoms'. Even holding the boxed set in her hands made her feel afraid. Not only afraid, though – it filled her with guilt, as she recalled her own part in creating the slides.

Hastily she replaced the slides, locked the safe with a sigh and left the small office.

A brief meeting with Mr Worswick had also been necessary to discuss the arrangements for the rest of the week. She had assured him that, with the help of her husband's several assistants, she would be more than capable of mounting the same spectacular show they had hitherto witnessed.

109

'The conventions of mourning must of force yield to one's commitments,' she had told him. 'After our programme has ended, I will enter full mourning, and pay my dear husband the respect he deserves.'

'Begging your pardon, ma'am, and without wishing to offend, but one of the reasons for your show's tremendous success during the past week has been the . . . commentary . . . provided by your dear husband.'

Georgina had bestowed upon him her most beatific smile, necessarily tinged with sadness. 'Oh, that's not an insurmountable obstacle, I can assure you.'

'But I don't think . . .'

'I repeat, it is not an obstacle. My husband will be very proud of his replacement.'

'But a woman's . . . voice, shall we say, will perhaps fail to . . .'

'Oh, you misunderstand! It will not be I who takes on the role. It will be someone who will be with us by tomorrow.'

'And who will that be, ma'am?'

'A man who will, of course, be fully conversant with the scripted commentary written by my husband, and more than capable of instilling the requisite fear in an audience.'

Next, she had retraced her steps along King Street to Ranicar's, a few yards away from the parish church gates. There she stood for a few minutes, gathering her thoughts and her emotions for the ordeal she would face once she set foot in this particular emporium. On the dark framed windows ran the legend:

RANICAR & SON
Family Mourning in Great Variety

She composed herself and walked up the few steps, where she was pleased to see one of the shop assistants waiting with the door open and a respectfully sombre expression on his face. She wondered if they had parramatta silk? She so hated bombazine.

*

A few flakes of snow were beginning to fall as the carriage disgorged its passengers on the steps of the Wigan Borough Police Station. Slevin had travelled on top alongside Violet, with Bowery keeping a watchful eye on the three men trussed tightly on the seats inside.

Within minutes Violet had been helped into Slevin's tiny office and given a steaming hot mug of tea. The journey had been excruciatingly painful for her, and she had winced with agony on more than one occasion as the carriage heaved from side to side.

Two of the ruffians were locked in the cells below ground level, while Billy Cowburn was escorted to a small room used by Sergeant Slevin for interview purposes.

There was a small wooden desk, blackened with age, and two wooden chairs. Set high in the wall facing the door was a small barred window, showing only the rooftops of the buildings opposite, and the darkening sky, now heavy with snow.

When his prisoner had been seated, with a glowering Constable Bowery standing behind him and longing for the man to prove intractable, Slevin sat opposite him and leaned forward.

'Now then, Billy. What's this all about, eh?'

'Tha's squashed me balls. They're black an' bloody blue.'

'I'll take your word for it. But why the rough treatment, Billy? Why react like that?'

'When I heard voices I thought that posh bugger had come back.'

'You mean, the man who was with your daughter yesterday?'

'Aye. Besides, when I caught sight o' that fat sod's uniform I just saw red.'

Slevin saw Constable Bowery shift his weight from one foot to another, as if he were taking aim.

'Some of your lads give me an' my mates a good hammerin' at Golborne.'

Slevin recalled the incident from the recent strike, where

a large-scale riot had broken out a few miles out of town, at Golborne Colliery. Every policeman from miles around had been despatched to quell the disturbance in any way they could. He himself had been there and cracked a few skulls himself. It wasn't his proudest moment.

'Let's talk about yesterday, then.'

'Our Vi says she fell downstairs.'

'I don't mean what happened at home. I mean what happened afterwards.'

'Afterwards?' Cowburn frowned. 'You mean when I ran off? Give them soft buggers the slip?'

Again, a movement from behind the prisoner.

'No, Billy. I mean first of all the time between Violet's . . . accident, and the time you eluded capture.'

Cowburn looked perplexed. 'I don't know what you're on about.'

'The man you chased?'

'Oh, that smarmy bastard. Aye, I chased him right enough. I think he shit himself he ran that fast. Any road, I lost him. But I'll know the bastard again. An' he'll know me an' all. Our Vi's nowt but a lass.'

'So when you escaped the feeble efforts of my constables to arrest you, where did you go then?'

"I wasn't hangin' round. So I went to George's. Lives in Scholes.'

'George?'

'Him with the scar.'

'Then what?'

'What d'ye mean, "then what"? Me an' him went out. Had a few drinks. Well, more than a few. I talked him into takin' a holy day so we could have another session. Met up wi' Rodge.'

'Oh. The third musketeer.'

'Third what?'

'Never mind. Where did you go last night? For a drink?'

Cowburn laughed. 'Where didn't we go? You don't go thirsty up Scholes.'

'I need to know where you were last night. Especially late on.'

Now Cowburn's eyes narrowed and he licked his lips nervously. 'What the bloody hell for?'

'That man you chased was found murdered last night.'

'What?'

'In a very brutal manner. Do you see now how important it is that you co-operate fully? You were heard by half of Mort Street threatening to gut him like a kipper.'

Suddenly Cowburn went even paler than normal, and the surly resentment that had burned in his eyes throughout the interview was now snuffed out, to be replaced by the cold chill of fear. His hand moved involuntarily towards his throat, as if he could already feel the rough fibres of a rope tightening around his neck.

*

'How's me dad?'

'Co-operating,' Slevin said as he sat down beside Violet. He spoke to her gently, seeing a very frightened and troubled girl, not much more than a child.

'He . . . he couldn't kill anybody, you know.'

He nodded, knowing full well that Billy Cowburn did indeed have it in him to commit murder.

'I really want to talk to you about Richard Throstle, Violet.'

She looked down at her hands that still grasped the mug, even though she had long since drained it of its contents.

'The man who was murdered. I need to know anything you can tell me about him.'

'Such as?'

'How long have you known him?'

She shifted in her seat. 'A few months.'

'Where did you meet him? Apparently he came from Leeds.'

'In Bolton.'

'Bolton? What on earth were you doing in Bolton?'

Again she moved in the chair and raised her eyes to the ceiling. 'I just went there . . . caught the train and went there.'

'Why?'

When she spoke he saw tears begin to form in her eyes. 'Since she left – my mother, that is – it's not been easy at our house.'

'Why did she leave?'

'Ran off wi' a soldier. One o' them sent here durin' the lock-out.'

'I see.' Yet another reason for Billy Cowburn's fury.

'We were starvin'. An' me dad was gettin' more an' more – well, you've seen what he's like. He'd sit in that chair for hours, just starin' at the flames. Then I had this idea.'

'What was that?' he asked, although he reckoned he already knew the answer.

'Nobody knows me in Bolton, do they?' she said, accepting the look in his eyes that showed understanding. And, she was surprised to see, some compassion.

'And that's how you met Mr Throstle?'

'Yes.'

'Was it simply a . . . a financial arrangement?'

She swallowed and looked out of the small window that overlooked King Street in the distance.

'Violet? Did you do it just for the money?'

'Oh, the money. I suppose. And it felt nice, you know? Havin' someone cuddle me an' make me feel wanted.' She looked at him with a new intensity, as though willing him to see inside her soul. 'Any road, he was the only one. Said he'd give me enough money as long as I kept meself for him. Just for him. Though there were some things I drew the line at.' She stopped suddenly and averted her gaze.

Slevin had the feeling she was keeping something back.

'Such as, Violet?'

'You don't expect me to describe them in detail, do you?'

But Slevin wouldn't allow her to hide behind feminine modesty.

'No, I don't want chapter and verse, Violet. But I am a policeman and a man of the world, so there's nothing you can say that can shock me, I assure you. Why don't you just tell me what sort of thing Mr Throstle demanded that you had the good sense to refuse to do?'

She shook her head violently. 'I can't.'

'We may have to charge your father with attempted murder, you know.'

'What?'

'Well, he did hold a knife to the throat of a police officer in the course of his duties.'

Violet shivered and started to sob.

'He would probably serve his time in Strangeways,' Slevin went on relentlessly. 'Now that *is* a cold place, and no mistake. They say there's more die in there of pneumonia than of starvation, but it's a close-run thing.'

When she raised her face to him it was streaked with tears, and he felt a pang of guilt, once more seeing the child she still wanted to be.

'An' if I tell you, you'll let him go?'

'If he's innocent of Throstle's murder, Violet. If he can prove where he was and what he was up to last night.'

She sat upright, placing both her hands on the desk top, and held her head high. Perhaps she was trying to disguise her shame at what she was about to relate by an appearance of strength. Slowly, she began to speak, and as her tale unfolded the temperature in the small office became very cold indeed. Slevin listened, first with calm patience, then with a growing sense of outrage.

Man of the world or not, when she had finished telling him, he was shocked to his very marrow.

*

115

Herbert patted Benjamin on the back as they crossed the street, the grim edifice of the Wigan Borough Police Station looming behind them, and said, 'That's the ticket!'

'I realise I cannot keep you caged, like a pet bird.'

'Of course not.'

'And that there are times when you need to be alone. I accept that.'

'Eminently kind and sensible.'

The snow was falling heavily by now, and people rushed past them with their faces buried deep in upturned collars or flimsily wrapped shawls, anxious to reach home. The pair walked quickly down the narrow passageway that led to the stage door.

Once inside, when they reached the auditorium they found most of the company already there, standing around on stage in small groups, their voices low and subdued. The euphoria of the previous night was now a mere memory.

'What's this?' Benjamin opened his arms and spread them wide.

Jonathan Keele, who as the oldest member of the company appeared to have been elected as its spokesman, stepped forward. 'Some of our group are a trifle worried, Benjamin.'

'Worried? About what?'

'You have heard about the murder, no doubt?'

'Murder?' This, apparently, was news to Benjamin. He looked quickly at Herbert, who merely shrugged his ignorance.

'In the Royal Hotel.'

'I see.'

'And according to my landlady, whose son works at the Royal, it was a murder of particular brutality.'

Benjamin frowned. 'Who was the victim?'

'Apparently he is the one who has been showing the magic lantern *Phantasmagoria* in the Public Hall.' Jonathan looked directly at Herbert. 'You knew him, didn't you, Herbert?'

'I read the posters, Jonathan. Don't we all?' Herbert smiled thinly at Benjamin, who had been watching him closely.

Some of the group shifted their weight uneasily.

Belle Greave spoke up. 'The point is, Benjamin, that it is a murder. And many of us are in, shall we say, less than secure lodgings.'

'But apart from Jonathan, who has always made separate arrangements, no one is alone,' said Benjamin. 'Every one of us shares an address. I would never leave one of my company out on a limb.'

The attempt at reassurance was hardly a success, judging from the worried expressions, especially on the faces of the female members of the company.

It was Herbert who spoke next. 'Wigan is hardly Whitechapel.'

Belle Greave added, 'It's hardly Belgravia, either.'

Several of the female members of the group murmured in agreement.

Susan Coupe then spoke, her face flushed with worry. 'I happened to meet James this afternoon. I had taken a stroll along the canal bank . . . Isn't that right, James?'

The others all turned to the leading actress and gave her curious glances, each of them wondering what on earth the girl was on about.

'Quite right,' Shorton agreed. He looked at Miss Coupe for permission to continue the story, and when she gave an assenting nod, he did so. 'I decided to escort Miss Coupe back to her lodgings, and I must say it was rather fortuitous that I did so.'

'Why?' asked Benjamin, articulating the question on all their lips.

'Because we were attacked.'

'Attacked?' The word spread through the company with consternation.

'Yes. Attacked,' said Susan. 'Some lunatic grabbed me and made to attack me.'

'What happened?'

'Why, James stood up to him, and after a few seconds the brigand ran off, clapping his hands together like a madman.'

'Did you inform the police?'

Shorton and Susan exchanged glances.

'No, we did not,' said Shorton.

'Why not?'

'Because there was nothing taken and it was obvious the man was simply deranged.'

Benjamin cleared his throat. 'I rather think we must inform the police if a . . .'

'There is no point, Benjamin.' It was Susan who interrupted him. 'What *is* the point is that we are staying in a dangerous place and we need assurances that we will be safe when we leave the theatre tonight.'

Benjamin gave his most paternally reassuring smile. 'I can assure each and every one of you that there is nothing to be afraid of. The Wigan police force is among the finest in the land. Why, only last night I met the chief constable himself, Captain Bell, who was at the opening night.'

'Perhaps he was applauding at the actual moment of the murder, eh?' said Jonathan Keele, with a wry glance at the others.

'He inspires confidence,' Benjamin declaimed grandly.

'And the murder took place much later!' Herbert added.

Jonathan looked at him coolly. 'How do you know that, Herbert?'

The young man gave a dismissive smile. He had been uncharacteristically subdued for a few minutes, but now he seemed to have recovered his equilibrium. 'Oh, one hears things by the by. Come, surely we can trust Benjamin to look after us? I doubt if a ghoul is prowling the streets looking for travelling thespians. As for the chappie who accosted our leading players, surely he recognised you and was seeking an autograph? I am told Edmund Kean's hand fetches three guineas.'

'We need to be very vigilant,' said Jonathan, giving Herbert a venomous look. 'And Benjamin, you need to ensure no member of the company leaves alone.'

'That is precisely my feeling, Jonathan.' He surveyed the group. 'Is that agreed, my friends? We must never be alone.'

Susan Coupe gave James Shorton a small nod.

'There is one other thing,' said Jonathan, who felt the meeting hadn't exactly gone to plan.

'What now?'

'In case you hadn't noticed, the theatre, from the tiny and totally inadequate privy at the rear to the grand sweep of the upper circle, is freezing.'

'In a few short hours this theatre will once more be full,' said the actor-manager with a dismissive wave of the hand. 'Audiences bring their own heat.'

'But we can see our breath as we speak!' said someone standing at the rear of the group.

There was a muttering of agreement, and Benjamin could sense the moment had come for firm action. The last thing he needed was a rebellious and miserable ensemble. 'I propose a grand feast at the Silver Grid Dining Rooms after tonight's show – with drinks included.'

It was a magnanimous and totally unexpected gesture and struck them like a bolt from heaven itself. They would normally have retired to the small salon in the theatre for a few desultory drinks before going back to their respective lodgings, the communal get-together being usually reserved for the last night, when they could finally relax and perhaps over-indulge before catching the train to their next engagement the following morning. It also had the added attraction of providing safety in numbers.

'That is a very generous gesture, Benjamin,' Jonathan Keele said, and turned to the others, who appeared to agree with their spokesman.

'Good. That's settled, then. Now we must get backstage and prepare to transform ourselves once more.'

Their protest drowned at birth, the company began to move off to the wings. Benjamin stayed for a while to savour the moment. Of course the dinner would make quite a dent in his pocket, but it would be worth it. Quite by chance, their little demonstration had played wonderfully into his hands. He couldn't have managed it better if he had scripted it himself.

6

Slevin watched Violet walk slowly and painfully down the station steps and into the swirling snow. He was about to return to the cells to resume his questioning of Cowburn when a small boy rushed from nowhere and touched his flat cap.

'You Slevin?' he asked, hardly able to catch his breath.

'I'm Detective Sergeant Slevin, yes.'

The boy reached into his pocket and took out a small envelope. He shoved it towards Slevin, who reached down and took it.

'It's from Dr Bentham,' he said to himself. 'Good lad.'

'Aye,' the boy panted. 'He said you'd be grateful.'

'How grateful did the good doctor say I'd be?'

'A bob?'

A response born more of wishful thinking than truth, Slevin reflected. 'Here's a tanner.'

With a dramatic sigh the young Hermes reached up, snatched the proffered coin and scooted back down the steps with a hasty 'Thanks!'

Back in his office, he slit open the envelope and read its contents. Bentham's style was curt and to the point. He wasn't a man who expended much energy on any of the social graces, his employment of a street urchin as a courier being a prime example.

Slevin,

Mixture standard Chlorodyne, though possibly a tad too much chloroform mixed with the morphine.

P.M. on Mr R. Throstle. Suffocation prior to death.

Asbestos dust in nasal passage and around throat. Cause of death: multiple stab wounds generating huge loss of blood. Removal of genitalia main cause of blood loss. Official Report to follow.

So, nothing unusual about the mixture Richard Throstle had obtained for his wife. The slightly excessive chloroform might explain why Georgina Throstle lay undisturbed while her husband was being butchered. Perhaps it was a blessing that she had lain senseless during that time.

But what was he to make of the asbestos dust found in the nose and around the throat? Had the murderer held something covered in asbestos to his face, ensuring the suffocation before mutilation? The suffocation hadn't apparently been sufficient to kill the victim, just render him unconscious so that the villain could go about the ghastly operation freely.

He felt sure there hadn't been anything remotely composed of asbestos in the room – but he would have the room checked once more.

He left the office and walked down the short flight of steps that led to the canteen. There he found Constable Bowery seated at a table drinking a mug of tea, holding court – as he usually did – with the younger and more impressionable constables.

'Constable Bowery!'

Bowery spilled some of the tea on the wooden table. 'You made me jump, sergeant.'

'Good. Perhaps we can conclude the interviews with our main musketeer.'

Within minutes, they once again faced Billy Cowburn, who was by now looking cold and miserable.

'Look,' he said, putting his blackened hands together as if in prayer, 'I chased the swine, an' if I'd have caught him I'd've wrung his bloody neck. No question, mood I was in. But what would you've done, sergeant, eh? You come home an' you find a bloody toff in your daughter's bedroom an' her half-naked! What did you think I'd do? Go down an' make him a bacon butty?'

Slevin, hiding his amusement at the unlikely scenario, gave a grave shake of the head.

'So I chased the bugger, halfway to Wigan. Then he jumps on a passin' tram an' all that swine does is give me a wave. Imagine that, eh? A bloody wave! I'd've shoved his arm up his arse sideways if I could've reached him. But I couldn't.'

'What about last night?'

'I . . . give them bobbies the slip. Then I went up to Scholes like I said. We went on a bender, me an' George an' Rodge. I told 'em about the bastard I'd caught with our Vi.'

'Where did you go?'

He let out an exasperated breath. 'Started off in t'Windmill, then t'Roebuck, then th'Harp, then t'Crown an' Sceptre, then t'Shamrock, then th'Angel . . . .then I lost track after that. Might've tried one in t'Clock Face farther down, but I'm not all that sure. I was a bit oiled by then.'

With over seventy public houses in Scholes, the three of them had no shortage of opportunities not only to get very drunk indeed, but also to devise some sort of brutal and bloodthirsty revenge on the defiler of Violet Cowburn. What was also significant was the drinking route these men took – they had started at the farther end of Scholes, but with each subsequent port of call they were moving closer to the town centre. And the Royal Hotel.

'What time did you get back to your friend George's house?'

He shrugged his shoulders and gave a snort of helplessness.

Back in his office, Slevin looked at Constable Bowery and thought for a long while before putting words to his thoughts. Eventually he said, 'He has the best of motives, doesn't he?'

'Aye, he does, sergeant.'

'And he admits that the three of them at least discussed the possibility of doing the deed.'

123

'And the more they yapped, the more they planned, I reckon.'

'Go on.'

'Well, they're not far from the town centre, not far from the Royal. They could've got in some way, through the kitchen at back, say, an' then crept upstairs an' sliced off his John Willy before you could say Bob's your uncle.'

It was dark outside now, and the snow had temporarily deteriorated into a sort of haphazard flurry. Slevin noticed the yellow flame of the gas lamp opposite, dull and flaring occasionally as the wind crept through the tiny gaps in the glass bowl.

'One thing puzzles me though.'

'What's that, sergeant?'

'There was no sign of Throstle's door being forced. The lock was intact, which it certainly would not have been if Cowburn and his allies had barged their drunken way in.'

'So how *did* the murderer get in?'

'Three possibilities. One, Mrs Throstle left the door unlocked after she got up to admit her husband. Perhaps she didn't relock the door in all the – shall we say, excitement? – at her husband's entry into the room. Besides which, she was rendered rather groggy by the Chlorodyne.'

Bowery narrowed his eyes to picture the scene Sergeant Slevin had described. 'Stroke of luck for the murderer if she left it unlocked.'

'Or whoever entered the room had a key of their own, opened the door silently while the husband and wife were lying there, Throstle in a drunken stupor and his good wife in a drugged sleep enhanced by the Chlorodyne and the chloroform it contained.'

'But where would anyone get another key to fit that lock?'

'Hotel manager, or any of the night staff. But I must admit that is highly unlikely. It would throw them under immediate suspicion if they asked for the pass key.'

'What's the third possibility?'

'That the murderer was already inside the room, had been there all the time.'

'What? You mean, like hidin' in a wardrobe or summat? Waitin' to pounce? That's a bit unlikely, ain't it, sergeant? I mean, she must have put her coat back in there when she got to the room. And even if she didn't, what if the Devil made a noise while Mrs Throstle was lying there an' before her husband came to bed? Nah. That's a risky one an' no mistake.'

'I said it's possible the murderer was already in the room, constable. I said nothing about anyone hiding in the wardrobe.'

Bowery frowned. 'But if he was already in the room, and not in t'wardrobe, where exactly would the murderer be then? Under the bloody bed!'

'Not *under it*, constable. No.'

A look of surprise spread over Jimmy Bowery's face as the implications set in.

'You mean his wife did him in?'

'As I say,' Slevin went on without waiting for his constable's machinery of logic to whirr into action. 'Three possibilities. And there may be a fourth we haven't even considered yet.'

'Bloody hell!'

'Still, let's take one step at a time. At the moment we have a suspect and possible accomplices in custody, don't we?'

'Do we keep him in, sergeant? Let the devil sweat a bit longer?'

Slevin nodded. 'I suppose we'll have to.'

He stood up and told Constable Bowery to sign off for the night. There was nothing they could do for the moment.

'Does that mean we can forget lookin' all round town for the card sharps, sergeant? Them as probably don't exist?'

'We'll leave them in the realm of fantasy for the moment, constable. Now go home.'

After Bowery left the room, Slevin stood at the window and saw, not the dying flakes of snow dropping listlessly from the blackness, but his own reflection gazing at him with more than a hint of accusation. He had promised Violet Cowburn her father would be set free and he had broken that promise. But it would be folly to release him just now.

He thought also of the grieving widow, Georgina Throstle. Was she even now alone and wretchedly bereft in the solitude of her hotel room? She had told him she would remain in town for the foreseeable future, until a resolution of some kind could be found and she could take her husband's body back to Leeds. Surely an onerous and melancholy task in itself.

But then he thought of her jewellery. The idealised image of a black-clad widow keening over her loss dissolved, to be replaced by a cold, heartless woman interested only in retaining her material possessions. Which was the true image? Or was it somewhere in between? With a husband who was at the very least a philanderer and probably (if what Violet Cowburn had told him was true) something much worse, was this a woman capable of such a gruesome act?

He had already seen the thick black lettering pasted across the advertisement for the Public Hall *Phantasmagoria:*

TONIGHT'S PERFORMANCE CANCELLED

OWING TO UNFORESEEN CIRCUMSTANCES.

SPECIAL MEMORIAL PERFORMANCE TOMORROW NIGHT!

VERY FEW TICKETS LEFT!

It was beyond his understanding how she could continue with any performance under the 'unforeseen circumstances'. And what on earth was a 'memorial performance' if it wasn't a despicable way of profiteering from murder?

Slevin left the room in darkness and was making his way along the corridor and out of the station when he heard the familiar voice of the chief constable booming behind him.

'Isn't it time you gave me your report on this damnable crime, Detective Sergeant Slevin?'

*

Outside room number four, the young boy adjusted the collar of his Post Office uniform, making sure his silver-plated numbers were visible, and knocked loudly.

He heard what sounded like drawers closing from inside the room, and then the door swung open to reveal a tall, graceful and beautiful woman dressed in black.

'Telegram, ma'am, at your service!' He snapped his heels together and sharply handed over the telegram. He gave her a sharp salute and stood back, hands clasped behind his back and chin held high.

Georgina Throstle opened the missive and read quickly. Then she frowned and whispered to herself the single word 'Tomorrow!' As soon as she uttered the word, the messenger's heart sank. They rarely gave a tip when the news was bad.

She mumbled something he couldn't catch and turned her back on him, pushing the door shut with a backward swing of her hand.

Georgina Throstle slumped in her chair and wept. A wave of fatalism overwhelmed her as the events of the previous twenty-four hours pulled her down into darkness. Her face was beginning to pulsate with each successive sob, and she looked around the table, searching for her salvation. Where in God's name had she put that bottle?

She stood and looked around. The pain was growing now, and she could feel the nerves tingling down the side of her face as if they were gleefully anticipating their reawakening.

Then she remembered. That awful, over-zealous policeman had taken it. She could feel her breath coming in spasms. First the telegram from Edward and now this.

She ran to the door and gripped the handle. But where could she go? Rush out and make a dash for the nearest chemist? It would hardly be seemly, clad as she was in these ridiculous widow's weeds.

No. She would control herself and stroll slowly, with a suitably sombre expression on her face, and she would instruct the desk to send out for an analgesic. What was the potion called? Chlorodyne. That was it. She drew the black veil over her face and opened the door.

She gasped as out of the shadows of the corridor a dark figure loomed over her, with one arm raised and ready to strike.

*

'Good Lord!'

Captain Bell had listened with increasing disbelief as Detective Sergeant Slevin recounted the tale he had been told by Violet Cowburn. That such evil existed in this world! Not only that, but the very idea of people paying money to see those vile images!

'We're entering a new Dark Age, sergeant,' he said at last. He peered intently at his sergeant for a few seconds. 'Do you believe her?'

'Yes, sir. I do. The girl doesn't have the imagination – nor, do I think, the wickedness – to invent such things.'

'But to suborn women, some of them young girls, for God's sake! No older than twelve, you say?'

Slevin opened his hands in sad assent.

'And have them pose in such abominable ways – for the delectation of wealthy and supposedly respectable gentlemen – why, I must confess I am speechless.'

'Miss Cowburn admits she posed in highly improper tableaux. And she says she saw several such girls, sweet, innocent little girls taken not only from the streets but from, shall we say, compliant families. Children with whom she was expected to consort.'

'That is the aspect of the whole affair that I simply cannot believe. No father with any spark of decency would agree to such a thing. There, at least, the girl must be romancing, eh?'

Slevin shook his head. 'I really can't say, sir. But whatever the truth about Mr Throstle is, at least he will do no more harm to

128

young girls. And this information may provide us with another motive.'

'Vengeful females?'

'Or their husbands, fiancés – or even fathers. You know how violently Cowburn reacted when he found his daughter *in flagrante*.'

'Where are these vile photographs?'

'I don't know. I intend to ask Mrs Throstle.'

'Good grief, man! You surely don't think *she* had any knowledge of such goings on, do you?'

Slevin shrugged. 'No idea, sir. But as I say, I intend to ask.'

Captain Bell took a deep breath and spoke in his most sonorous tones. 'Remember that she is a bereaved woman, sergeant.'

'I will be discreet, sir.'

'And sensitive, Sergeant Slevin. Discretion wrapped in sensitivity. Is that understood?'

'Of course, sir.'

*

It was almost six-thirty – sixty short minutes to curtain-up – and Benjamin felt an uncomfortable dryness in his throat.

Where the devil was Herbert?

He had gone around the various dressing-rooms and he was nowhere to be found. Jonathan Keele, fully made up and pacing the corridor with head bowed and hands firmly pressed against his midriff, merely shook his head when Benjamin asked if he had seen the wayward boy, while Susan Coupe sat facing her mirror with a distant expression on her face.

'He's probably gone out for some fresh air,' suggested Belle Greave.

'Fresh air?' Benjamin had boomed. 'In Wigan?'

He stormed onto the dimly lit stage and peered through the curtain at the auditorium. It was already beginning to fill. At other times he would have beamed with satisfaction at the sight and the fact that these patrons had braved foul weather to be here tonight. But there would be no point if one of the main characters went missing. Young Toby, Herbert's understudy, was capable and willing enough, it was true. But he had come to regard Herbert as a sort of talisman, a physical assurance of success, despite his sometimes mercurial behaviour.

He was just about to inform Toby of his elevation when he heard the stage door slam.

'Herbert! Where in damnation have you been?'

Herbert stopped and spread his arms wide. 'What do you mean?'

'Curtain in less than an hour! This is most unprofessional.'

'I can be ready in half the time.'

'But where have you been?'

'Oh?' Herbert walked slowly towards him. 'And what happened to the concept of trust? Of free flight?'

'It has nothing to do with trust, everything to do with the performance.'

Herbert seemed to be on the point of replying when he held back. Instead he took a deep breath and came up close to the actor-manager, laying a hand on his shoulder. 'I have been out saving your bacon, Benjie, if you really must know.'

'My bacon?'

'I have been in the Silver Grid. You promised the company a feast after tonight's performance in the ice-house. Remember?'

He remembered the promise, certainly, but he clapped his hand to his forehead as he realised he had done nothing about it. 'My boy!' he said. 'It had completely slipped my mind.'

'It would have been quite the thing if the whole group of us had turned up to find the place either in darkness or unprepared for our arrival. A feast, dear Benjamin, takes some preparation, does it not? Rather like a play.'

'I am sorry, Herbert. It was just . . . it wouldn't have been the same if you weren't . . . . I worried. Forgive me.'

'Of course.' He smiled warmly. 'Now I cannot stand here gossiping, Benjie. I could well miss my entrance!' With that, he turned swiftly around and marched to his dressing-room, his habitual swagger even more pronounced.

As he made his way back to his dressing-room for the final touches to his make-up, Benjamin could now smile at his earlier panic. Everything was right with his world once more.

*

A sentiment shared, earlier that evening, by Georgina Throstle.

Admittedly, she had been alarmed to the point of screaming when she saw the dark figure apparently about to strike her as she opened her door, but her obvious shock had elicited an immediate expression of regret and concern 'for my unwarranted intrusion, ma'am'.

The man's voice had been soothing. She stood in the doorway and struggled to regain her widow's composure.

'Please forgive me, ma'am. I have come only to offer my most sincere condolences.'

She gave a slow nod of acceptance.

'I realise this is a most distressing time, but if there is anything I can do, I would be more than happy.'

As he stood there in the doorway, his shadowy features gradually revealed themselves. He was of average height, with hair of light brown and rather elegantly flowing locks that seemed to blend seamlessly with his small moustache and beard. He wore rimless spectacles, and his eyes were deeply set beside a sharp aquiline nose. The suit he wore, however, was smeared with dust and had seen better days. She had seen the man about the place, and recalled how he had waved to Richard the previous night when they got back from the Public Hall.

'I'm sorry,' she said when her breath had returned. 'But who are you?'

He smiled and gave an apologetic bow. 'My name is Jenkins. I was honoured to make your husband's acquaintance a few days ago here in the hotel. I am a resident. We shared a few drinks in the hotel bar last night, and he told me so much about you. I have only just returned from a business trip to Manchester. I was most distressed to hear of . . . what happened.'

'That's very kind of you.'

'Well,' he said, after a brief hesitation. 'I must say farewell. I have a ticket for *The Silver King*. It's a play. And my business clothes are hardly suitable for the theatre.'

'Yes,' she gave a wan smile. 'I have seen it advertised.'

He turned to go. 'I can only repeat. If there's anything I can do, I would be delighted. It cannot be easy for you. I presume your family are on their way?'

She frowned and cast an involuntary glance to the table behind her. 'My brother will be here tomorrow evening.'

'We must be thankful for that. There's nothing like the support of one's family at a time like this . . . Well, I must be going. Good evening, Mrs Throstle.' He gave a small bow and walked off down the corridor, taking precise and slow steps, as if afraid that haste would be an indecorous way of leaving a recently bereaved widow.

She was about to close the door when she saw a figure approach Mr Jenkins at the top of the small flight of stairs that led down to the hotel foyer. In the dimly lit corridor it was impossible to make out the man's features, although she felt sure she knew him. He said something to her recent visitor, who glanced down at his fob watch in what she supposed was a pointed display of irritation – he did, after all, have a play to go to – but he gave the man a curt nod, and they both walked into the foyer and out of sight.

When she closed the door and returned to her seat at the dressing-table, her curiosity was piqued, so much so that she realised with surprise that the pain in her face had quite gone.

*

'I won't keep you long, sir,' said Detective Sergeant Slevin, observing the man's impatient frown and the deliberate way he took out his fob watch and flicked its gold casing open with an irritated flick of thumb and forefinger.

Once they were inside the manager's office, Mr Jameson, who had told the detective of his elusive guest's presence when he entered the hotel in search of Mrs Throstle, tactfully withdrew 'on his rounds' and left the two of them sitting in the two armchairs by his desk.

'Well, sergeant?'

'Well, Mr Jenkins. You're quite an elusive character.'

Jenkins smiled and held up his hand. 'Admitted! I travel quite extensively, and Wigan is my current base, you see. It's central to most of my towns.'

'Your towns?'

'Hosiery doesn't sell itself, sergeant.'

'Quite. Can you tell me what you and Richard Throstle talked about last night?'

Jenkins stroked his beard before replying. 'Ah yes. Terrible business. He was most companionable. Had some stories to tell about some of the places we have both visited.'

'And was that the entire gist of your conversation with him last night?'

Again, Jenkins stroked his beard, but there seemed to be a definite discomfort now as he shifted his position in the armchair. 'That and other things, you know.'

'What other things?'

'I got the impression that he was . . . deeply unhappy.'

'Unhappy? In what way?'

Jenkins shrugged. 'I don't think it decent to speculate.'

'But surely if you sensed that he was unhappy, then you must also have gained some awareness of its cause?'

'He said something to me – now you must understand, sergeant, that at the time he was rather the worse for wear, and whatever he was saying must therefore be treated with a certain amount of caution.'

'Well?'

'He asked me a curious question. He asked me if I was happily married.'

'Why is that curious?'

'Because of what he said next. "Do you love your own wife?"'

Slevin frowned. 'Surely the two questions are the same?'

Jenkins shook his head. 'No. You see, he put undue emphasis on the words "your own". "Do you love *your own* wife?"'

Slevin still didn't follow.

'Are you suggesting that he and his wife were estranged in some way?'

'Well, yes and no. I got the distinct impression there was more to it than that. I felt he was hinting, in that leery drunken way, that not only did he not love his own wife – he had feelings for someone else's.'

This was a departure, Slevin thought. Throstle had been seeing young Violet Cowburn, but she was to all intents and purposes a common prostitute, and therefore he would have felt nothing for her. But if what Jenkins was saying was true, then it was possible that the man had been conducting an illicit affair with another woman, one who was married. Married women meant husbands. Was Throstle killed by a vengeful husband seeking redress in the most gruesome of ways?

'Is there anything he might have said that could shed some light on the identity of this . . . other woman? If indeed such a person exists.'

Jenkins again pondered the question. 'Nothing of substance. But he did say that he couldn't wait to get back to Leeds. I got the impression that whoever he was talking about might actually live there.'

Slevin took out his notebook and pencilled in a few words.

'Will that be all, sergeant? Only I will be late for the theatre and I still have to change. The four-thirty from Manchester Piccadilly was not the most comfortable of journeys.'

'What time did he leave you?'

'We went to our respective rooms – I am on the third floor – at the same time. That would be around twelve-thirty, something like that. Mr Golding – you have met him, I presume? He is an Inspector of Mines. He had joined us for a few drinks and the three of us left together. To think that a few hours later a murderer was abroad . . .'

'Quite. Well, sir, you have been most helpful. Thank you.'

They both stood and shook hands.

Jenkins turned at the door and said, 'This will be quite a story for my wife, you know. She thinks mine is the dullest profession in the world!'

*

Within minutes, Slevin was standing by the window in Georgina Throstle's hotel room. The widow herself was also standing, her visitor having refused the invitation to sit down.

'When men refuse to sit, it is because they have something unpleasant to relate and wish to be away as soon as the news is imparted,' she said finally when he had fallen silent after the usual civilities.

'You're quite right, ma'am. Unpleasant to relate.' He sighed. 'We have received some disturbing information regarding your husband's . . . predilections.'

'Predilections?'

'It has been brought to our attention that he has been in the habit of taking photographs of a rather . . . salacious nature.'

'*Salacious* now? And who provided this intelligence?'

'I can't say.'

'So some anonymous personage makes accusations of the vilest nature against a man who has been brutally murdered, and you decide to investigate allegations against the victim rather than pursue the perpetrator of the crime?'

This wasn't proceeding in the way he had planned. 'I apologise if this seems insensitive, ma'am. However, I need to know if you can shed any light on the allegation.'

. 'Well, it depends what you mean by light, detective sergeant. If by light you mean truth, why then I think I can. The allegation is nothing more than slander of the vilest kind. A post-mortem attack on a man's good name, a man who cannot now defend himself. But I assure you that I can. There is absolutely no truth in this preposterous suggestion. I should know. We have worked very closely together over the years since I devoted my life to his passion.'

'The magic lantern shows?'

'Precisely. I was very happily working as a governess when he began. In those days he had a small photography shop not a hundred yards from the Upper Head Row. Then he decided to expand his business. Rather than have people come to his premises for portraits, why not go to the people? Use the marvellous projectors to show not only individuals but scenes? And not only scenes. Why not develop whole legends to accompany them? A far cry from the early days of lantern slides, when they were simply hand-painted and illuminated by oil lamp. This current show, his *Phantasmagoria*, is in many ways outdated. There aren't many these days. But Richard feels the time is right for a revival, and if he can display subjects more topical, more immediate to his audience, then he will create an entirely new form of entertainment. It was his dream.'

She had inadvertently lapsed into the present and future tenses, and he recognised the beginnings of despair in the way her voice was steadily rising, not in hope but in hopelessness.

'You say he photographed individuals and used them in his shows?'

'Yes.'

'Females? Children?'

He watched as she flushed a deep scarlet. Guilt? Or disgust at what his words implied?

'Always chaperoned. Richard was most anxious to observe all the proprieties.'

He thought he detected a note, not of defiance, but of anxiety, in her voice now. 'You see, ma'am, a suggestion has been made that he has taken photographs of an intimate nature. Of young women and . . . children.'

She raised a hand to her mouth.

'And if that is the case, well, as you can appreciate, it gives us a motive for what happened to your husband.'

He watched her move slowly to the chair by the dressing-table and sit down. When she next spoke, she addressed his reflected image through the looking-glass, in which he could see her hands clasp and unclasp.

'There aren't the words to express what I feel about your insinuations, sergeant. I can only state what is the truth and hope that will be the end of the matter. My husband was the kindest and most solicitous of men. That we have not been blessed with children has always been a source of regret for both of us. Now it is a source of deep and irretrievable loss to me. But I can assure you, sergeant, that he would never harm or abuse in any way any of God's children. Now, if you will excuse me?'

He bade her farewell and left the room. He stood in the darkened corridor for a few minutes, exploring every nuance of what had been said beyond the door. Could she really have known nothing about her husband's undoubted philandering? He didn't think so. In which case the closing reference to his sainthood was merely the gabble of a self-deceiving widow. Or the words of a devoted wife who nevertheless knew of her late husband's faults. Or, far worse, the testimony of a willing accomplice.

He smiled, remembering her face as she spoke to him through the looking-glass. Aren't images reversed in those things? Perhaps they have the same effect on words, too. What is the opposite of a saint? he asked himself as he finally strolled down the corridor. It was time to go home.

*

Although the performance didn't hit the emotional heights of the opening night, it went off passably well, gradually growing in stature and earning a standing ovation at the end. Once the theatre had emptied and only the company and a few of the stage-hands remained, Benjamin gathered them on the stage and spoke briefly to them all, once again thanking them for their efforts especially 'in the teeth of such inclement conditions.' He couldn't help but notice the way some of them were trying valiantly not to shiver.

'And now, let us repair to the Silver Grid and an excellent supper.'

Benjamin noticed Herbert walking alongside Susan Coupe and James Shorton, talking earnestly to both of them. An irrational feeling of jealousy overcame him, and he moved quickly through the departing company to bring himself alongside the trio. 'I am told they are absolutely delightful,' he heard Herbert say just as he got near them.

Susan Coupe gave Benjamin a scowl. Was she annoyed at his sudden appearance? Or annoyed with the young man she so obviously disapproved of? Certainly there was a half-flush on her cheeks.

'Ah, Benjamin!' said Herbert, turning and throwing a manly arm around his shoulder. 'I was just singing the praises of American audiences. What do you think of American audiences?'

'Most enthusiastic,' he said with a disarming smile.

'I was telling Susan that you were there on Irving's last tour.'

Benjamin felt quite proud, not of his tour with Irving but of the fact that Herbert should be talking about him in these terms.

'I would love to go to America!' Herbert said to him with a sly smile.

'You shall. Perhaps we all shall. Wouldn't that be splendid? The Morgan-Drew Broadway production of *Othello*.' He held his arms aloft as if he could already see the huge advertising posters before him.

'If you leave us for Mr Irving, Susan,' said Herbert with a smile, 'we may well get there before you.'

'Susan will become the most critically acclaimed actress of her generation,' Shorton affirmed with conviction in his voice.

'Well,' said the would-be *grande dame* with lowered eyes, 'I shall try.'

'That's the spirit!' said Herbert. He gave Benjamin a strange look that lasted just half a second, but Benjamin caught it. However, he couldn't quite grasp what it signified.

*

An hour after the Morgan-Drew Theatre Company had enjoyed their supper in the specially reserved room on the first floor of the Silver Grid, and after Benjamin had personally organised a fleet of hackney carriages to convey every one of them home to their lodgings, a solitary figure proceeded along the mainly deserted streets of the town.

By the side of the Public Hall, a narrow passageway led onto the back yards of a long row of terraced houses. The figure looked quickly around, saw that no one was watching, and darted into the dark alley. Ten yards down, on the left, the rear exit door to the hall was firmly closed. There was a dull sound of wood splintering, damp, mouldy wood that had long since yielded to the ravages of time, rendering the break-in a simple task.

An oil lamp swayed as it was carried forth out into the great hall itself. There, halfway along the rows of seats, stood the range of cameras mounted on tall tables, their lenses all pointing towards the makeshift white screen at the rear. A row of cylinders lay against a wall, the words 'Oxygen' and 'Hydrogen' stamped in black lettering along their sides. The intruder gave a sigh, and moved towards the apparatus, walking steadily and with a purpose that could have been seen quite clearly in the grim set of the mouth – if anyone had been there to see it.

*

A sudden sound woke Benjamin Morgan-Drew. His eyes felt heavy, leaden, and he realised that perhaps he should not have indulged himself quite so much at the Silver Grid.

There it was again. A curse. Most definitely. He turned over and tried to peer at his watch. But it was too dark in the lodging-house room, and there seemed to be little or no moonlight to afford even a glimmer of light. He lay back and closed his eyes once more. Then, with the insidious inevitability of an incoming tide, he recalled the argument earlier.

The reason why he was sleeping alone.

The one thing we can be grateful for, he told himself, is that sleep is the perfect analgesic, allowing us respite from even the most unpleasant of thoughts. He had not meant to allow the night to turn sour after the meal, but the extra glass or two had transformed honey into vitriol and he had become maudlin, fancying a slight every time Herbert engaged another in conversation . . .

Another curse! Surely that wasn't Herbert's voice! Herbert had consented to share the hackney back to Mrs O'Halloran's, although he had stormed upstairs like a recalcitrant child and insisted on going to his own bed.

Yet the cursing came from the stairs, and it was getting closer. Herbert's voice. Most definitely. He was just about to leave his bed, see what on earth was happening, when he heard a door open, and the tired drawl of their landlady's voice asking what the bejasus he thought he was doing at this time of the night? Surely Herbert hadn't sneaked out again? Perhaps he had simply wandered downstairs for something to eat?

There was a drunken mumble, a few harsh words, then the slamming of a door. Benjamin lay back once more, and prayed for the lovely oblivion that sleep would bring, if only for a few hours.

7

Georgina Throstle eschewed convention and decided to eat in the small hotel dining room the following morning. The room was half empty, and she had no difficulty finding a table for herself. Although she felt a trifle uncomfortable, and was sure that the eyes of everyone were focused on the black fabric of her dress, she herself did some surreptitious surveillance to see if her concerned fellow guest of the previous evening, Mr Jenkins, was in the room having his breakfast. But she saw no sign of him.

After she ordered a single round of toasted bread and a small bowl of porridge, she asked the waiter if Mr Jenkins had already breakfasted.

'Never see him, ma'am.' The waiter spoke in hushed tones, cowed a little by the black of her mourning dress.

'Well, thank you. And I'd like my toast very lightly done, please.'

The waiter gave a respectful bow and left. She noticed him say a few words to the hotel manager, who had happened to enter the room at that moment, and he came over to her with a sombre, solicitous expression on his face.

'If there's anything I can do, Mrs Throstle . . .'

'No, thank you.'

'I gather you were asking after Mr Jenkins? It's just that Mr Jenkins hasn't taken breakfast at all this week. He uses the Royal merely as a base. He travels quite extensively, so he informs us.'

'Really?' She uttered the word with a touch of *ennui*.

'If there is anything I can do . . .'

'Yes, as a matter of fact, there is.'

'Oh?'

'My brother is due to arrive this afternoon.'

'Your brother?'

'The Reverend Edward Malvern. You should have received a telegram confirming his booking.'

'Ah, yes. I seem to recall a Reverend Malvern due to arrive later. I hadn't realised he was your brother.'

'Please see that he is accorded every attention.'

'That goes without saying.' He paused, then added, 'He will be a comfort to you, I'm sure.'

'And if you could show him to my room as soon as he arrives, I would be most grateful.' She gave him a cold smile.

'I'll see to that personally,' he said, and offered what appeared to be a relieved bow before he moved to the other side of the room.

Georgina accepted the porridge, when it arrived, with a cold grace. She knew that she would have to come to some sort of decision – the Throstle Magic Lantern Company was in a parlous state now that Richard, for all his faults, had gone. He could present the *Phantasmagoria* as no one else could, and even the temporary measure she had in mind couldn't obviate the necessity for a more permanent strategy. She felt her spirits sink even lower when she considered the prospect of her sainted brother Edward at the helm. As Richard had expressed on more than one occasion, it would become merely an evangelical road-show, touring the country and espousing prayer and the benefits of mortifying the flesh, an ironic change of direction if ever there was one.

Perhaps the person she had arranged to meet later might offer some glimmer of hope – he was certainly keen enough, and under no illusions as to the nature of Richard's more 'exclusive' ventures. She would have to be very careful though.

A part of her insisted that she could have nothing now to do with that seedier world, those nether regions into which she herself had once plunged. It was a thing she didn't like to reflect upon, and so, with that spiritual self-preservation that had always been one of her strengths, she firmly locked those dreadful memories deep at the back of her mind, rather like the incriminating box of slides even now secreted in a safe across town.

'Ahem!'

She looked up from her thoughts and her porridge and saw Mr Worswick, the manager of the Public Hall, standing beside her. He had a most anxious expression on his face.

'Yes, Mr Worswick?'

'Mrs Throstle, I . . . am so very sorry to disturb you at such a time.'

Whether he was referring to her recent bereavement or the cold porridge before her she couldn't tell. Yet she couldn't help feeling irritated by the man. 'Then why do you?'

'It's a . . . matter of some urgency.'

'Then tell me urgently what it is.'

'It's the Public Hall, ma'am. We had an intruder last night.'

Her heart leaped. 'What happened?'

'We . . . we don't know. Someone broke into the hall and . . . disturbed a few things.'

'Was anything stolen?'

'Stolen?'

'From the safe?'

'Nothing. The safe had been tampered with, but it was unopened.'

She breathed a sigh of relief and dabbed at her lips with a napkin. 'Were the machines damaged? The projectors? The gas cylinders?'

'No. They were still intact, as far as we could tell when we checked everything this morning. It was the cleaners who sent for me, you see.'

'So if the equipment is all right . . . ?'

144

He coughed again, looking even more uncomfortable. 'They wrote something, Mrs Throstle. On the walls.'

'Wrote something? What did they write?'

'It was vile filth.'

'Specifically?'

He looked around at the other diners, who seemed to be oblivious of his presence. 'There was a reference to your presentation. It said it was the work of the Devil.'

'Is that all?'

'Isn't that enough? We have a show tonight, and it will be the devil of a . . . please forgive me. But it will be very difficult to erase all the writing – the villain used some of the fluorescent paint your husband employed for the background scenes on the canvases.'

'You are the manager, are you not?'

'I am, ma'am.'

'Then you will manage to have the walls cleaned by tonight.'

'But . . .'

'My brother arrives later. He is a man of the cloth. It wouldn't do for him to see such abominations. Do you understand?'

He nodded, gave her a gracious bow, and left.

All this bowing! Georgina looked at the congealed mess in her bowl and pushed it away from her. This was a curious thing. Why would anyone want to break in and daub such things on the walls? Were people so childishly superstitious? Did they really believe the projections of hobgoblins and suchlike were a manifestation of evil? With a sad shake of the head she left her table, her fast unbroken.

*

Samuel Slevin was told about the intrusion at the Public Hall as soon as he arrived at the station and decided to take a look for himself at the damage. Constable Bowery, who had just settled down to his morning mug of tea, uttered a whispered curse when Slevin ordered him to accompany him.

It was a matter of minutes to the hall, and when they arrived they were met by Mr Worswick, the manager, who showed them the walls inside the large hall where the letters had been drawn.

'Thought you said they were glowin', Bowery said, disappointed at the dull white of the lettering.

'When it's dark, constable,' Worswick explained.

'Well? What do you reckon?' Slevin asked as they both gazed up at what was written along the walls:

AMEND YOUR WAYS AND YOUR DOINGS

EVIL COMMUNICATIONS CORRUPT GOOD MANNERS

THE WAGES OF SIN IS DEATH

'Looks like a threat to me, sergeant.'

'Perhaps whoever did it was annoyed they couldn't open the safe.' Worswick nodded to his office, where the safe was stored. 'So they thought they'd cause some other damage.'

Slevin nodded.

With a slight smile, the manager walked quickly over to his cleaners, who were scrubbing away at the paint with very limited success.

'I reckon whoever did this killed Throstle,' said Bowery, slowly and sagely shaking his head.

'So they kill him, then issue a warning,' said Slevin. 'Is that it?'

Bowery thought for a moment. 'Well then. They wanted us to know why he was killed.'

'They kill Richard Throstle, then let us know why they did it. Is that what you're saying?'

'Looks like it, sergeant.'

'If our murderer did this, then he was taking a chance, wasn't he? I mean, if you think you've got away with the crime, why take another chance to get caught?'

Bowery looked perplexed. 'So who did this then?'

'Perhaps it isn't a warning to Throstle.'

'Who then?'

'Well, his grieving widow intends to continue the presentation tonight, does she not?'

'You mean this could be a warning to her?'

'It could be, constable.'

'So she's in danger, then?'

'She may well be.' He glanced at the manager, who was still talking to one of the cleaners. 'Mr Worswick?'

'Yes, sergeant?'

'May we use your office? For a few moments' deliberation?'

'Of course.' Worswick waved a hand in the direction of the small office by the stage area, and the two policemen headed for its open door.

Once inside, and having made sure the door was shut and they could not be overheard, Slevin sat at the desk and graciously allowed his constable to perch on a stool that stood by the far wall, a stool far too small for Jimmy Bowery's considerable weight.

'Tell me what you think,' Slevin said, steepling his fingers.

His colleague tried to sit erect and show some gravity of demeanour, which wasn't an easy matter when the two circumferences of base and backside didn't match. 'Well, first off, I think that Mrs Throstle isn't as upset as she should be.'

'Go on.'

'Like you say, sergeant, she seemed more concerned with her own baubles than her husband's.'

Slevin suppressed a smile. 'So how did she do it? We know the mechanics of the mutilation. And the suffocation. A pillow pressed hard on the face would suffice. Although there is the question of the asbestos dust. There is nothing in that room that possesses such dust. I checked last night. But what I mean is, how *could* she do it? Do that to the man she was married to and presumably in love with? Surely a knife in the gullet would have served the same purpose?'

'Might be mad, eh?'

'No, constable. There's a meaning to the crime, surely.'

Bowery gave that some deep thought. 'His charley was sliced off for a reason?'

'Yes.'

'That means he's been up to no good with it.'

'It may well mean that, constable.'

'And if Mrs Throstle found out . . .' He stopped, and it was as if a great illumination had spread across his mind. 'And we know he was doin' what he shouldn't a been doin' wi' young Violet Cowburn, don't we?'

'Yes.'

'Then there's Billy Cowburn. He could've broke in, I suppose.'

'He could. Only the door was intact. Whoever got in the room did not break the door down.'

'So if Cowburn's alibi holds up, an' he was gettin' rat-arsed in Scholes, then he couldn't be the one any road.'

'I suppose not.'

'There, then!'

'Where, then?'

'Mrs Throstle finds out he's been seein' other women, an' while he's sleepin' yonder all peaceful, picks up a knife an' whips off the offending member. Bob's your uncle!'

'I see. And then she proceeds to open every drawer in the place to make it look like the motive was burglary, eh?'

'Exactly.'

'Then there's just one more thing and we can proceed to the Royal and clap her in irons.'

'What's that, sergeant?'

'Presumably if she picked *up* a knife, she then put it *down*. If she did, then where is it? Where is the murder weapon, Constable Bowery?'

'Hid it?'

'Where? We searched all over that room. Not only was there

148

no knife, there was no sign of blood anywhere else apart from the vicinity of the body. Surely if she'd hidden it in the room there would be some traces of blood, even if by some miracle of prestidigitation she managed to remove it later.'

'Hmm. That's a bit of a bugger.'

'It is.'

*

By the time Benjamin got downstairs, Herbert had already left.

'I had a few words with Mr Koller,' said Mrs O'Halloran. 'Sure he woke half the neighbourhood with his shoutin'!'

'On behalf of the company, Mrs O'Halloran, I must apologise.'

'An' why must ye, Mr Morgan-Drew? Ye've done nothin' wrong. An' the one that did the wrong apologised this mornin'. So we'll say no more on the subject. He's only a boy, after all's said.'

'That's very magnanimous of you.'

'I had a cousin like him,' she said, sitting down beside Benjamin at the breakfast table and spending the next ten minutes regaling him with all manner of anecdotes pertaining to the recklessness and relative innocence of the sowing of wild oats.

'An' ye can bet there'll be a pair of sparklin' blue eyes somewhere along the way,' she said finally with a nudge.

'Oh, Mr Koller doesn't have time for any of that. He's much too busy with the performances. It takes over, you know.'

'Well, he said something about meeting someone this mornin', so I just presumed . . .'

'Meeting someone?'

She shrugged and gave a flirtatious smile. 'He was very mysterious!'

'Was it someone from the company?'

But he knew the answer to that. Herbert wasn't the sort to become close with anyone – apart from himself, that is – involved in the company. Certainly he had never seen him really *engage* with anyone. But what if he had? What if he were even now meeting someone they both knew and they were laughing at him, an ageing roué, as they strolled through the park? Or what if Jonathan Keele had been right all along, and Herbert was meeting the man he had seen him with only the other day? Herbert had said he was the owner of the Magic Lantern Company, and of course the man had later been found brutally murdered in his hotel bed, but was Herbert telling the truth? If he was, then he might well be called upon to answer some questions from the police. If Herbert had been lying, if the man Throstle was simply the first person he thought of – a name seen on a poster, perhaps – then was there another man altogether, whom Herbert was even now in conference with? Furthermore, was this person linked with what Herbert had been up to last night, when he was supposed to be in his room, sulking?

*

All morning, Susan Coupe had had the strangest feeling that she was being watched. It was ridiculous, she knew, and once she had posted her letters at the main post office in the centre of Wigan, she would stroll into Mesnes Park to meet James, as they had agreed before they parted last night. So, having spent a considerable time composing her letters – including a particularly long and excitable missive to her sweet cousin Mary, with whom she shared some (though of course not all) of her deepest secrets – she wrapped herself up well and walked into town.

The first sensation of being followed that she had was a laughable one. It manifested itself as a prickling along her spine. Turning quickly around as she came to a small curve in the sloping road, she thought she saw someone dart into a shop doorway. But surely that was a mere customer, anxious to get out of this bitter chill? When she heard the sounds of a group of women laughing nearby, she scolded herself and moved on. On the corner with Lower Standishgate, she paused as a tram, filled with passengers on their way into town, shunted its way to a stop. Several of the passengers disembarked and pulled their shawls or their coat collars tightly around them to ward off the cold.

She moved quickly, occasionally turning her head to see if anyone was indeed following her. But she caught sight of no one, and walked up the slope towards Market Place, tightly clutching her small bag containing the letters.

But as she stopped to place the letters in the post box, she heard someone behind her say her name. When she turned around, she breathed a sigh of relief and said, 'Oh, it's you!'

*

The Reverend Edward Malvern stood before the steps of the Public Hall and perused the poster, a sneer slowly spreading across his face. He was dressed in a sombre-hued frock coat with black armbands, and wore a top hat covered in smooth black silk. In his right hand he carried a small suitcase.

He crossed the street in the direction of the Royal Hotel. Entering the foyer, he gave a curt nod to a young man who was sauntering through the reception area with what could only be described as a smirk upon his face, and who responded with a most impertinent 'God bless!'

He introduced himself to the young man on the reception desk and was immediately greeted by the manager, Mr Jameson, who told him he had been awaiting his arrival, and that his sister – 'Dear Mrs Throstle, such a noble and devoted wife' – had asked for him to be escorted to her room as soon as he appeared.

'I think not,' said the new guest.

'I beg your pardon?'

'It is customary, is it not, for guests to be shown their room upon arrival?'

'Well, yes, your reverence, but . . .'

'If you inform my sister that I have indeed arrived, then perhaps you can also let her know that I will visit her as soon as I have settled myself and prayed. That will be in an hour. What is her room number?'

'It's number four, your reverence.'

'Excellent. Now, my room, if you please.'

Jameson took his case and led the way himself. He would have been rather put out by the reverend gentleman's manner, if he didn't have something else preying on his mind at that moment.

*

Herbert was nowhere to be found. Wigan town centre wasn't exactly extensive, and there were only so many tea rooms and public bars he could have visited. But wherever he looked, Benjamin drew a blank. Surely he hadn't gone farther afield? The town boasted three railway stations, but it was highly unlikely that Herbert would have suddenly, and without warning, decided to take a train to any of the neighbouring towns. But if he had stayed within the confines of the town centre, then where on earth could he be?

With an increasing sense of unease, he walked into Market Place and along the slow decline that led to Standishgate. To his right, as he faced the northern end of town, he saw the Royal Hotel. He had made his mind up to cross the road and walk through the portals of the hotel, giving the reception area a cursory glance before venturing into the adjoining hostelry. But as he waited for a frustrating parade of horse-drawn carts filled with agricultural produce to wend their way past him, he saw a familiar figure touch his forehead and address a clergyman before emerging from the building and setting off down Standishgate at a brisk pace.

From the expression on Herbert's face, whatever his business had been inside the hotel, its conclusion had been entirely to his satisfaction.

*

'Sergeant?'

Slevin looked up from the scraps of paper he had been writing on in an attempt to put some order into his thoughts. From the circled name, Throstle, stretched several strands, apparently unconnected, and yet . . . Violet Cowburn was most definitely linked – she had enjoyed carnal relations with the deceased only hours before his death, and her father, Billy Cowburn, had a circle around his name linking him with both Violet and Throstle. Georgina Throstle, the bereaved widow, was of course connected, yet the double line linking her with the victim indicated the added detail of her complete absence of alibi. She was lying next to him, for pity's sake, when it happened! Yet Violet had an incontestable alibi – she was enjoying the dubious hospitality of the Royal Albert Edward Infirmary at the time. Her father, too, might well have an alibi if he could give them names of witnesses who saw him out drinking when the crime took place. At the moment he was languishing down in the cells, trying desperately to unfog his memory of that drink-sodden night.

Who else was there? Slevin felt sure that the story young Violet had told him of Throstle's immoral and disgusting activities had some basis in truth: Mrs Throstle had vehemently defended his reputation last night, but then she would, wouldn't she? So if Violet's tale were true, someone else – an enraged father or lover, perhaps? – could be guilty of the crime, a crime which, by its very nature, strongly suggested vengeance of a particularly personal kind.

He drew another circle, with a line leading back to the victim's name in the middle of the page. But he could as yet think of no name that would fill the empty space.

'Sergeant?'

The voice, more insistent this time, and accompanied by a sharp rap on his office door, forced him to look up.

'Yes, Paintbrush? What is it?'

'There's a bloke to see you at the sergeant's desk,' answered Constable Turner.

'What bloke?'

'Says he's the manager of the Royal.'

'Well, bring him here then!'

The young constable muttered something Slevin couldn't quite catch, and disappeared from view.

Mr Jameson was brought in a minute later. He looked distinctly unhappy, and nervously fingered the bowler he held in his hands.

'Mr Jameson?'

Once Constable Turner had closed the door, the man seemed to relax slightly. 'Detective Sergeant Slevin,' he began. 'This is most awkward. But I would be remiss in the prosecution of my duties if I didn't do all that I could to assist the police.'

'Of course.'

'It concerns a rather . . . delicate matter.'

'You can rely on my complete discretion, Mr Jameson.'

'It concerns Mrs Throstle, the recently –'

'Yes?'

'An hour ago, I happened to be walking around the hotel. It is my usual custom. My *rounds*, as I call them. And it goes without saying that I have been paying Mrs Throstle's room particular attention, in case any small service is required. As I say, an hour ago I was on my rounds when I happened to pass her room. Mrs Throstle's. I . . . overheard something.'

'What?'

'Raised voices.'

'Who was her visitor?'

'That was, initially, the problem, you see. I hadn't been aware she had any visitors. Certainly none had announced themselves. We were expecting her brother, of course, the Reverend Edward Malvern. But it disturbed me, you understand? To hear anyone raise his voice at such a time as this . . .'

'*His* voice? Her visitor was a man?'

'Alas, yes.'

'What were they talking about?'

Jameson shrugged. 'I couldn't hear specific words, only their general tenor. And volume.'

'What did you do?'

'I knocked as gently as I could on her door.'

'Did she respond?'

'Not at first. I could hear some . . . well, it sounded like whispering.'

'Then what?'

'She came to the door and asked me what I wanted. I told her I was at her service if she required anything. I caught sight of her visitor in the looking-glass. It faces the door, you know, although I am sure he didn't see me observe him.'

'Who was he?'

Mr Jameson suddenly, and with a renewed enthusiasm, reached into his side pocket and pulled out what appeared to be a small book of very few pages. He handed it to Slevin, who looked at the cover with keen interest. It was a programme for *The Silver King*, the melodrama that was playing at the Royal Court Theatre.

'If you look at the second page, sergeant, you'll find a list of characters in the play and the names of the actors playing them. I was invited to the opening night in recognition of my position.' He seemed to throw out his chest a little as he imparted the information. 'And the man I saw in Mrs Throstle's room was playing that part on Tuesday night.'

He reached down and pointed to the line:

HENRY CORKETT – *Ware's Clerk*.........Mr Herbert Koller

*

Edward Malvern stood with both hands clasped firmly behind his back and glowered down at his sister. The expression on his face was a familiar one to those who regularly sat in his church and waited with a timorous sense of foreboding for the sermon to begin.

Georgina Throstle merely sat there, both hands folded neatly on her lap in a demure attitude of compliance. She had known before she opened the door that Edward's arrival in Wigan had little to do with the bringing of fraternal or even priestly comfort but more with the delivery of censure.

It had been ever thus. When they were children, he had forced her to sit before him as he stood on a stool giving her the lesson of the day that he himself had received at school, testing her on salient and abstruse points and punishing her roundly for any lapse in concentration.

'An abomination!' he had screamed on more than one occasion. It was a word he had heard in Bible class and had particularly liked.

At eighteen she had taken a position as governess, and the relief she felt as she left the house for the last time was matched only by the sheer sense of exhilaration at the dizzying prospect of freedom that the future held. A future that contained Richard. And how she had sinned since then!

'I have thought long about what my first words should be to you, Georgina.'

His voice was low, whispered.

'You know, of course, that your marriage to that charlatan was a source of great torment both to myself and our father.'

Who art in heaven, reflected Georgina, but wisely kept the thought to herself.

'And it has been a constant agony for me to stand by and see you become more and more embroiled in his manic schemes.'

'I seem to recall you were more than willing to provide some funds for Richard to develop his business?'

'For a higher purpose than hitherto has been the case,' he said coldly. 'Richard knew the focus of his shows would have to change dramatically if I were to support him. But we both know he would have rejected the idea. Now, lamentably, the Lord has seen fit to remove this man from the world and cast him into the pit of hell. It is a chastening fate, sister.'

She glanced up at him for the first time. 'These are your practised words of consolation and fraternal love, are they?'

He bridled, clasping his hands even tighter behind his back.

'I see your marriage has taught you incivility.'

And many other things, dear brother!

'I came because it was my duty to do so. I will not leave until I have discharged that duty.'

'And what is your duty?'

'Well, it most certainly is not to offer you absolution for your sins. I am no Roman cleric. Your sins are deeply imprinted upon your soul. Like brands on a cow. No, sister. I am here to offer you comfort. And to take you back to Leeds. To live with me.'

'With you?' She moved her head back a little in an involuntary gesture of shock.

'It is my duty to take care of you. Here – proof positive.' He handed her a small package, wrapped in brown paper.

'What is it?'

'Your medicine, which you asked me in your telegraph message to bring.'

'Thank you.' She took it and placed it on the table beside her. 'What about Ellen?'

'My wife has naturally concurred with my suggestion. She agrees it will be a boon to her household.'

Georgina smiled thinly. 'I see. You wish me to live with you, as it were, in service.'

'Nonsense! You will merely undertake those duties that are seemly for a bereaved widow. You will be in mourning for two years, and in that time there will be ample opportunity to grieve and reflect.'

Georgina was about to reply when there was a knock at the

door. Without waiting for her permission, he turned and swung it open. A man stood there with an apologetic smile on his face.

'Who are you?' Edward asked curtly.

'My name is Detective Sergeant Slevin, sir. And who might you be?'

Edward turned and glared at his still-seated sister. 'Her brother.'

'Ah. A most distressing time for both of you, sir, I have no doubt.'

'What do you want?'

'A few words, if I may?' Without waiting to be invited, Slevin strode past the open-mouthed brother and stood before Mrs Throstle. He thought he detected the trace of a smile on her features. 'My apologies, ma'am, for this intrusion.'

'My sister is in no condition to speak with anyone, let alone the police.'

'Under normal circumstances I would be in full agreement, Mr...?'

'Reverend Malvern.'

'But of course these are not normal circumstances. You are doubtless aware of how your brother-in-law met his demise?'

'Yes.'

'Well, it's my duty to discover the one responsible and bring him to justice.'

'By harassing his widow?'

'I am not harassed, sergeant,' Georgina Throstle said quietly. 'I assure you.'

Edward shot her a glance before muttering 'Excuse me!' and leaving with a slamming of the door.

'I apologise for my brother, Sergeant Slevin. As you can see, he is –'

Slevin held up a hand. 'No need, ma'am. He is concerned and protective, I'm sure.'

The look in her eyes gave the lie to his words.

'But I am here to ask you a rather delicate question, and perhaps it is best that your brother has left us.'

'Go on.'

'I am reliably informed that you have recently entertained a visitor . . . Can you tell me who your visitor was and why he was here?'

'This is more than a little intrusive, sergeant.'

'It is necessary.'

'He is someone who knew my husband. Came to offer his condolences.'

'And his name?' If she gave him a name different from the one he knew, then she would be hiding something, and that in itself would require further investigation.

'His name is Mr Herbert Koller. An actor with the touring company at the Royal Court.'

'I see. And what was the nature of his acquaintance with your husband?'

She shrugged. 'I have no idea. They knew each other, and he came to offer his condolences and his support. It was most kind of him.'

'I see. There was no . . . shall we say, unpleasantness?'

She blinked at him, then glanced away for a second before returning his gaze. 'Whatever has given you that idea?'

He shrugged. 'Someone heard raised voices.'

'Not from this room.'

'Then they must have been mistaken.' He gave a short bow. 'Well, Mrs Throstle, I apologise for the intrusion. I hope you gain comfort from your brother's presence in town. Is he staying here at the Royal?'

'He is.'

'For how long?'

'I can't say. I am hoping he will make all the arrangements for my husband's return to Leeds.'

'I'm sure he will. Good day, Mrs Throstle.'

'Good day, Sergeant Slevin.'

*

Jonathan Keele sat in Mesnes Park and watched the swans glide by. On either side of the tall, proud parent swam six or seven tiny cygnets, their movements more rapid and frenetic. Yet they all followed the parental lead as he led them to a small clump of rushes on the far bank.

Suddenly, he heard a great hissing as something disturbed the swans, a water rat perhaps, and the whole family swung effortlessly around and took a different route through the water. The last he saw of them was the smallest of the cygnets struggling to keep up as they disappeared beneath the dark archway of a railed footbridge. Gradually the ripples died away until the water was smooth and undisturbed once more.

Just as it had been when little Catherine had sunk beneath the surface.

He shook his head, but the maudlin thoughts only veered in another direction.

Would he leave such a small and indistinguishable trace? When he shuffled off this mortal coil, would the only thing left be yellowing playbills and curled programmes? Perhaps a faded eulogy in *The Era*, a thespian curiosity, of interest only to the bored historian of tomorrow anxious to find any reference, however slight, to Irving, or Miss Terry, or Miss Bernhardt?

He touched the swell of his gut and sighed.

'Jonathan?'

The voice startled him, and he sat upright on the wooden bench.

He turned to find Susan Coupe and James Shorton standing now between him and the stream.

'You seem to be in another place,' Susan said.

He noticed that her eyes were red, as if she had been crying.

'In a manner of speaking, I was.'

'Jonathan, is there anything wrong?' Susan Coupe's voice was full of concern.

'Wrong?' He dragged his gaze from the darkness of the water that flowed beneath the bridge. 'Why, of course not.'

'You seem somewhat preoccupied.'

Jonathan Keele laughed, a chesty, hearty sound. 'You could say that, my dear!'

Shorton placed his hand on Susan's as if to give her some reassurance. Jonathan wondered what it was that had upset the girl.

'Will you walk back to the theatre with us, Jonathan?' Susan asked.

'And you can tell us just what you intend to do with the great fortune you will be given tomorrow,' Shorton added.

'Tomorrow?' he asked, standing up with a great effort.

Susan smiled fondly. 'Your benefit performance! Surely you haven't forgotten that?'

He shook his head and allowed her to link his arm with hers. He had, indeed, forgotten. With everything that was on his mind at the moment, his benefit was the last thing to occupy it.

*

As Benjamin entered the theatre by the stage door, he was surprised to find someone standing by the small cubicle that was normally occupied by old Norman, the stage-door custodian.

'Can I help you?' Benjamin asked.

Detective Sergeant Slevin gave his warmest smile and introduced himself. 'I wish to speak to a member of your company.'

'And who might that be?'

'Mr Herbert Koller.'

Slevin saw the man swallow hard.

'Herbert? But what could you possibly want with him?'

'I'd rather discuss that with him, sir. A confidential matter, you understand. I thought I might find him here.'

'Yes. Yes, of course. But as I am his manager, so to speak, I think I have a right to know why he is of interest to the police.'

'Just a few questions, sir. Then I will be on my way.'

Benjamin looked around nervously. 'He isn't here.'

'So I gather. Can you tell me where he might be found at this time? His hotel?'

'We do not stay in hotels, sergeant. The expense of a lengthy tour such as ours would be . . . well, suffice it to say that we use rather more modest accommodation. Lodging-houses.'

'I see. And where might Mr Koller's lodgings be found?'

The spark of defiance seemed to die in Benjamin's eyes. 'I'll take you there if you like. I share the same lodgings.'

'That won't be necessary, sir. Just the address will suffice. I think I can find it.'

'Find what?'

Both men turned around and saw three people standing in the doorway that Benjamin had left open. There, standing between a young man and one very much older, was the most beautiful girl Samuel Slevin had ever seen. The dark hair beneath her bonnet had a few wisps out of place, and they caressed her smooth ivory cheeks that were slightly reddened from the cold.

Benjamin quickly made the introductions.

'But who are you here to see, sergeant?' said Susan Coupe, approaching him with a cool look of curiosity in her eyes. 'Is it to track down the lunatic who accosted myself and James here yesterday?'

'Lunatic, miss?'

'A madman who kept clapping his hands before our faces and who stared so wickedly into James's eyes.'

'Ah, Clapper!' He gave an apologetic smile. 'A local character. No real harm in him. Alas, no, I'm here on quite different business.'

'Which is?'

'I have all the information I need, Miss Coupe. Just the address, sir?' He turned to the actor-manager, who gave an elaborate sigh and muttered the address in Darlington Street. 'Thank you. If you will excuse me, miss?' He gave a small bow and immediately felt foolish, a feeling increased when she smiled and held out her hand for him to kiss. He took it, felt its softness, the slender, almost bird-like bones that lay beneath the pale flesh, and touched it lightly with his lips, all the time knowing full well that in some strange way he was being mocked by this confident, statuesque vision. As he closed the stage door behind him, he heard Morgan-Drew say, 'Really, Susan!' and the vision replying, 'He fascinates me.'

*

With her enigmatic words still ringing in his ears, Slevin walked jauntily along Darlington Street, pulling his coat collar close around his neck to ward off the bitterly cold wind. Flecks of snow flew wildly around his head.

When he reached the address he had been given, although he knocked quite loudly, and several times, there was no answer. Yet he could have sworn he heard voices beyond the door. He moved to the curtained window and peered through, but the curtains were thickly woven and afforded no glimpse of what lay beyond. When he returned to knock again, he was more than a little alarmed when the door immediately flew open and a large woman stood there with a look of concern on her face.

'Good afternoon,' said Slevin.

He was about to introduce himself when she said, 'If you're the doctor you're bloody quick an' no mistake. Only sent for you five minutes ago.'

'Doctor? No, ma'am. I'm Detective Sergeant Slevin of the Wigan Borough Police.'

'Police? Hell's teeth! What do you want wi' me?'

'Not you. A guest of yours. Mr Herbert Koller.'

She narrowed her gaze and nodded, stepping aside and indicating that he should enter. 'Well then, an' isn't that a coincidence?'

'What is?'

'Well, here's you lookin' *for* Mr Koller, an' here's me lookin' *after* him.'

'What do you mean?'

'It's Mr Koller I've sent to the doctor for.'

'Why?'

'Because he collapsed in my front room not ten minutes ago. An' I've the divil to rouse the poor soul!'

When Slevin entered the front room, he saw the one he was seeking lying prostrate on the floor before a roaring fire. There was no sign of movement from Mr Herbert Koller.

8

Mrs O'Halloran watched from the doorway as Slevin and the doctor, who had arrived some ten minutes after the policeman, laid her lodger on the bed.

'How are you feeling now?' the doctor asked Herbert.

'Rather weak,' said Herbert, giving a sickly smile to show courage in adversity.

'I shouldn't wonder. But I think you will be fine in a day or so.'

Mrs O'Halloran uttered a groan. 'An' him due to perform tonight. What will poor Mr Morgan-Drew say?'

Herbert gave a small cough. 'We have a more than adequate understudy who can step into the breach, Mrs O'Halloran.'

As the doctor left, Mrs O'Halloran gave Slevin only a few minutes with the invalid.

'It's all I require,' he said, and waited for her to close the door.

'Well?' came the frail voice from the bed. 'How can I be of help, sergeant?'

'You paid Mrs Georgina Throstle a visit earlier.'

For a few moments, Herbert closed his eyes, licking his lips and breathing in shallow gasps. 'Mrs Throstle?'

'Yes.'

'I . . . went to pay my respects. Her husband . . .'

'She says you knew him.'

Slowly he opened his eyes once more. 'I have met him.'

'Where?'

'Here. In Wigan.'

'What were the circumstances of your meeting?'

165

'It was a . . . a chance meeting. In a public house. The Shakespeare. You know it?'

The public house in question was a matter of yards away from both the Royal Court and the Public Hall, and was a popular venue for theatre-goers and actors alike.

'What happened?'

'Nothing. We . . . swapped stories. You know the sort of thing. Audiences. Scenery. Equipment costs. We were almost in the same business. But not quite.'

'How often did you meet him?'

'Only once.'

'But you felt you needed to offer his wife condolences following such a brief encounter?'

Herbert once more closed his eyes but continued to speak. 'The world of make-believe, sergeant . . . it lives by rather more bohemian rules. One doesn't need a formal introduction or a lengthy acquaintance to –' He broke off and began a short coughing fit.

'I've been informed that you and Mrs Throstle had sharp words.'

'Nonsense!'

'Reliably informed.'

Herbert screwed his eyes shut to suggest a searing pain. 'I may have been voluble in my condolence,' he said after a few seconds. 'I am used to declaiming rather loudly from the stage, you see. Sometimes one gets carried away.'

Slevin looked down at him and stood up. It was obvious that he would extract no more useful information from the man, and so he bade him farewell. As he stepped onto the landing, Mrs O'Halloran was standing at the top of the stairs. She beckoned him silently to follow her downstairs. When they reached the hallway, she said to him in a low voice, 'Doctor says he wants a word. He's outside.'

Curious, Slevin thanked the landlady and walked out onto the pavement. A small carriage was waiting there, the driver hunched into his heavy coat and muffler, the doctor seated inside looking impatiently at his watch.

'You wanted to see me?' shouted Slevin through the open window.

'Ah yes. Can I give you a lift, sergeant?'

'I'm going back to the station.'

'Very good. I am visiting a patient on Market Street. Please.'

He held open the door of the carriage and Slevin climbed in. As they trotted away from the house, the doctor leaned back and smiled.

'Well, sergeant. What do you think of our patient?'

'Mr Koller? We've only just met.'

'Same here. Strictly speaking, he isn't my patient. But of course, under the rules of the Hippocratic Oath I am bound to say nothing.'

'I understand.'

'I will merely make an observation.'

There was a mischievous twinkle in the doctor's eye, and he placed his hands together, pointing them towards his travelling companion. 'Well, my observation is this, sergeant – I am reliably informed by his good landlady that Mr Herbert Koller is a very good actor. Do you agree?'

'Oh, I agree wholeheartedly,' he replied with a grim smile. 'A very good actor indeed.'

*

Benjamin was glad that Jonathan had knocked on his door and spent the following half-hour in his company. There was something reassuring about the ageing actor. They had known each other for many years, and often, at least until this particular tour, when they were appearing in the same production together, they would find the time to settle down in some corner of a public house, or occasionally take an invigorating stroll and simply enjoy the delights of gentle conversation. He knew that the old man valued not only his company but also the support he had offered five years ago, when his dearest granddaughter had died in such tragic circumstances. Jonathan had stayed with him in Cheyne Walk for a month, and, by dint of often painful conversations and long, meditative silences before a roaring fire, he had helped him accept at least the fact, if not the manner, of her passing.

Now, in the small dressing-room, the conversation had developed along casual and familiar lines until Jonathan suddenly stooped over and gripped his stomach with a heavy groan.

'Jonathan? Are you all right?'

The old man closed his eyes briefly before opening them once more. This time, there were tears beginning to form there.

'What on earth is wrong?'

A heavy sigh seemed to draw all the breath out of the man, and he took several seconds to respond.

'My apologies, Benjamin. I hadn't intended that.'

'Intended what?'

'These . . . moments are becoming more frequent.'

The expression on Benjamin's face told its own story.

'I am ill.' He spoke the words simply, his voice low and tremulous.

'How ill?'

'I have a matter of months.'

There was a lengthy silence before Benjamin said, 'I am so sorry.'

'No need. You see, in a way I welcome it. It is both a punishment and a reward. Isn't that a remarkable thing?'

'How do you mean?'

But before he could answer, there came a timid knock on the door.

'Yes?' Benjamin snapped.

The door opened and Norman, the doorman, peered around and looked at the actor-manager with worry etched deep in the lines of his face.

'Sorry Mr Morgan-Drew. Summat of a problem.'

'What sort of problem?' He glanced at Jonathan, who now sat slumped back in his chair, the effort taken to break such shattering news having taken its toll.

Norman bit his lip. 'Young lad at the stage door. Says Mrs O'Thingy sent him.'

'Mrs O'Halloran?'

'Aye. Her. He says she says there's summat up wi' Mr Koller.'

'Up? What's *up*?'

'She says he's indisposed.'

'What!'

''S'what she says. Tell Mr Morgan-Drew that Mr Herbert Koller is indisposed.'

'How?'

Norman shrugged. 'Dunno. Didn't say.'

'Where is the lad now?'

'Gone. Delivered his errand an' then rushed off. Didn't wait for no reply.'

He turned to Jonathan, who had remained motionless. 'Jonathan, I . . .'

'Of course,' came the faint reply. 'I understand.'

'We must continue this, and you will tell me more. Is that clear?'

Jonathan patted him on the hand and gave a feeble smile. 'Go!'

Within minutes Benjamin was inside a carriage, even though Darlington Street was within walking distance. He sat on the edge of his seat as he was driven, 'with all haste', to Mrs O'Halloran's lodging-house.

As soon as the carriage pulled to a halt and the cabbie was paid, he rushed through the door and was met by a concerned-looking Mrs O'Halloran, who quickly ushered him upstairs with a promise to bring them both a 'hot cup o' tay'. Her Irishness came to the fore in times of crisis.

When he entered, the room was dark and Herbert seemed to be asleep. Taking great care not to step on any creaking floorboard, he moved slowly to the bed, where he sat in the chair thoughtfully provided by Mrs O'Halloran, and sat down. He did indeed look pale.

Gradually, the patient opened his eyes and looked directly at the ceiling. 'Father?' he said in a hoarse whisper.

'No, Herbert. It is I. Benjamin.'

Herbert turned and gazed up. 'I became very faint. Barely made it back.'

'Where have you been?'

'I went for a bracing stroll.'

'Anywhere in particular?'

'Oh no. Meandering, you know. Then I found myself staggering around the market, holding my head and almost delirious with the pain.'

'The important thing is that you are here now,' said Benjamin. He turned his eyes away, unable to maintain eye contact with this most brazen and duplicitous of liars.

'Yes, it is. You aren't crying, are you, Benjie?'

'Only inside, dear boy.'

'Because I'm quite all right. All I need is one night's rest . . . I'm sure young Toby is ready and more than willing to fill the breach. Have you broken the news to him?'

'No. Not yet. I was hoping . . .' He allowed the word to drift into the ether, like a spirit leaving its carcass behind.

'And I shall be fit as a fiddle tomorrow night. It's very good of you to be so understanding, Benjie.'

'Oh I understand, Herbert. I really do.'

*

Georgina sat facing the door that led into the dining room. It was almost six o'clock, and the place was already filling. Sitting opposite Georgina, Edward was finishing his clear turtle soup.

Over his stooped shoulder, she saw the door open and Mr Jenkins peered in. Was he looking for her? He caught sight of her and gave a small wave.

'You are determined, then?' Edward said, glancing up from his bowl.

'On what?'

'This outrage tonight.' He was now staring at her with recrimination in his eyes.

'It is no outrage to fulfil a promise.'

'A promise made by your late husband. To continue with this ridiculous slide show is monstrous. He died two nights ago. You are in mourning!'

'Indeed I am. And what better way to show my devotion than to do exactly what my dear Richard would want, no, expect, me to do?'

Her brother gave a curt nod as the waiter came to remove their soup bowls. 'I have been informed that some damage has been done to the place.'

'Damage? Oh, you mean the childish scrawls by some ill-bred local.'

'It is not ill-bred, as you say, to quote scripture.'

'It is ill-bred to break into a public building and deface its walls.'

'Some would argue that is no worse than what takes place during your shows. I mean, really, Georgina! These Phantasmagorias cater for the lowest and the most superstitious. They are as outdated as burning at the stake.'

'That's as may be. But they are very well attended.'

'You mean they are profitable. That seems to have been the thrust of everything Richard did. And you are apparently now infected with that self-same lust.' He gave a heavy sigh. 'I shall stay here tonight, in my room, and read. Tomorrow we can discuss the future.'

'In what sense?'

'The sense we have already spoken of.'

'And you have already been given my answer.'

'But where else can you go? Surely you can see that as a woman in deep mourning your options are, shall we say, severely restricted?'

'I have certain plans.'

'Plans?'

'Not only to continue with Richard's business, but to develop it.'

'Develop? By all the saints, woman, what do you intend to do? Throw in a séance and conjure up the very spirits you now only portray by projection? What about resurrecting the dead and putting them on display in well-illuminated glass coffins? I'm sure that would be a novel development!'

She was about to retort when the waiter brought their main course.

'What is this?' Edward demanded of the waiter. He pointed to the contents of his plate.

'Calf's head, your reverence.'

'And what is that liquid?'

'Piquant sauce, your reverence.'

'I asked for the dish plain.'

'But it comes with the calf's head, your reverence. Says so on the menu.'

Edward sat with his back fully erect. 'Please take it away and bring me a plain calf's head. Without the sauce. That is what *plain* means.'

'Yes, your reverence,' said the waiter, with a blank expression on his face.

Georgina reached up to touch the side of her face.

'The pain again?'

'Yes. It's beginning.'

'Then you must take your medicine. You must take the medicine that was prescribed for you by your doctor and which

172

I have taken the trouble to bring for you all the way over the Pennines. Not that vile mixture Richard obtained for you.'

'It helped with the pain.'

'As the Lord can.'

She looked down at the contents of her dinner plate – pigeon with a small selection of vegetables. Her appetite was waning as the pain in her face grew. Suddenly she felt overcome – not by the pain, not yet at any rate, but by the prospect of the coming presentation, and all those people, and the uncertainty of what was to come over the next few months.

One step at a time, she told herself with a long, deep breath. And the first step was tonight, and the arrangements she had made for the show.

'I shall go to your room,' Edward said.

'Why?'

'For your medicine.'

'Yes, thank you,' she said, surprised at the frailty in her voice. This particular attack was threatening to be quite a vicious one. 'Yes, please, Edward. Hurry.'

*

Slevin sat in the front row of the empty theatre and listened to Benjamin Morgan-Drew talk about the theatre. Although he had been to the theatre on many occasions, both here in Wigan and farther afield, and although he would never admit as much to Constable Bowery, he preferred the more raucous and spontaneous atmosphere of the music-hall, where whatever had been previously rehearsed often took unexpected and hilarious turns, and the entire hall became a palace of pleasure. The theatre was for special occasions, which he and Sarah could enjoy together.

'It's been my whole life, sergeant,' Benjamin said by way of concluding his potted autobiography.

"Do you think Mr Koller will feel the same way?"

'How do you mean?'

'Well, he strikes me as someone who might feel . . . less dedicated.'

'You mean because he is ill at the moment?'

Slevin shrugged. 'He is an interesting fellow, though.'

'Interesting?'

'Well, for one thing, he is acquainted with the widow of the man who was so brutally murdered a few days ago.'

'What?' This apparently was news to the actor-manager.

'He went to meet her this morning. I simply wanted to ask him why when I went to see him.'

'And what did he say?'

'That he was simply offering her his condolences.'

'Offering condolences to a woman he did not know?'

'He informs me he was acquainted with the victim. Mr Richard Throstle.'

He was surprised when Morgan-Drew stood up and walked to the roped-off area where the orchestra would be playing in an hour's time. He put both hands on the rope and gripped it tightly.

'Mr Morgan-Drew?'

'I'm sorry. Of course it would only be natural for him to offer his . . . condolences.'

'Quite.' Slevin stood up and walked over to stand beside him. 'Where was Mr Koller on Tuesday night?'

'Pardon?'

'After the performance.'

'We went to a civic reception. At the town hall.'

'And after that?'

'Back to our lodgings. Mrs O'Halloran's.'

'You returned together?'

A slight hesitation. A deep breath. 'Yes.'

'And he remained there all night?'

'Of course he did. What are you implying, Sergeant Slevin?'

174

There was a cough from behind the curtains, and a young man appeared. 'Mr Morgan-Drew?'

'Toby? What is it?'

'Sir, they're having a bit of trouble finding my cigar.'

'What?'

'It's not in the box.'

'Good grief! Am I to take over props now? Perhaps I should get a lucifer and light all the footlights while I'm at it?'

The young man withdrew sharply.

'Problems?' Slevin asked.

'That was Herbert's understudy for tonight. Young Toby Thomas. Good-hearted young lad but nervous as a kitten. God knows how he'll go on when he lights his cigar. The damned thing's almost as big as he is – if he ever finds it, that is.'

'Does he have to light a cigar? I mean, can't you cut that out?'

Benjamin wheeled around, fully restored to his role now. 'It's essential to the moment! Young Corkett – whom Toby will be playing – is a brash young Cockney who has come into some large winnings on the horses. He flaunts his new-found wealth in a public bar by setting fire to a five-pound note and lighting a huge cigar with it. Essential, sergeant! Now if there's nothing else . . .'

Slevin shook his head, and Benjamin walked quickly to the steps leading up the wings and exited in search of a cigar. He could hear the sounds of activity behind the curtain – objects being hastily moved, curses muffled but heated, footsteps rushing from one end of the stage to another. He decided to follow Morgan-Drew's example and take a look backstage, telling himself it was purely out of interest and that the prospect of seeing Miss Susan Coupe once more was the farthest thing from his mind. As he squeezed himself past what appeared to be a row of skittles in the bar of a public house, he caught sight of the unfortunate young Toby scratching his head and peering into an open box which Morgan-Drew was holding an inch below his nose.

'And just what is that?' he was asking, nodding impatiently at something inside the box.

'A cigar, sir.'

'A *real* cigar, not an invisible one?'

'A real one, sir. But I could have sworn the box was empty.'

'When I made my debut on tour, boy, I was physically ill seconds before my grand entrance.' Benjamin's voice was kindlier now, more understanding. Slevin wondered if it were relief at finding the missing cigar, or genuine concern for the young actor's edginess. The rest of their conversation failed to penetrate, however, because he caught sight of a colourful dress, patterned with floral designs and swaying slightly as Miss Susan Coupe flitted onto the far reach of the stage.

'Benjamin?'

Morgan-Drew swung around and smiled. 'Yes, Susan?'

'James would like everyone to do him a great favour while he is making up.'

'And what is that, my dear?'

Slevin saw her face, the smooth ivory perfection, and wondered what it would be like to touch her skin. Soon, he knew, it would be coated with make-up and nature would be spoilt. Her next words broke sharply into his reverie.

'Well, it should already be inside his coat pocket for the opening scene, but he cannot find it anywhere.'

'What?'

'His revolver, Benjamin. It seems to have disappeared.'

*

They found him staggering from an alleyway halfway down Cooper's Row. He was clutching his stomach and groaning in obvious pain, but when a couple of mill girls went over to him to offer some assistance, he growled at them like a wild animal. As soon as they saw who it was, they backed away.

'It's only Clapper!' one said.

'What's up, Clapper? Gut ache?'

They walked off arm in arm, giggling, to catch up with the rest of the girls who had just ended their shift at Trencherfield Mill. The unfortunate Enoch Platt put one arm out and leaned against the wall of the alleyway, taking deep breaths but wincing as the bitterly cold air sliced through his wounded lungs.

'Bastard!' he yelled at no one in particular. 'Two-headed bastard!' He limped forward, still holding his gut and muttering curses to everyone who passed him by. Some of them moved away quickly, while others stood their ground, one or two even making a tentative move to help, but those who got within a foot of him were afforded the same growl as the mill girls, and they moved on with a shake of the head. 'Two eyes!' he screamed. 'Two eyes! An' two heads an' all! Devil's here, right enough! Devil's bloody here! Not down yonder any more!' He raised a hand above his head and pointed his forefinger downwards, saying once more, 'Devil's bloody here! Two eyes an' two heads!'

With a dizzying sway, he launched himself forward, slipping on the snow-covered cobblestones and crashing into a group of colliers, their blackened faces and whitened eyes seeming to bring him to an abrupt halt. Immediately, and in spite of his obvious agony, he brought his two hands together and began to clap in their faces. Slow, loud claps.

Then he stepped past them with a final clap, looking at them all and walking backwards now. He stepped from the kerbstone, and failed to understand why the colliers were shouting at him, one of them rushing towards him with arms outstretched. But it was too late. The rear of the steam engine caught him on the shoulder and he was shunted into the middle of the road, where the tramcar it was pulling swallowed him up beneath its iron wheels.

*

Herbert Koller saw the commotion at the very top of King Street, but decided it was of no concern to him. Mrs O'Halloran had been most perturbed at his sudden appearance on the landing dressed in his suit and greatcoat and appearing set for a night on the town. 'Sure ye're delirious, Mr Koller.' she had said. 'Ye were at death's door not two hours ago.'

'Mrs O'Halloran, I did knock, but Death must have been out. At any rate, I think a stroll around town might be just the ticket. All this snow and this bracing cold air. I might return a different man.'

And so she had stood on her doorstep and tutted and fussed, but he had sauntered out in his greatcoat with his muffler wrapped tightly around his face, looking so full of life that she gave a shrug of resignation before closing her door.

Now, having strolled along Warrington Lane and into the centre of town via Millgate and Station Road, thus avoiding the hazardous walk past the Royal Court, he stood at the top of Market Place, looking down towards Wallgate and its junction with King Street. Whatever was going on down there was certainly attracting the interest of many passers-by, and under different circumstances he would have allowed his curiosity to get the better of him and gone to see what all the fuss was about. He was tempted when he caught sight of two policemen running across from the railway station, but he knew that if he went to investigate, there was the very slight chance that Benjamin, or someone else from the company, might have been drawn out of the theatre to see what was happening.

Benjamin! He smiled and turned to his left. If he knew what his darling boy was up to tonight! With a jaunty spring in his step, he headed towards his destination, and thought happily of the rewards that would soon be his. He was about to keep his side of the bargain, and he was sure she would reciprocate.

*

It was difficult for Slevin to explain to Constable Bowery back at the station the chaotic scenes he had left behind him at the Royal Court Theatre.

When Miss Coupe had announced the news about the missing revolver, he had held his hand up and asked everyone to remain where they were, for now this was 'a police matter.' It had disturbed him somewhat when everyone around him, including the delectable Miss Coupe, had fallen into fits of laughter at his expense, his embarrassment only compounded when Morgan-Drew explained that the revolver was, like the cigar, merely a prop, and was used in the opening scene when Will Denver, drunken and rendered penniless because of his excessive gambling, draws out his revolver and hints at suicide.

'It is nevertheless missing,' Slevin had said, his voice slightly higher than normal, 'and this is therefore a possible theft.' It was straw-clutching at its worst, he knew, but he couldn't stand there and say nothing, not with Miss Coupe now stifling her giggle behind a delicately slender hand.

She watched while he and the others scrabbled around the stage looking for the missing prop. He came to a large trunk, its lid open to reveal an untidy heap of breastplates, helmets, swords, plumes and what looked like a scarlet blanket.

'That's a toga,' came a voice behind him. He turned around to come face to face with Miss Coupe. 'We're doing *Julius Caesar* next week. In Liverpool.'

'I . . . I see.' He felt his face flush once more, caused both by his recent embarrassment and his proximity to such a beautiful creature. He saw her eyes. A deep blue, intense and alluring. He wondered how many hearts she had already broken.

'You must think we're all mad.'

'Not at all.'

He recalled the words he had heard her use about him earlier – 'he fascinates me'. The memory robbed him of the power of eloquent speech, and he was, for the moment, reduced to the most abrupt of responses.

'Did you find Herbert?'

'Pardon?'

'We were present earlier when you were enquiring about him.'

'Oh, yes. Yes, I found him.'

'Unwell, I gather.'

'Apparently so.'

She looked at him with an enigmatic smile before continuing.

'We were all sorry to hear he was poorly. But Toby deserves his chance.'

'Is Mr Koller often unwell?'

She frowned, thrown by the question. 'Of course not. Herbert, you might say, is in the pink of health.'

There was something about the way she said it that aroused his curiosity.

'Have you known him long, miss?'

'Herbert? A matter of months.'

'And, forgive the question, but do you know of his relationship with the man who was murdered here in town? Mr Richard Throstle?'

'Throstle?' echoed a voice from the darkness.

Slevin was startled by the intrusion. Then he saw the man he had met briefly, the older actor, Jonathan Keele.

Jonathan stepped from the darkness and beyond one of the flats. 'What's this about Throstle?'

Slevin, irrationally piqued by the old man's appearance, explained briefly the circumstances of the murder while omitting its more lurid aspects. 'It appears Mr Koller knew the victim.'

'Yes, I know.'

'You knew?' Susan Coupe lifted a hand to her lips.

Jonathan smiled. 'I had seen him with Throstle. At least Herbert said it was he. They were dining together. I got the impression they knew each other quite well.'

'Oh?' Slevin said.

'I saw Herbert pass him some money. Apparently he denied it to Benjamin, but I know what I saw.'

Susan Coupe looked horrified. 'This town,' she said in a whisper. 'Murderers. Madmen. Black-faced colliers.'

'Susan,' said Jonathan in a kindly voice, 'hadn't you better go and turn into Nelly Denver?'

'You'll excuse me, Sergeant Slevin?'

He nodded and she moved off into the dark recesses of the stage.

'Is there anything else you can tell me, sir?'

'Only that he isn't to be trusted.'

'Koller?'

'Yes.'

'Why not?'

Jonathan thought for a moment, choosing his words carefully. 'There is a breed of young men for whom nothing will ever suffice. They are driven by some inner demons . . .' His words trailed off and he stood there, a pained expression on his face.

'Thank you,' Slevin said after a few seconds' silence. 'Then I shall resume my search for the missing revolver.' He moved to a row of sealed containers made of shiny metal.

'It won't be in there,' Jonathan said.

'What are they?'

'Stage effects for our next production. Shakespeare's *Julius Caesar*. Benjamin will play the lead, of course. Some contain pots of dust to smear on our breastplates in the battle scenes to make us look battle-weary. A great believer in verisimilitude, is Benjamin. Here are very realistic strips that look for all the world like scars and knife wounds. And of course,' he stooped and patted one of the containers, 'the special capsules filled with fake blood. There's a lot of blood in Shakespeare, haven't you noticed?'

Slevin said that he hadn't particularly, no. Apart from *Julius Caesar*, the only other Shakespeare he and Sarah had seen was *A Midsummer Night's Dream*.

'Oh the public like blood. As long as it isn't their own.'

From the other side of the stage, someone shouted 'Found it!' and a great hurrah went up.

'The show will go on,' said Jonathan. 'Poor Benjamin will be relieved. Despite the best efforts of some people.'

'What do you mean?'

The old man shook his head and mumbled something about getting himself ready, leaving Slevin suddenly alone.

'Queer lot, if you ask me,' said Constable Bowery after he had listened to the account of Slevin's visit. 'First a cigar buggers off, then a gun.'

'Well, strictly speaking, the cigar didn't "bugger off". It was found where it was supposed to be. Young Toby was simply nervous, that's all.'

Slevin leaned back in his chair and glanced up at the clock above his desk. Seven-fifteen.

'So, Constable Bowery. Your visit to Springfield and the delectable Violet. Yield results, did it?'

Bowery, who had been sent to Mort Street earlier, shrugged. 'Well, she seemed glad we'd let her old man go at last. Without charges.' He let the latter statement hang in the air before continuing. Slevin recalled the curses of the three sober and bitter brigands as they barged their way out of the station earlier. Billy Cowburn and his musketeers would even now be celebrating their release, no doubt glorying in their intransigence.

'Dunno if it means owt, sergeant. She'd never heard of Herbert Koller, not by name, any road. But she said Throstle told her summat once that made her think he had friends who were actors.'

'What was it?'

'Told her if she'd agree to do some more poses for him, he'd have her specially trained. Said he knew a bloke what could help. Said this bloke was just what he needed, 'cos it meant London. That's why she kept lettin' him . . . You know. On account of his promise to take her to London with him. Make her famous among the toffs.'

'But she never heard his name?'

182

'No, sergeant.'

Slevin looked up at the ceiling and thought for over a minute. Then he suddenly slammed both hands down on the desk top. 'Right!' he said firmly. 'Get your coat on, constable.'

'Where we goin' now?'

There was just enough weariness in Bowery's voice to forestall the sharp response already forming on Slevin's lips. It was late, and his constable had had a long and tiring day.

'I'm treating you, Jimmy!'

As soon as he heard that particular form of address, Bowery's heart sank.

'What to?'

'You tell me you enjoyed it so much I think it's time for an encore.'

'What?'

'We're off to the Public Hall, Jimmy. To watch this amazing *Phantasmagoria*, and perhaps keep an eye on the grieving widow. We can't ignore the scrawled slogans, can we?'

Bowery's shoulders slumped as he followed the reinvigorated sergeant down the corridor and out of the station. The snow was falling thickly now, heavy flakes that came down in swirling gusts, stinging their faces with a bitter chill, and they both hunched forward into their coats, hands shoved into deep pockets.

*

'Don't you talk about rope, Spider! If it comes to hanging, it won't be me, it'll be you!'

Toby Thomas, pinioned from behind by Harry Montford, who was playing Cripps, stared defiantly at the arch-villain Spider. The entire theatre was hushed and expectant as *The Silver King* built to its climax in the fourth act. The band of villains was disintegrating before their eyes and it was glorious to watch, especially when they knew the wronged Will Denver, disguised as the simpleton Dicky, was listening to their every self-incriminating word.

'Curse you!' roared Henry Parks as the Spider. 'Will you never give me peace till I kill you?'

Toby raised his head high so that the entire auditorium could hear his next words. 'Yes, as you killed Geoffrey Ware!'

James Shorton leapt onto the stage to the consternation of the group of villains gathered at Coombe's Wharf. 'Ah!' he screamed euphorically, the misery of false accusation at last in sight of being destroyed by the truth. 'Innocent! Innocent! Thank God!'

He made a dash for the door, flourishing a crowbar, and, pursued by the others, escaped through the wings with the words 'The whole world shall not stop me now!'

The quick curtain brought a tumultuous round of applause.

Backstage, the atmosphere was similarly jubilant. 'Marvellous, my boy!' Jonathan Keele placed a hand on Toby's shoulder and beamed at him. The boy was perspiring and holding a cloth to his face, careful not to ruin his make-up.

'Thank you, sir.'

Benjamin walked past, making sure everyone was in place for the opening scene of the final act, set in Skinner's villa. The euphoria that was evident on everyone's face was curiously absent from his. Some reflected sagely that it was Mr Morgan-Drew's way, that the joy could only be unconfined when the final curtain fell and he could then relax and exult. Yet Jonathan knew different. No matter how well young Toby might perform as the sharp-tongued Cockney, it would never be enough to compensate for the absence of Herbert Koller. He could see, hidden deep behind those black-rimmed eyes, a sadness that was rendered almost unbearable by his sense of betrayal.

He knew that no words could soothe what his old friend was feeling. So as they passed briefly behind the curtain, Jonathan merely nodded and gave a smile of support, but he knew full well that the smile he got in response was merely an act.

*

A mere fifty yards away, Herbert Koller, the absent Corkett, was actually enjoying himself. He stood behind the raised screen in the Public Hall and spoke in the deep, sonorous tones Georgina Throstle had told him to adopt. He took a peek at the audience, which was almost exclusively drawn from the labouring classes, and smiled. Did superstition still hold sway among these people, he wondered.

'Now the dead, unhappy at their forced incarceration, begin to rise. They attempt to rise to heaven, but look! How they are hurled back by the thunderbolts flashing through the sky! Now look how the rotting flesh hovers through the fog and the filthy air . . .'

Herbert felt a hand on his arm. It was Georgina Throstle. She gave him a sharp look. 'Slow down!' she whispered. 'You make it sound as if they are being transported to Hell by steam locomotive!'

Herbert gripped the sheets of paper tightly and thrust them into her face. 'You dare criticise my pacing!'

'If it moves faster than the railways, yes. Remember what you are here for.'

He lowered his script. He daren't antagonise the woman now, not until he had what he had come for. And soon, in a matter of half an hour, he would succeed.

Although he was unaware of their presence, Detective Sergeant Slevin and Constable Bowery were well aware of his. They had sat through the last thirty minutes listening to his voice and watching the projected images soaring high above them. Bowery had told Slevin not to be afraid, it was all done by lantern projectors. He had even patted the sergeant's knee to reassure him of his presence and support.

'Do that again,' Slevin had whispered, 'and I'll snap every one of your fat fingers. Do I make myself clear?'

'Yes, sergeant.'

Nevertheless, Slevin had to marvel at the way the images were created. He could hear the occasional gasp from those around him, but he felt somehow detached from the fear infecting the rest of the audience, probably because of the constant, nasal drone of the narrator. He didn't like Mr Herbert Koller, and now he could see why the young actor had feigned illness this afternoon: perhaps Mrs Throstle had offered him a large sum of money, more than he would be paid by the company, to fulfil her final engagement in town, and therefore avoid forfeiting the contract and missing out on the sizeable income to be gained from the large attendance.

Was this arrangement the reason for their raised voices, as reported by the hotel manager, Mr Jameson? Had they been arguing over the size of his fee?

His thoughts were interrupted by Herbert Koller, now speaking in a new, more measured pace.

'Picture a dark and lonely cottage . . .'

A slide was projected onto the screen, the inside of a filthy hovel. Onto the scene was suddenly projected another: three old hags peering wildly at the audience. Above the screen, a horned devil rose with a ferocious expression on its vile features.

'Picture three wicked dams, all staring with the vilest of intentions at their next victim. And their beloved fiend, the one with the cloven foot and the serpent's tail, he has heard their evil chants and now he prepares to come among them, to come among us . . . every one of us . . .'

Slevin watched with admiration as the figure projected above the screen now seemed to dissolve and change its features as it moved slowly around the room. All eyes in the audience were now gazing upwards, following the slow, insidious path of the demon that could, at any moment, swoop down and possess their living souls.

Then something caught his eye, and he switched his attention to some movement beside the main screen. More of the audience now turned to see this latest horror: the dark shape of a woman walking towards them, with her hands clasped to her neck and the sound of a guttural, rasping screech forcing itself from her throat. He marvelled at the ghoulish realism of the vision: it did actually appear to be a woman of flesh and blood! But what made everyone gasp was not the sound, but the dim glow that was pouring from her mouth.

The commentary ceased. There was no voice now to describe the horror the audience was witnessing. All they could hear was the low hiss from the gas and the scrape and shuffle of the woman's feet staggering along the aisle towards them. One or two of those near the back began to applaud, thinking the performance was over and expressing their appreciation of this final vision. Yet those nearest to her saw that this was no projected image; this was no illusion. It was Slevin who stood up and pushed his way past those seated beside him. It was Slevin who realised now that this was no planned part of the show. And it was Slevin who reached Georgina Throstle in the very moment when she finally yielded to the agony of her burning throat and slumped to the floor, a dull green glow bursting from her wide-open mouth.

Now the horror was real.

9

The four operators of the slide projectors were finally allowed to go home. It was well after eleven. Slevin felt it highly unlikely that any of them had been involved in the death of Georgina Throstle, but he nevertheless had to go through the formalities of interview and statements, and he decided to carry those out on the premises. The audience – none of whom had come into direct contact with the deceased woman – had left. Some of them had even grumbled, complaining that, as the slide show had been prematurely ended, surely they were entitled to some recompense.

Mr Herbert Koller, on the other hand, had disappeared.

Once the confusion had turned into horror, there was a veritable Babel of noise, of barked orders and screamed obscenities, and in the midst of all the uproar, the young actor had apparently taken the opportunity to make his exit.

'Find him!' Slevin ordered, giving the gathered policemen a brief description along with the address of his lodgings in Darlington Street.

The body had been removed and taken to the mortuary at the Royal Albert Edward Infirmary. Slevin had politely sent a request to Dr Bentham for a post-mortem as soon as was humanly possible – he wanted to know the exact cause of the woman's death. Then one of the policemen reported to him that the office by the stage had apparently been broken into and the small safe prised open with a crowbar. All of its contents had been removed. With the situation rapidly going out of control, Slevin braced himself for the hurricane of charges that would blast his way when he next came face to face with his chief constable: 'You were present at a murder *and* a burglary, detective sergeant?'

Worswick, the manager of the hall, had assured him that Mrs Throstle had seemed in good spirits (considering her recent tragic bereavement, of course), on arriving at the Public Hall. She had seemed most anxious for Mr Koller to be shown every courtesy, and had asked if, at the conclusion of the night's demonstration, he would make available his office for a little personal business.

'Were Mrs Throstle and Mr Koller left alone together at any time?'

'Of course not.'

'What refreshments did Mrs Throstle take?'

'None that I am aware of. She told me she had dined earlier.'

'And Mr Koller? Was he left alone at any time?'

'I don't think so. No, I am quite sure he wasn't. He seemed rather anxious to get on with the commentary and be done with the whole thing. Nerves, I suppose.'

'Of course. Thank you, Mr Worswick.'

'Er, there is one thing I should perhaps mention, Sergeant Slevin.'

'What's that?'

'Mrs Throstle had asked that I make a certain package available for her at the conclusion to tonight's performance.'

'Package? What kind of package?'

'Something she and her husband had stored here in our safe. I promised that I would see to it personally.'

'What was in the package?'

'I have no idea. But it was around twelve inches square. Quite bulky.'

'I see.'

'It's quite fortuitous, in a sense.'

'What is?'

'Well, the safe being prised open like that.'

'And how is that fortuitous?'

'It's obvious that whoever broke in was not only responsible for Mrs Throstle's ghastly end, but also after the night's takings.'

'A fair conclusion.' Slevin wondered how on earth this could in any way be seen as fortuitous.

'But you see, I failed to carry out her instructions.'

'What?'

'When the young man at the entrance came with the evening's receipts, I counted everything, gave the fellow his wage for the evening, and put the money in my bag.'

'Your bag? Why not the safe?'

'We have already been the victim of one break-in, as you are aware. And the safe was interfered with on that occasion, too. I felt it was only a matter of time before the miscreants returned with the necessary tools to open it. I intended to take the money home with me rather than leave it here overnight and wait for the banks to open.'

'So you think the words scrawled on the wall were a subterfuge?'

'I am by nature a suspicious and precautionary person.' He reached down and picked up the brown leather bag he had placed on the floor. 'Having put the money in my bag, I then opened the safe and removed the package. I put it into my bag, which I then placed beneath my desk. Who would think of looking there, eh?' He opened the bag and pulled out a brown paper parcel.

Worswick proudly handed Slevin the parcel, which was surprisingly weighty. Slevin wondered if it contained money. If so, there was a princely sum wrapped up here, he thought. He thanked the manager and moved over to where Bowery was speaking with a few of the other constables.

'Any of you men got a knife?'

One of the constables pulled out a shiny silver object and handed it over. Slevin slit the edges of the parcel so that he could peer inside without ruining the entire package. Then he cut down the left hand side until the contents were exposed. He handed the knife back and tore the rest of the packaging away to reveal a dark red box, divided into four compartments. On the front of the first compartment were etched the words 'Rose Blossoms' in fine italic script. In each compartment appeared to be six or seven square frames, measuring around three inches, and edged in dark grey. Slevin lifted one from its slot. As he held it up for them all to see, they noticed the frame contained a piece of glass upon which were imprinted diminutive figures too small to distinguish.

'What the blazes is that lot?' Bowery asked.

'Unless I'm mistaken, Constable Bowery, these are magic lantern slides of a most specialised nature.'

'What sort of specialised?'

'Remember what Violet Cowburn told us?'

Bowery leaned closer to the glass image. 'Blow me, sergeant! You mean there's *that* sort of stuff on here? But you can hardly see it.'

Slevin pointed to one of the slide projectors standing a few yards away. 'That's their job. To magnify the image.'

'What stuff would that be, Jimmy?' said Constable Turner, one of those remaining behind to keep guard on the premises. He moved nearer, until Bowery pressed a hand against the young constable's chest.

'Nowt that would interest you, lad. What's on these here slides would give you nightmares for a week, and no mistake.'

Slevin turned and called over to the manager, who had just finished counting the contents of his bag for the fourth time. 'Mr Worswick! I wonder if you can help?'

He walked over to the manager and whispered something in his ear. Whatever he had said, it was met with a frown, then a contemplative closing of the eyes, then finally a decisive nod and the words 'Of course.'

'Right!' said Slevin, returning to the gathering of constables. 'I want every one of you to take up strategic points all around the perimeter of the building.'

'What?' said Paintbrush.

'He wants us all outside,' Bowery explained. 'Guarding the place.' He ushered the others outside, but as he got to the exit door he turned and gave his sergeant a rueful look that expressed in more than words his disappointment at not being included in this next phase of the investigation.

'Right!' Slevin said, when the door had banged shut, leaving only himself and the manager in the vast hall. 'You know what to do.' He handed the wooden box and its contents to Worswick, who walked quickly over to the nearest projector.

'I've watched them during the week,' Worswick said. 'One of the assistants showed me how they use these gas cylinders to produce sufficient heat to light the block of limelight inside. It's just a matter of getting the right mix . . .'

Cautiously, Slevin stepped back.

'The ones on wheels,' said the now engrossed manager, 'are pushed to and fro to give the illusion of movement, making the ghastly images seem to move closer or farther away.'

'I don't need movement to see what's on here,' Slevin snapped.

'Ah!' Worswick declared as the combined gases lit the block of limelight. 'Success!'

A bright white light was cast onto the screen before them. Slevin took a deep breath as he handed the first of the slides to Worswick.

*

Later, much later, Slevin sat in the darkness and watched his son's chest as it rose and fell with a regular rhythm. The curtains were closed, but a tiny gap between them allowed a shaft of moonlight to rest exactly where his small hand lay above the bedclothes. Beyond the window, the snow was swirling manically, caught up in angry gusts of wind.

'What is it, Sam?' Sarah had asked earlier. 'What's on your mind?'

He couldn't tell her, of course. He had simply reached across to pat her hand and say he was simply tired. Now, as she lay asleep next door, he sat beside little Peter, trying to let the sound of his son's breathing banish the dreadful images that lay floating around his brain like a phantasmagoria out of control.

But it was impossible. The more he became aware of Peter's breathing, of his presence, of his future, the more he felt his heart sink under a cold and heavy weight. Although he tried most desperately, he simply couldn't shake from his consciousness the sights he had seen tonight, the degradation he had witnessed on those abhorrent slides. Worswick had been physically ill and begged leave to retire to his office, leaving instructions on how to change the slides and maintain the focus of the image, so that Slevin watched the bulk of the images in a dreadful silence pierced only by the unheard screams and pitiful pleas of those poor children up there on the screen, whose smiles and poses were so obviously forced that it was a matter of wonder how the photographer got them to remain still for the length of the exposure.

But it was the final set of slides that made him shake with loathing: worst of all was the face of a young girl who could have been no older than eleven. It was the way her eyes looked up at the man forcing himself on her that made him retch with disgust. The man's face was of course out of shot, but he could see hers clearly. Innocence and depravity framed for ever in a hellish vision of evil. That there were men who delighted in viewing such things! Her eyes gazed upwards, where heaven should be, but where only wickedness leered back.

He had felt an overwhelming wave of pity for the poor child, a sensation that still flooded his entire being now as he gazed down at another such innocent.

He knew with certainty what he would do to the monster who perpetrated such vileness. But he also knew that what he had in mind had already been done, for Richard Throstle had been the man in the slide, the man defiling the innocence of childhood.

He saw the shaft of light slowly fade as a cloud drifted across the moon. Tomorrow, he promised himself, this will all be concluded.

*

'Phosphorus poisoning?'

'Just so.'

Slevin looked at Dr Horatio Bentham and shook his head. They were standing on either side of the covered remains of Georgina Throstle. Her brother Edward had been brought down to the mortuary to provide the formal identification of the body, and had flatly refused to leave her side until he had recited innumerable prayers for the sanctity of her 'sinful soul'. Now, as the Reverend Edward Malvern was waiting in the visitors' room under the watchful gaze of Constable Bowery, Slevin looked at the pitiful outline of a woman he had spoken to a matter of hours ago.

Bentham pointed to the contents of a large crucible, fortunately also covered by a cloth.

'It's quite easy to detect, post-mortem,' he explained. 'All we do is lower the lighting and watch.'

'Watch?'

'The organs glow, you see? Phosphorus is a very illuminating poison. It caused the glowing from her mouth you described to me earlier. Still, I conducted a few tests to make sure. Oxidisation by nitric acid, mainly.'

'How could she have taken it?'

Bentham shrugged. 'Orally, of course, but the means . . . well, not my area, really. More in your line.'

'Isn't phosphorus used in match-making?'

'Yes. But you'd have to crush a number of matches to provide a fatal dose, and there are other agents involved in making matches. I think rat poison's your man. Probably Rodine.'

'But what about the taste? Wouldn't it be impossible to disguise?'

'Difficult, but not impossible. You see, phosphorus has a sharp tang of garlic, so the food or drink you need to mix it with has to be quite strong, strong enough to mask the taste.'

'I see. Is there anything else, doctor?'

'Oh no, I don't think so. Not with this one at any rate.'

'What do you mean?'

Bentham raised a finger and gave him a mischievous smile. 'If I hadn't got your message about this unfortunate lady, I had planned to contact you anyway. It may be something or it may be totally unconnected, but I think you might at least wish to take it into consideration.'

'And what might that be?'

The surgeon escorted him to another part of the mortuary, a long, dark room that seemed somehow much colder than the examining room they had just left. Bentham lit a small gas lamp fixed to the wall and picked up a small oil lamp which he also lit. Its tiny flame danced eerily as they moved quickly down a narrow passage with darkened alcoves spaced to right and left at regular intervals. These alcoves, he knew, were the penultimate resting-places of those unfortunates who were awaiting some sort of interment at the expense of the parish. Poor, desolate souls whom no one came forward to claim and for whom no one came forward to grieve. He shuddered and kept close to the feeble yellow light before him.

'Here we are!' Bentham announced like a museum guide.

Slevin followed him into one of the alcoves on the left. He saw the edge of a hard wooden slab and a pair of whitened feet with a piece of card tied to one of the ankles.

Bentham read aloud the name on the card. 'Enoch Platt.'

'Clapper!' Slevin said.

'You knew him?'

'Oh yes. A character about town, you might say.'

'Well, this fellow was run down by a tram in the centre of town.'

'Accident?'

'Oh, indubitably. Several witnesses, you see. He just staggered out into the path of the tram and, well, that was it.'

'So what has this accident to do with my investigation?'

'A coincidence. Involving the man's clothes.'

'His clothes?'

'Yes. One of the assistants was about to throw them away – they were dreadfully filthy – when she began to sneeze. Before I could admonish her – we were in an examining room, after all – she said it was hardly surprising, considering she'd just inhaled a mouthful of the vilest dust.'

Slevin grew more alert.

'So I took the trouble of examining the man's clothes.'

'And you found asbestos dust?'

Bentham resembled an actor whose best line had been stolen and used by another. 'As a matter of fact, I did. Your Mr Enoch Platt had asbestos dust all over his midriff. It matches exactly the dust I examined on the body of Mr Richard Throstle.'

*

The police constable who had been despatched to Mrs O'Halloran's lodging-house the previous night had searched the bedroom where Mr Herbert Koller was staying. There was no sign of him, although he had evidently not planned to leave the town, for his clothes were still in the wardrobe and his suitcase was beneath the bed. When the policeman left, Mrs O'Halloran sat in her front room waiting for the arrival of Mr Morgan-Drew, who would doubtless know what to do. It had been a terrible misjudgement on Mr Koller's part to leave his sickbed. Perhaps he had grown delirious and done something that was completely out of character?

When the actor-manager arrived, he had already seen the policeman standing outside and was alarmed to be told the reason for his presence.

'But did he say what they wanted to speak to Herbert about?'

'Not a word, Mr Morgan-Drew.'

Benjamin sat there, pondering the situation. But as the night grew on, he had no alternative but to accept Mrs O'Halloran's advice and go upstairs to bed. He was certainly not foolish enough to go out and look for him. After the lies Herbert had told earlier that evening, he would never deign to pursue him again. He lay down in his cold bed and waited for the tears to come.

It was after one o'clock when he heard the sound and sat up in bed.

He moved across to the bedroom window. He lifted the curtain and peered down into the darkness of the back yard. At first he saw nothing. Then, from the privy halfway down the back alley, he saw a murky shape detach itself from the doorway and run to Mrs O'Halloran's back wall, where it raised an arm and was about to hurl another snowball at his window. Quickly, Benjamin undid the catch of the window and swung it open.

'Herbert!' he called in his quietest stage whisper. 'Herbert? Is that you?'

The figure froze and stooped low; from behind the brick wall came the familiar voice. 'Let me in, for God's sake! I'll die of frostbite out here!'

'One minute!' Benjamin said and closed the window.

He crept downstairs and went to the kitchen, where he carefully unbarred the back door and opened it. A second later, Herbert, shivering, slid inside and urged his saviour to close the door and take him to his room.

A few minutes later, as they lay together in bed, Benjamin could feel the chill on his skin, and a gloomy heaviness settle in the pit of his stomach. Despite his noble defiance, his vows of earlier, he was once again in thrall to this mendacious young god. But he knew that, for the time being at least, there would be no point in hurling recriminations or even in asking questions. He would let him thaw out first.

*

197

The two constables stood before Sergeant Slevin and tried to get their story straight. He had asked to see all those policemen who were present at the previous night's accident at the top of King Street, an accident that had necessitated the closure of the street and the diversion of all horse-drawn vehicles. For half an hour the situation had been quite chaotic, and the unfortunate constables had borne the brunt of all manner of hostility. They had even come under attack from a flurry of snowballs.

'We never saw where he came from,' said one of the constables. 'Bugger just turned up on King Street.'

'Well some of them as saw the accident reckon he slunk out of the alley.'

'Did any of them see him with anyone else?' Slevin asked.

'One bloke told me Clapper was seen talkin' to some lasses. Mill lasses.'

'Nah!' said his colleague. 'He weren't talkin' to 'em – he were yellin' at 'em. They came up an' said he'd had a right go at 'em.'

'What did he say to them?'

The first constable screwed up his face to concentrate. 'Dunno, sergeant. They said it were gibberish. But the bloke who told me, well, he knew Clapper. Or Enoch. Worked with him down the pit an' he reckoned Clapper were scared. Kept sayin' to this chap that the Devil had got him.'

'Got him? How?'

'God knows. But he also said summat else. Kept sayin' summat about somebody havin' two eyes an' two heads. Tried to get some sense out of him, but by that time Clapper was well gone. Don't make any sense, does it? Two eyes an' two heads, he said.'

'Anything else?'

The two constables shook their heads and Slevin dismissed them. As they left, the forbidding figure of the chief constable replaced them.

'Another murder, sergeant? Are you collecting corpses, by any chance? How do you know when you've got a full set?'

'Mrs Throstle was poisoned by phosphorus, sir.'

'And it appears she was murdered under your nose.'

Slevin leaned forward and opened a thin folder. He took out a single sheet of paper and handed it to his superior. 'Dr Bentham's preliminary report, sir. You'll notice the reference to times of ingestion. He surmises that the poison – probably Rodine – was somehow given to the victim a few hours before her death.'

'Had a chap commit suicide in the army with the blasted stuff. Mixed it in his curry and had the gall to eat it in front of us. Once he'd done, he said it was the best curry he'd ever tasted and he would see us all in Hell. Medic said later his innards glowed like a firework display.'

'There seems to be a link between the two shows,' Slevin said, ignoring the digression. 'That is, the play at the Royal Court and the *Phantasmagoria* at the Public Hall.'

'Really, sergeant?'

'One of the actors, a Mr Herbert Koller, feigned sickness last night and missed the performance. Instead, he stood in for Mr Richard Throstle and gave the commentary to the lantern slides. He had apparently known Throstle personally and was possibly involved in some business deal with him.'

'Mr Koller, you say?'

'Yes, sir. Are you acquainted with him?'

'We have met. Where is the fellow now?'

'I have constables keeping an eye on his lodging-house in Darlington Street. If he turns up there, they'll bring him in, have no fear.'

'Anything else I should know about?'

Slevin told him about Enoch Platt's accident, and the curious coincidence of the dust matching the asbestos dust on Throstle's body.

'Asbestos dust, you say?'

'Yes, sir.'

The chief constable was frowning. 'It takes me back, sergeant. To India and the Punjabbers.'

Slevin looked up to the heavens for help. Not another reminiscence!

'We used asbestos dust, you see? Smeared it all over our costumes during our famed production of *Ivanhoe*. The dust is used to show someone has been travelling, or fighting, or both.'

Slevin recalled the tubs of powder he had seen backstage at the Royal Court. Another connection between the two productions.

'Two eyes and two heads, you say?' Captain Bell was shaking his head sadly. 'What on earth does that mean? Poor imbecile had two eyes and no head. Not to speak of, anyway.'

He smiled at his comment and bade his sergeant farewell.

Two eyes and two heads. Now what indeed had Enoch Platt meant by that?

A sharp knock at the door made him jump. Constable Bowery breezed in with the air of a man confident that the news he brought would excuse any breach of etiquette.

'Sergeant! That Jameson bloke's at the main desk.'

'The manager of the Royal?'

'Aye. Reckons he has summat we should know about.'

'And what might that be?'

'He knows someone who had a bit of a confrontation with Clapper not ten minutes before the poor sod was killed. Says he saw Enoch go up to one of his guests and grab him by the throat. Says he stared into his eyes and yelled out that he was starin' into the eyes of the Devil.'

Slevin glowered impatiently at his constable. 'Who was the guest?'

'Bloke called Jenkins, sergeant. Jameson says he sells hosiery.'

*

It was a problem Benjamin Morgan-Drew had faced several times in his life, although never as intensely as this. Never before had he felt such a burning desire for another human being as he did for Herbert Koller. Now, as the two of them lay together, communicating by the softest of whispers, he knew that his feelings were at war once more. Herbert had lied. He had lied about being ill and he had lied about where he had been. Lies and more lies.

'You have to speak to the police,' he said, regarding the ceiling with burning eyes.

'You mean the ones who want to throw me in prison? The ones who wish to see me dangle at the end of a rope?'

'That sounds like a line from a bad melodrama, Herbert. You know it won't come to that.'

Outside the bedroom door they heard Mrs O'Halloran pass noisily along the landing. She had knocked once, and when Benjamin told her he did not require breakfast, she had huffed her way downstairs muttering incomprehensible oaths.

'How well did you know Mrs Throstle?'

'I've already told you. I have confessed my duplicity, Benjamin.' He sighed and repeated the tale once more. 'I met her husband and he asked me if I would be interested in working for him, delivering his vile drivel in public halls to stinking masses across the country. I refused, of course. My loyalty is to you and the company, as you know. But how could I refuse the request of a poor bereaved widow?'

Benjamin gave a sad smile. Trust Herbert to turn an act of betrayal into one of nobility. 'What, then, do you propose to do? Hide here in this room until you are discovered? Let me accompany you to the police station and explain exactly what your arrangements were with Mrs Throstle. The fact that you were present at her unfortunate demise is neither here nor there. What reason would you have for killing her?'

Herbert turned onto his side, away from Benjamin. 'And then I would be free to rejoin the company?'

'Of course. You will be Henry Corkett tonight!'

He watched Herbert take a deep breath and give a slight nod of acquiescence. If he could persuade Detective Sergeant Slevin of the boy's relative innocence, then perhaps he would see a new Herbert. It was a slender hope, he knew, a candle lit in a blizzard, but any hope at all is better than the dark shadows of despair. He'd seen enough of them.

*

Slevin's men had been in Georgina Throstle's hotel room since the early morning, and it hadn't taken them long to find what they were looking for. Once he had been apprised of the discovery, Slevin arranged to speak with Mr Jameson in the manager's office about the encounter between Enoch Platt and Mr Jenkins, the hosiery salesman.

'Last evening, while some of our guests were dining, I saw Mr Jenkins in the foyer,' Jameson began. 'He seemed a little – shall we say? – flustered, but I bade him a good evening as he left and turned to resume my duties. Suddenly I heard a strange sound – a clapping sound – and I noticed a man dressed in filthy rags, standing on the steps below Mr Jenkins and clapping in his face. He moved aside to get past, but the man blocked his way. He then grabbed Mr Jenkins by the shoulders, as if he were staring into his eyes. Of course, I rushed to the entrance and immediately demanded he release Mr Jenkins. He kept his eyes fixed on his victim and yelled out, "The eyes of the Devil! The eyes of the Devil!" And then some nonsense about two heads.'

'What happened then?'

'Mr Jenkins grabbed him, and there was a struggle. By now quite a crowd was gathering – I did what I could to help, but I can assure you, sergeant, it was most unseemly. With the help of some of my staff we finally managed to extricate Mr Jenkins. I offered to send for the police, but Jenkins said it was of no consequence and we were to let the imbecile go.'

'May I speak with Mr Jenkins?'

'Unfortunately, no. Mr Jenkins never returned to the hotel last night. His bed has not been slept in. Not only that, his wardrobe is empty. His clothes have gone.'

'So he has left without paying?'

'Perhaps,' said Jameson with a shrug. 'But there is a further mystery to compound matters.'

'Go on.'

'It is rare for a guest to leave without settling his account – rare, but it does happen. But there is something singular about this occurrence. You see, this morning we found his suitcase in the room.'

'All packed and ready to leave, no doubt.'

'No, sergeant. The suitcase was not packed at all. In fact, it was quite empty.'

'Empty? But that's –'

'Yes. It's puzzling, isn't it?'

Slevin thought long and hard, trying to assimilate two very disparate pieces of evidence. An empty suitcase and a man with two heads. Suddenly, he gave the hotel manager a beaming smile. 'Not impossible at all, Mr Jameson. But logical. Oh yes. As logical as a man with two heads!'

*

The Reverend Edward Malvern sat facing Sergeant Slevin in the hotel manager's office.

'Naturally I want to assist the police. The perpetrator must be brought to meet the full rigour of the law before justice is pronounced.'

'He will be, your reverence, you can rest assured on that.'

'But there are practical matters I need to attend to, you understand, sergeant.' Malvern gave a frosted smile. 'I must be allowed to collect my sister's possessions and take them back to Leeds with me.'

Slevin nodded. 'Soon, your reverence.'

'But you have already searched her room for goodness knows what. And that is tantamount to defilement! Surely you see there is something profoundly distasteful in strangers rifling through her personal belongings?'

'They are policemen doing their duty, your reverence. And there is something even more profoundly distasteful in allowing a murderer to elude justice by failing to uncover all possible evidence.' He spoke sharply, and Malvern, who evidently was unaccustomed to such pointedness, remained silent.

'Now, your reverence, would you kindly tell me what took place last night before your sister left for the Public Hall?'

'We dined.'

'That's all?'

'Would you like me to describe what we ate, sergeant?'

He had meant it as merely as an ironic riposte to what he thought of as unnecessary questioning. He was therefore surprised when Slevin said, 'In detail, please.'

'Are you mad, sergeant? What possible use –?'

Slevin held up a hand. 'Your sister was poisoned by phosphorus, sir. It is a vile-tasting substance that needs a disguise. Something to take the taste away. Perhaps the food she ate last night.'

'Preposterous!' Now the reverend looked the detective fully in the eye. 'Are you suggesting that someone in the hotel kitchen poisoned my sister?'

'Unlikely.'

His eyes widened as he put his next question. 'Then are you implying that –?'

'I imply nothing.'

'That I . . . what did I do, sergeant? Lean over and drop the substance onto her pigeon? If it is as vile-tasting as you say, then pigeon is hardly a strong enough disguise now, is it?'

'No, it isn't.'

'Well then!'

'Your sister suffered from neuralgia.'

Malvern's eyes narrowed. 'Yes. Yes, she suffered greatly. My father used to say it was a curse from Heaven for her disobedience.'

'Disobedience?'

'Yes. She had been a governess, a position he found for her and for which she ought to have been profoundly grateful. But she had spent barely a year teaching the wretched child, a girl who grew very attached to her, I might add, when she ran away with Throstle. The girl grew surly and inconsolable, and both her family and my father never forgave her betrayal. Nor did my father ever speak to the man responsible for her fall from grace. Despite my efforts to improve him, Richard Throstle was a vile and calculating man, God rest his soul.'

'I see.'

Malvern looked at Slevin for a while, then with some hesitation asked his next question. 'Why do you ask about her neuralgia?'

Slevin smiled and stood up. 'Because she apparently had an attack last night. During dinner.'

Malvern swallowed hard. His shoulders seemed to sag a little before recovering themselves and being restored to their former rigidity. 'Perhaps she did.'

'And you kindly offered to go to her room to collect her medicine.'

'How did you –?'

'The waiter saw you leave and return with a small medicine bottle.'

'It was an act of charity on my part. I offered to bring it. But what does my kindness to my sister in getting her medicine have to do with her death? I hardly think –'

'We have examined the bottle of medicine in your sister's room. It contains not only her prescribed medication, but perhaps a very dangerous amount of rat poison. Once it has been examined we'll know for certain. Ironic, isn't it, that she died as a result of taking something designed to alleviate her suffering?'

Malvern was open-mouthed. 'Are you suggesting it was I who . . .'

'I'm suggesting nothing, sir.'

'But that is preposterous, man! I am her brother!'

'And she lacked the obedience you desired. She wouldn't return with you to Leeds and so you punished her.'

'I am a man of God!'

The detective sat back and scrutinised him. 'Tell me about the room.'

'What room?'

'Your sister's.'

Edward looked confused. 'It's a bedroom in a hotel.'

'Yes. But where was the bottle of medicine?'

Edward thought for a moment, as if he were trying to recreate the scene in his head. 'On the small table beside her bed.'

'And this was the same bottle you brought over from Leeds?'

'Yes. She has a standing prescription with her doctor.'

'Was there anything unusual about the bottle?'

'What do you mean?'

'Had it been tampered with in any way?'

'Of course not! Who on earth would tamper with it?'

'The murderer?'

It was Edward's turn to sit back.

'Was the door locked when you got to her room?'

Edward had to think before answering. 'I rather think it was unlocked. In fact it must have been, for she gave me no key.'

Slevin thought about that for a second.

There was a knock on the door and Constable Bowery entered, whispered something in Slevin's ear, and left.

'Well, I think that will be all for now, your reverence.'

Malvern stood up and glared at the policeman, irritated at being addressed like some recalcitrant schoolboy.

'Then I am under no suspicion?'

'Let's say you are low on my list.' Slevin rose to his feet and faced the man. 'My men have scoured your hotel room from top to bottom, and examined every single item of clothing, every utensil you brought with you, while you have been here with me.'

'My . . . all my belongings? *Scoured*, you say?'

'Indeed, your reverence.'

'Why?'

'Looking for phosphorus traces. It glows, you see. And smells of garlic. And you will no doubt be relieved to know that we found nothing of interest to us. No drops of phosphorus carelessly spilled in your suitcase. No specks on your clothing, nor on your floor, nor anywhere in your room.'

'But I could have told you that!'

'Perhaps I should have asked, then,' Slevin said with a smile, allowing the reverend to leave the room in high dudgeon, his martyrdom assured.

*

When Mr Benjamin Morgan-Drew stepped out of Mrs O'Halloran's lodging-house and told the constable standing conspicuously out-side the front door that the man they were looking for was willing to pay Sergeant Slevin a visit, having spent the night there, the news wasn't received with any sense of satisfaction. It meant that one of the four constables who had shared the watch had slipped up and allowed Mr Herbert Koller to gain entry. Luckily, it would be difficult for Slevin to discover who exactly was responsible.

Within half an hour, the constable, Mr Morgan-Drew and Mr Koller were walking through the snow along Darlington Street.

Detective Sergeant Slevin would be with them soon, said the duty sergeant when they arrived at the station. He asked the two actors to wait in the visitors' room until they could be seen. As they sat down in the bare room with just a single deal table and four chairs, Benjamin and Herbert noticed a large and forbidding shape outside the frosted glass window of the door. It looked as though the police were taking no chances this time.

Furtively, Benjamin reached down and gave Herbert's hand a gentle squeeze.

'This will soon be over,' he said in a low voice. 'Then we can return to normal.'

'Normal!'

There was something strange in Herbert's voice, a combination of incipient hysteria and bitter sarcasm. Benjamin took a deep breath and said, 'I may have a surprise for you tonight, Herbert.'

'Surprise? What kind of surprise?'

Benjamin shook his head. 'The very nature of a surprise is its unexpectedness.'

Before Herbert could probe any further, the shadow in the frosted glass moved to one side and the door opened. Detective Sergeant Slevin walked in.

'Good morning, gentlemen. I'm glad we have found you, Mr Koller.'

'You didn't find me. I revealed myself.'

'Quite.' Slevin turned to Benjamin and said, 'And, Mr Morgan-Drew, I should like to thank you for bringing your companion here today.'

'It was nothing, sergeant.'

'And, with your duty done, you may now of course leave.'

'Leave? But I wish to stay.'

'Ah, but I wish to speak to Mr Koller in private.'

'And I am here to provide him with support.'

'Which you can provide by waiting outside. I have instructed Constable Bowery to provide you with a cup of tea.'

As he had been speaking, Slevin had slowly edged the actor-manager towards the door, which now opened to show the beaming face of Constable Bowery.

Once they were alone, Slevin sat at the table opposite the young man and began without preamble.

'You ran away from the Public Hall last night when Mrs Throstle died. Why was that?'

Koller shifted in his seat. 'Because I saw you.'

'Am I so alarming?'

'You knew I had faked my illness yesterday afternoon.'

'Faking an illness is no indicator of guilt where a murder is concerned.'

Herbert gave a thin smile. 'I just thought you might interpret it otherwise. I admit I was shocked when she collapsed the way she did. I suppose I simply panicked.'

'Did you happen to find yourself in the manager's office during the confusion, Mr Koller?'

Herbert suddenly looked pale. 'What on earth for?'

'Well, there's a safe in there.'

Now he gave a nervous guffaw. 'So which am I? A murderer or a safebreaker?'

'Neither. Or both.'

'I can assure you I went nowhere near the safe.'

Slevin placed his hands palm down on the table to indicate a change of tack. 'Your relationship with Mr Throstle. Let's pursue that a little further, shall we?'

'We already have pursued it, sergeant. I barely knew the man.'

'But we are informed that Mr Throstle was making promises. Young women were given the prospect of . . . professional coaching, training from someone who possesses all the confidence and skill of a professional actor. Throstle planned to develop these . . . models for his own, highly exclusive purposes.'

'What has that to do with me?'

'Mr Throstle gave my informant the impression that he already had such an actor lined up to provide that support. Were you that person, Mr Koller?'

Herbert slowly shook his head. Slevin could see that the poise, the confidence had returned, but beneath the veneer lay something else. What was it? Relief? Or regret?

'Models, you say? Modelling what?'

'Shall we use the term "posing", then?'

'Posing for what?'

'I think you know, Mr Koller.'

'But you see, that's the thing, sergeant. I really have no idea what you are talking about. I'm an actor, not an artist. Artists have models, don't they? But actors, well, we merely strut our hour upon the stage, then we expire, signifying nothing.'

Slevin had the impression that Koller was mocking him, but he persisted.

'Your relationship with Mrs Throstle was purely financial, then?'

'Of course. She made me an offer and I accepted. Shamefully bad form, I know.'

'But why would she do that?'

'She needed a male voice for the lantern show. A trained male voice.'

'Quite. But why ask you? And if she did ask you, then she must have known you, mustn't she?'

'I suppose so.' Herbert's voice was more wary now as Slevin's slow, inexorable logic began to sink its teeth into him.

'And if she knew you, then she must have been told about you by her husband.'

'Possibly.'

'And you were seen giving her husband a certain amount of money.'

That threw him. He swallowed hard and looked down at his hands. 'Who told you that?'

'That is irrelevant. Did you or did you not give Mr Richard Throstle some money?'

'No. Certainly not.'

'I see. Of course, another suggestion might be that Mrs Throstle knew you, and her husband did not.'

'What?'

'In which case, you may have been of assistance to her in other ways than merely vocal.'

'What are you suggesting?' Now he was genuinely afraid of what Slevin was saying. He shifted nervously in his seat and clasped and unclasped his hands.

'Let us imagine, shall we, that you and Mrs Throstle knew each other. Let's also imagine that she asked you to do her a small favour. Say, kill her husband.'

'My God!'

'And now let us imagine that, for some reason, the two of you had a serious disagreement. A disagreement that was overheard by someone in the hotel.'

'But I never . . .'

'In which case, you would have no choice but to resolve the disagreement to your satisfaction by killing her.'

'No!'

'You were working with her last night. There was plenty of opportunity to slip the noxious substance into her system by a drink or a small piece of confectionery.'

'Nonsense! This is madness! Madness!'

'You knew her, you had business with her husband, you may well have been the angel of death in their bedroom when he was so brutally slain, you argued with her before her death and you were with her minutes before she died. To complete this miserable picture of guilt, you then compounded your involvement by attempting to steal what was in the safe before running away. Do you see how very black things look for you, Mr Koller?'

Herbert clenched his hands into fists and slammed them both on the table. 'I have killed no one! You must believe me, sergeant!'

Slevin leaned back. The arrogance had now gone. Instead, he was facing a young man trembling as the shadow of a noose dangled above his head.

'Mr Koller, before I arrest and charge you for the murders of Richard Throstle and Georgina Throstle, do you have anything to say?'

Herbert slumped forward and put his forehead on his balled fists. 'Yes,' he said hoarsely. 'There is something I think you should know.'

*

As he spoke, Herbert Koller's voice lost much of its air of superiority. Occasionally he wrung his hands, anxious for his words to be believed.

'I met Throstle in Manchester. I knew a few chaps there, and they took me along to a private showing. You have no idea how monotonous it can be, touring the country with the same people and having the same conversations, and . . . So, I was intrigued by Richard Throstle. He told me about his ambitions. God, how refreshing it was to speak to someone with ambition! He told me he wanted to expand his business – not the phantasmagoria nonsense, you understand. He said there was a fortune, an incalculable fortune, to be made if he could find the right person to assist him.'

'Assist in what way?'

Koller licked his lips. 'London was his golden opportunity, and he intended to set up business there. But he needed someone who could . . . provide him with a steady supply.'

'Of what?'

'Young women. And, on occasion, young men.'

'And you could provide this supply?'

'London is a place of plenty, sergeant. I would be providing a service and sharing in the profits.'

'With little thought for the victims of your enterprise?'

'They would be paid handsomely. I hardly think that they would regard themselves as victims.'

'What about children?'

'What do you mean?'

'Richard Throstle included children in his . . . presentations.'

Koller shifted uncomfortably. 'I know nothing of that. He

asked me to provide young women, and, for an even more specialised audience, young men.'

Slevin watched him carefully and decided to probe further. 'You saw no slides of children being defiled?'

'Certainly not! The idea appals me.'

'So the extent of your involvement with Mr Throstle was as procurer and investor?'

'We may quibble over your terminology, but yes.'

'And the money you say you didn't hand over to Mr Throstle?'

Koller blinked. Slevin didn't seem to be the type to give up. At last he said, 'It was evidence of my good faith. I saw him as a lucrative prospect.'

'Unfortunately, he was murdered. If what you say is true, then you had a very good motive for keeping him alive, not dismembering him.'

'Of course I wanted him alive. I had given him money.'

'So tell me again about your meeting with his widow.'

'I went of course to express my condolences.' He saw Slevin's lip curl, and added quickly, 'And to see if she intended to continue his work. I reminded her of my investment. She said she could not be held responsible for her husband's private arrangements.'

'Hence the raised voices.'

'Yes. Although we did come to an agreement of sorts. I would help with the *Phantasmagoria* and she would consider my proposals. She fully intended to continue his work.'

'And that is the whole truth, Mr Koller?'

'The whole truth, Sergeant Slevin.'

*

Slevin returned to his office and sent for Constable Bowery.

'What can I do for you, sergeant?'

'First, we have let Herbert Koller go.'

Bowery's eyes widened. 'But he was there last night, the bugger ran away, and he –'

He was counting off on his fingers reasons to keep Koller in custody when Slevin interrupted him.

'Don't, constable. You'll run out of fingers.'

'So why, then?'

'He told me things that make the situation a little clearer.'

'What things?'

Slevin took a deep breath and began to repeat the gist of what Koller had told him. 'But Herbert Koller is lying,' he said finally, 'He was telling me what he wanted me to hear. You see, I know the real reason he wanted to foster Throstle's acquaintance. And I don't think it had anything to do with business opportunities in London, or anywhere else for that matter. Nor do I think it had anything to do with his ridiculous suggestion of suborning young females to pose for immoral photographs.'

'So what was his reason?'

Slevin narrowed his gaze and looked away.

Bowery, oblivious to the gesture of evasion, went on. 'But he's lying, so you let him go?'

'Yes.'

'Why?'

'Because I want to catch the murderer of Richard Throstle and Georgina Throstle. For that I need proof. And because I have solved the mystery of the two heads.'

'What?'

'I'll explain later. But that's the reason I wanted to see you, Jimmy. I want you to accompany me to the theatre tonight.'

'The theatre? A bloody play?'

'Indeed.'

'I've never been to a play in me entire life, sergeant.'

'First time for everything. In any case it's an order, constable. Here in a suit at six-thirty sharp. Got it?'

'Yes, sergeant.'

*

'Are you sure you will be able to do this?' Benjamin asked Herbert.

Although they were only thirty minutes from curtain-up, he had asked Herbert to spend a few minutes alone with him in his dressing-room, away from prying eyes and well-wishers. Everyone had been glad and relieved to see Herbert when he was brought back to the theatre – almost everyone, that is. Jonathan Keele had turned away as soon as the two of them bustled in through the stage door, and Toby Thomas had used his acting talents to the full when he went over to congratulate Herbert on his return. The young understudy had been gratified when James Shorton and Susan Coupe took the time to offer their whispered commiserations, and told him that his chance would come to prove to the wider world what a great actor he could be.

Now, with the buzz of excitement building in the theatre, Herbert reached over and patted Benjamin on the leg.

'You worry too much,' he said.

'I do everything too much,' came the cryptic response.

'You said you had a surprise in store for me?' Herbert gave him a wicked smile, and his eyes glittered in anticipation.

Benjamin touched his face. 'You have such smooth features,' he said in a gentle whisper. 'I have never seen such beauty, you know.'

Herbert reached up and slowly pulled his hand away. 'Benjamin? The surprise?'

'Ah yes. The surprise. I will wait till later. Once you have given another of your great performances. Regard it as an incentive.'

Herbert gazed at him curiously. 'You are being deliberately evasive, Benjie, but I forgive you. As long as the surprise is worth it! And now, may I return to my dressing-room?'

'Of course.'

They embraced tentatively before parting.

Benjamin stared at the closed door for a long time before

turning to make his own final adjustments. Somehow, as he looked at the face of Detective Samuel Baxter in the looking-glass, he saw an expression that made him flinch – what did his eyes contain behind the mask?

It was time.

He averted his gaze, unable to maintain the introspection, and donned his coat, flicking away the remnants of dust from the previous night's performance.

*

Susan Coupe was once more Nelly Denver, the faithful and long-suffering wife of a man falsely accused of murder. As she too faced herself in the looking-glass, she thought of the heavy irony of her role: a stage marriage to the man she loved above all else in this world, and yet that was all it was – a sham, something to play at for a few hours before shedding the clothing and wiping clean the make-up so that once more she could become herself, a person whose hopes depended on the whims of others. James's wife, for instance. It was loathsome and insupportable that she could even contemplate holding him to ransom for the sake of a few paltry pounds, even threatening to contest the divorce.

That James loved her, she had no doubt. Hadn't he proved his devotion to her time and time again? His expressions of adoration had sustained her more than he could ever know during those dark moments of despair.

Soon they would be back in London, and she knew the following months would be hard, perhaps far more difficult than even she could contemplate, and she realised that if they were ultimately to be together, then she would have to show strength, a strength she hadn't shown for a very long time. She saw the determination resolve itself on her face. Wasn't Nelly Denver, at heart, a strong and resilient woman? And didn't Will and his beloved Nelly live happily ever after? Perhaps it was a good omen. Perhaps life would reflect art. The next few years held a wealth of possibilities, not least the promise of an American tour with Henry Irving himself. She closed her eyes and saw the future, as she and James strolled down Broadway, listening to the calls of the street vendors and the rattle of the carriages as they swept past on their way to Central Park.

She opened her eyes and set her mouth firmly. Nelly Denver had a resilience that would see her through. Slowly she stood up, ready for her call.

*

His benefit night. Jonathan Keele couldn't help smiling, although the smile was a bitter one. Tonight he was celebrating his many years on the stage, and due to receive a financial nod of gratitude for his lifetime's efforts. His bitterness was not born of a sense of his own mortality. No, he thought, as he caught sight of those kindly eyes belonging not to himself but to the devoted servant Jaikes, everyone has to die. It was the order of things, the immutable order of things.

But then he thought of little Catherine, so young, so innocent, and so tortured. How was her death immutable? Couldn't he have done something? Stepped in before the melancholia dug itself deep inside her muddled brain?

He thought of Benjamin, and the simple faith he hid behind his mask of experience and business. Yet he was so vulnerable, a man who loved not wisely but too well!

Now the boy Koller had once more succeeded in fooling the foolish.

Jonathan stared in the looking-glass at Jaikes, the devoted servant, who had helped sustain the family of the fugitive Denver until the man returned as John Franklin, the Silver King, his fortune made in the silver mines of Nevada. Melodrama was nothing more than the fulfilment of wishes, he thought, a dramatist's way of perpetuating the myth that good will prevail and the wicked shall be damned.

217

He thought of the cancer, insidious and unforgiving inside him.

Jaikes looked back at him, and Jaikes shook his head.

*

James Shorton adjusted his cravat so that it hung limply at his throat. Wilfred Denver's first appearance was important in establishing his drunken, dissolute nature, and he made sure that everything about his entrance to the Wheatsheaf at Clerkenwell was as it should be.

He thought of Susan. Would he lose her when they returned to London, where he would be forced to face his wife? He knew Elizabeth would fly into the foulest temper and make the direst threats. She would spend her days ensuring he had little chance to enjoy the cause of their separation until she extracted every last penny of her entitlement.

Or was that too melodramatic? The scorned wife turned virago?

He closed his eyes and an image of Susan began to form itself. A blessed relief and the most glorious of signs! There she was, her delicate features, her smooth cheeks and those deliciously tender lips, slightly parted and waiting for him . . .

Dear Lord, was it possible that he and Susan could be together?

He opened his eyes and touched the loose cravat. He had to remain firm. He was her protector, her knight in shining armour, and he would slay any dragon that stepped in their way. Including Elizabeth.

*

And what about Herbert? How did he regard himself during those last moments before curtain-up?

He wasn't a man given to introspection, yet he congratu-lated himself on getting out of a very hazardous situation. Detective Sergeant Slevin was no fool, and he had realised, even

218

as Benjamin spoke his words of comfort and undying support that morning, that it would take a superlative effort of will and artifice to convince all and sundry of his innocence. Slevin had to be given something, of course. An admission of guilt, or at least of potential guilt, should have been enough to slake his thirst for justice, so while he had cleverly admitted the desire and the intention to commit a crime, he had also made it clear that he had at last seen the error of his ways and would henceforth walk the path of righteousness.

He gazed at the cocky, confident Henry Corkett in the looking-glass and gave him a sly, rascally wink. There was something of any actor in the part he played, he knew that. Henry Corkett, the young clerk, began the play with a wealth of money from his winnings at the races. For a brief moment he would stand there glorying in all his new-found wealth, even to the point of burning money to light his huge cigar, until that dourest of detectives, Baxter, stage-whispered his admonishment. He loved that scene because it gave him a glimpse of the luxury, the sheer exultant pleasure, of unbridled wealth.

He knew that, in order to gain such wealth, he had to continue with his plan. The fact that he had been thwarted abominably the previous night by the most disgustingly bad luck only served to make him work harder to gain what he wanted. There would, of course, be some deception involved, but he was more than passably good at that, wasn't he?

Another roguish wink. You sly dog, you!

*

Five people preparing for a performance.

Death, too, his patience growing thin, waiting in the wings.

10

Constable Bowery squeezed into his seat and gloomily regarded the crimson velvet curtains. 'Doesn't seem natural, sat here watchin' a turn an' no pint to slurp.'

'*The Silver King* isn't regarded as a "turn". It's a play. A full-length five-act melodrama that has stunned audiences all over the world.'

The words 'full-length' seemed to depress Bowery even more. He shifted in his seat, getting himself settled for what was doubtless going to be a very long night.

'I don't see why we had to come, sergeant.'

Slevin shook his head slowly, suggesting that the reason was much too complicated to explain. Yet, if the truth were known, he couldn't really explain their presence either. They had to be here, of course, because he had worked out much of what had happened and why, but he could easily have carried out his duties and made his arrest backstage. Why sit here and watch the whole play before taking action?

He had tried to avoid any examination of what his motives for being here as a mere spectator could be. But he knew, deep down, what those motives were.

Ever since he had set eyes on Miss Coupe, he had been struck not only by her beauty, which was prodigious, but by her vulnerable and innocent eyes. Was it too much of a betrayal of Sarah to sit through one of her performances and simply admire her from afar? Looking at Miss Coupe began with what he might like to characterise as detached admiration, but at what point would that slide into desire, conjuring up concupiscent images?

As the orchestra struck up their opening strains, he recalled other concupiscent images he had recently seen. The vile filth that had filled the screen in the Public Hall, the face of that young girl as she lay there, naked and completely at the mercy of her defiler, and the way she gazed up at him with all the pain of hell in her eyes . . .

'Sergeant?' Bowery's voice broke into his thoughts. 'You all right?'

'Yes,' Slevin said with a catch in his voice. 'I will be.'

*

The music reached its climax and the lights began to fade around the auditorium. Before them, the footlights grew brighter with a sharp hiss as the gas was raised and the curtains slowly drew apart to reveal the opening scene of *The Silver King*.

It was strange, thought Slevin, as Jonathan Keele made his entrance, how very different he looked from when they had spoken. He moved with more agility, and his voice had a richness, a grandeur almost, that was in sharp contrast to the hoarse crackle that had previously marked his speech.

'Well, he's a bit wild,' said Keele, 'but there ain't no harm in him.'

A few moments later, there was a noise of confusion and disturbance as James Shorton made his startling entrance through the gate leading to the skittle alley of the Wheatsheaf. Will Denver was obviously drunk, and his clothing was dishevelled and full of the dust of the road, as if he had spent too much time stumbling his way from the racecourse where he had lost heavily yet again.

'Home!' he yelled, and Slevin noticed how the word echoed around the theatre with the force of Shorton's voice. 'What should I go home for? To show my poor wife what a drunken brute she's got for a husband? To show my innocent children what an object they've got for a father?'

'Is he actin', sergeant? 'Cos he looks drunk as a drayman to

221

me!' Bowery stared at the stage, having evidently set aside his distaste of the theatre for the moment.

Slevin shook his head. 'Oh he isn't drunk, constable. He's simply acting.'

'Well, I've collared soberer buggers than him.'

Benjamin Morgan-Drew entered as Samuel Baxter, detective. He looked cautiously around the room before going to the bar and taking hold of a large pewter pot of ale. Denver had taken out a revolver and was gazing down at it as a source of comfort, a possible way out of his financial mess.

'If you don't know what to do with that,' Morgan-Drew said in a low voice, 'I'll take care of it for you.'

But Shorton sullenly returned it to his pocket.

Suddenly a brash young chap, Henry Corkett, sauntered arrogantly into the room, an unlit cigar dangling from his mouth, brandishing a thick roll of banknotes.

'Have some champagne!' Herbert Koller called to all and sundry in the room, waving his money around. 'Tubbs! It's my shout. Champagne for everybody!'

Morgan-Drew sidled up behind the extravagantly confident young man and whispered, 'You young ass! Put those notes in your pocket and go home to bed!'

But the policeman's words had obviously fallen on deaf ears, for Corkett took out a match, struck it and held it to a banknote he had peeled from the wad in his hand.

The audience gasped as he lit the cigar with the banknote and inhaled deeply, the strong swirl of smoke curling upwards into the darkness above the stage.

'There!' Koller declared. 'That's a five-pound note! That'll show you what I'm made of! Money ain't no object to me . . . object to me . . . object . . .' Koller broke off in a fit of coughing, and stared down at the cigar with a look of mounting horror and revulsion on his face.

Slevin saw Morgan-Drew move towards him, and some of the

other actors on stage, including Shorton, who was supposed to be drunk and slumped in a chair by the bar, ran quickly to help the young actor, now clutching his throat and retching in a manner that left Slevin in no doubt about what he was witnessing.

'He's bloody good, sergeant! Bloody good!' Bowery was watching keenly, his hands gripping the back of the seat in front.

But Slevin knew this was no part of the act. The way Morgan-Drew held Koller's head and tried to drag him from the stage, and the way the others clustered around, told him that something very serious was taking place before their eyes, and it had nothing to do with make-believe. The actor-manager shouted something to the wings and suddenly the curtains began to draw to a close.

'That was bloody quick!' said Bowery. 'They've hardly begun.'

'I think they've actually finished,' Slevin whispered urgently as others around them began to murmur in confusion and protest at the unexpected turn of events. He stood up and forced his way along the row of seats, with Bowery following him into the centre aisle and down towards the steps leading to the side of the stage.

Slevin caught sight of the manager of the theatre, running down the side of the auditorium with an anxious look on his face and uttering feeble assurances to the members of the audience nearest him.

Once the two policemen reached the wings, they were met with a scene of utter confusion. Slevin forced his way through a tightly knotted group of actors and stage-hands gathered around the now prostrate Herbert Koller, who was writhing in speechless agony on the floor of the stage, with Benjamin Morgan-Drew cradling his head in his lap and screaming at him to take deep breaths.

'Let me through!' Slevin ordered. The crowd parted to allow both Slevin and Bowery access to the young actor. It was a horrific sight. His eyes were bulging and his cheeks were flushed a deep red, while his mouth seemed blistered and contorted.

'Has anyone called for a doctor?' yelled Slevin as he kneeled beside Koller.

Jonathan Keele stepped forward. He had been standing a little apart from the group. 'Benjamin has sent for one.'

Slevin looked up at the old actor, a curious expression on his face. 'Will everyone please stand farther back!' he ordered. 'Give the chap some air.'

They all did as they were bidden, apart from Benjamin, who flatly refused to let go of Herbert and was frantically stroking his moist, clammy forehead.

Slevin began to loosen the cravat around Koller's neck, simply out of a desire to do something, anything, that might alleviate the man's suffering.

Beyond the closed curtains they could hear yells and protestations, voices raised in anger and confusion. The manager of the theatre, who had stepped onto the apron of the stage, was informing the audience of an 'unfortunate accident' and asking them all to 'leave in an orderly and dignified manner'.

A few minutes passed, during which Koller's breathing became more and more strained and his eyes slowly began to retreat, to flicker and glaze in surrender. Slevin, checking his pulse, felt it beat so rapidly that he wondered how long it would be before his heart simply exploded. Then, as one of the stage-hands announced the arrival of a doctor, and as a small, wiry individual rushed from the wings to examine the patient, Herbert began to shake uncontrollably and Benjamin could no longer hold his head in his lap.

'He is convulsing,' the doctor announced. 'Please! Let me . . .'

But before he could finish the sentence, the spasms stopped. Someone sobbed, and Benjamin let forth a feral howl that startled everyone.

Herbert Koller was dead.

*

Slevin had given strict orders that no one was to leave the theatre after the audience had been ushered out. He had a dozen men surrounding the building within ten minutes, and another half-dozen constables placed in strategic positions inside the theatre itself. The doctor had formally confirmed that Herbert Koller was dead, and Slevin himself had draped a cloth over the corpse, which lay there still.

There had been protests when Slevin also gave orders for the entire cast and stage-hands to be assembled on stage a matter of yards away from the body, which lay there in its makeshift shroud, a macabre reminder of what they had all witnessed.

'But this is abominable!' James Shorton stood before the detective sergeant and glared at him. 'To force us all, especially the ladies, to stay here with . . .' He glanced sharply at the corpse, then briefly at Miss Coupe, whom he had been consoling.

'I assure you all that you will be allowed to leave within a very short time. I merely wish to ask a few questions which will help my investigations.'

'Into what, exactly, sergeant?' asked Jonathan Keele, who now came and stood beside Shorton.

'Into what we have just witnessed.'

Benjamin, who all the time had been standing before the body with his head bowed and hands clasped in an attitude of prayer, spoke for the first time since Herbert had died. '*Odi et amo*,' he said in little more than a whisper.

'What's that?' Slevin turned to Keele, who was shaking his head sadly.

'It's Latin, sergeant. A line from Catullus. "I hate and I love."' He searched Slevin's eyes until he saw the significance of the quotation dawn on him.

'I see,' he said, and gave a curt nod.

Slevin then strode purposefully to the centre of the stage and stood with his back to the closed curtains. He surveyed the scene: the painted backdrop, the wooden bar, the scattered stools

225

and tables, the frightened and resentful company of actors and actresses.

'According to the doctor, who has now left to make arrangements for the transfer of the victim to the local infirmary, Herbert Koller appears to have been poisoned.'

The word seemed to send a ripple of shock, of fear, through the entire company.

'Constable Bowery?' Slevin called out.

Bowery, who had been standing in the wings, made his entrance. He held something in his right hand, and when he reached stage centre he held it out for Slevin to take. They all looked at a small narrow box, around ten inches in length, which the detective slowly opened.

'Those are Herbert's cigars!' said one of the group.

'Indeed they are. And as each one of you is responsible for providing your own props – is that the correct word? – then it is safe to assume that Mr Koller purchased enough cigars to last the entire run of performances. He lights how many cigars during each show?'

'One,' said Jonathan Keele.

'And he always makes sure he has his cigar with him before coming on stage?'

'Of course. He places it in a small box by his dressing-table.'

'So the cigar he had for tonight's performance will have come from this batch. Obviously. And now, Constable Bowery?' Slevin held his hand out once more, as Bowery reached into his side pocket and pulled out a piece of cloth, which he handed to his sergeant. Slevin unfolded the cloth to reveal a cigar similar in length to the ones in the box. 'This is the cigar he was smoking tonight just before he collapsed. The doctor thinks it will be found to contain poison. Cyanide, probably, from the rather distinctive odour of bitter almonds on the late Mr Koller's mouth.'

There were several gasps.

'And of course there are only two possibilities, aren't there? Suicide or murder. We can immediately discount accidental poisoning, as cigar manufacturers tend not to use cyanide in their processes. Those of you who knew Mr Koller well will doubtless realise how preposterous the idea of suicide is. So that leaves us with murder.'

He allowed the word to resonate among them, and watched their reactions carefully. He knew of course that these were actors, people trained in the art of disguise and concealment.

Well, he was good at his profession, too.

'Mr Morgan-Drew? Would you do us the honour of joining us?'

Benjamin looked up, as if aware of their presence for the first time. 'Yes,' he said quietly. 'Yes, of course.'

Slevin watched him move slowly, almost painfully, to join their gathering. He gave the shrouded body a parting glance.

'Good. Now, I hope this won't take long, and I appreciate your patience, but we are dealing with the death of one of your company and I am sure you wish to discover the truth about the way he died. We need to ascertain exactly what happened here tonight. There is only one question you need to consider: Who saw anyone enter or leave Mr Koller's dressing-room? My constables will take down your statements and then you will be free to leave. Again, thank you for your understanding.'

'You surely don't think anyone in the company could have done such a thing?' said Morgan-Drew. His eyes were moist with tears, but he spoke now with the outraged tones of a father whose children are being falsely accused.

Slevin held his gaze steady before replying so that everyone could hear. 'Do you think anyone from outside this company would know where Herbert Koller kept his cigars?'

The question was met with a stunned silence.

*

227

Once the last of the statements had been written down in slow, laborious longhand, Slevin announced that everyone could leave with the exception of Benjamin Morgan-Drew, Jonathan Keele, James Shorton and Susan Coupe. Although several eyebrows were raised among the rest of the company, they filtered out through the wings feeling a mixture of relief and anxiety. Herbert Koller's body was still *in situ*, and Slevin appeared to be in no particular rush to be rid of it. He knew everyone was acutely aware of its shrouded presence, and if it became useful as his own peculiar prop, then he would not hesitate to use it.

'Is there any particular reason the four of us should remain, sergeant?' Jonathan Keele asked.

Slevin noticed him place a comforting arm on Morgan-Drew's shoulder.

'I wanted to ask some rather more pertinent questions, without the presence of an audience,' said Slevin with a thin smile. 'Mr Koller was a man of ambition, wouldn't you say?' He addressed the question to no one in particular, but it was Benjamin Morgan-Drew who answered it.

'He was an actor. By definition, all actors are ambitious.'

'But his ambitions stretched beyond the stage, did they not?'

Morgan-Drew shrugged.

'Yes, you're correct,' said Jonathan Keele, ignoring the sharp glance from his old friend. 'It's time for the truth, Benjamin.' He half-turned towards the body. 'Once the performance is over we shed our disguises, do we not?'

James Shorton said, 'Is it really necessary for Miss Coupe to remain? I mean, it is most distressing to be here with . . .' He too turned towards the body.

Slevin looked at Susan Coupe's eyes and their gentle, demure regard. 'This won't take much longer, sir. I assure you.'

Shorton moved to Miss Coupe's side. Slevin saw his hand grasp hers gently.

'Mr Koller, as I say, was a man of ambition. And when he

met Richard Throstle, it appeared to him to be a heaven-sent opportunity to realise that ambition.'

'How?' Shorton asked.

'By making money. As simple as that, Mr Shorton. You see, Herbert Koller was driven by his desire to make a great deal of money, and he knew full well that the stage was only a limited source of funds. No, if he wanted to make the sort of money he had his heart set on, then it had to be away from the stage. So when he met Throstle in Manchester, he . . .'

'What?' Benjamin almost yelled the word.

'Koller met Throstle in Manchester.'

'When?'

'According to Mrs Throstle, about a month ago. You were performing in Manchester at that time, I believe?'

'Yes. At the Prince's Theatre.'

'He met Throstle – we don't know how – but they struck up what you might call a professional friendship.'

Benjamin seemed unable to take in what he was being told. 'But how could this Throstle character make Herbert's fortune?'

Slevin coughed and looked quickly in the direction of Miss Coupe. The indelicacy of what he was about to reveal was not lost on him, but he was obliged to continue. 'Mr Throstle had, shall we say, made certain modifications to his slide shows. For certain audiences he gave presentations of a rather more salacious nature.'

Shorton pulled Susan Coupe closer to him.

'Without going into detail, I can say that the slides in such shows were vile and degrading. But there are men in our society who take pleasure in witnessing the subjugation and the humiliation of others. Some of his models were willing participants, it must be said, but most were innocents – young innocents – who suffered greatly at the hands of such a monster.'

Jonathan Keele inhaled deeply, as if he were about to dive into icy water. Beside him, Benjamin stood motionless, gazing not at

Slevin nor any of the others, but at the shrouded body of the boy he had once loved. Susan Coupe was sobbing quietly, Shorton's arm holding her to his chest.

But Slevin could not stop now. Not until the guilty one confessed.

'One of Throstle's victims discovered that he was here, in Wigan, showing his gruesome *Phantasmagoria* at the same time as *The Silver King*. That victim had suffered greatly, but now it appeared that Fate had sent its message. Throstle was here, and the opportunity might never arise again. So, what to do? How to get close enough to this vile man in order to exact revenge?'

Jonathan Keele stepped closer to Slevin. 'There's no need to continue, Sergeant Slevin.'

'Why not?'

'Because I am now making my confession. I killed Richard Throstle.'

Benjamin lifted his head, which he had bowed low as the policeman had been speaking. 'What nonsense is this?' he exclaimed. 'Jonathan?'

The old actor turned and gave him a smile. 'No nonsense, I assure you.' He turned to Slevin and gave a heavy sigh, his shoulders sagging in resignation. 'It would be best if you took me away from this place, sergeant. These people have suffered enough.'

'I'm afraid I can't arrest you, Mr Keele.'

'Whyever not?'

'Because you are too old.'

Jonathan Keele raised his eyebrows in amusement. 'Too old? I hadn't realised there was a statute in law that precluded the arrest of old men.'

'No, sir, but there is a statute precluding the arrest of innocent old men.'

'What?'

'When I said you were too old, I meant exactly that. In order to get close enough to Richard Throstle to commit the crime, the murderer had to do what actors do every single time they walk on stage.'

'And what is that?' Shorton asked.

'Why, they put on an act, Mr Shorton. Just as you did when you became Mr Jenkins, the travelling salesman.'

As he said the words, Susan Coupe collapsed in a heap. Shorton caught her just before she hit the hard wooden floor, and he laid her down with great tenderness, brushing the hair from her eyes and saying her name over and over again. Gradually, her eyes flickered back to life.

'What is this?' Benjamin asked, looking at Jonathan Keele for an explanation he couldn't give.

Miss Coupe sat up and was helped to one of the chairs from the set. As Shorton made sure she was comfortable, Slevin looked on with a mixture of regret and pity in his eyes.

'You see, Mr Shorton is deeply in love.'

Both Benjamin and Jonathan now regarded the two lovers, Shorton on one knee beside a now weeping Miss Coupe, and on both their faces a look of understanding was slowly registering.

'I remember Mrs Throstle telling me that her husband would do anything to help a damsel in distress. A most noble man, she said.'

'Noble?' Shorton sneered.

Susan Coupe placed a restraining hand on his arm and spoke for the first time since they had been left alone on stage. Her voice was surprisingly clear, despite an initial hesitancy. 'It seemed as if I was stepping into the infernal regions, sergeant. My fellow travellers thought it was something akin to an attack of the vapours upon seeing black-faced colliers. I ask you! But the first face I saw when I walked through the station portals here in Wigan was indeed the face of a devil, the face of a man I thought I would never see again. He didn't recognise me, of course. I was no longer the child he ...'

She was looking directly at Slevin, and once more he found himself catching his breath. But he wasn't looking at a young woman whose beauty and whose acting had lit up the world of the stage from Wigan to London. He was instead looking into the eyes of a small girl whose defilement had for ever been recorded on a set of lantern slides, the most heart-rending expression of terror he had ever seen on any victim, alive or dead. He had recognised her doleful eyes immediately, magnified a hundred times for the seedy delectation of depraved men.

Susan Coupe brushed aside the ministrations of her lover now. She held her head high, a defiant and somehow pathetic gesture, and spoke in the steady tones of a well-rehearsed soliloquy.

'I was introduced to Mr Richard Throstle by his friend and my governess, Georgina Malvern, who was later to become his wife. An unholy alliance! She told me he was looking for photographic models to illustrate a new set of slides he was calling his "Life Model Series". They are slides that tell a story. You will no doubt have seen similar, Sergeant Slevin.'

Slevin nodded. He and Sarah had sat in the Public Hall and watched such narratives as *Beware, or the Effects of Gambling* and *The Little Hero*. They had taken Peter to see the latter, a moral tale of a young stowaway and his wicked stepfather. They were a world away from the contaminated filth Throstle was creating.

'Once he did what he did to me, he said I was to tell no one, for how could my parents live with the photographs he had taken of me? Would they still love me if they saw what I had been a party to, what I had allowed to happen of my own free will? They said they would shield my wickedness from my parents, and Throstle would ensure my features would be blurred for the final slides, but only if I said nothing.'

Her voice, which hitherto had been controlled and measured, now broke, but she held herself erect and continued.

'I had told James nothing of this. How could I? But when he saw the way I had reacted that day we arrived in Wigan, it didn't take him long to reach the truth – there can be no secrets between lovers, can there?'

Benjamin flushed and looked away for a few seconds.

'So,' said Slevin, 'you devised a plan, a plan of revenge.'

'Yes.'

'Which involved Mr Shorton here presenting himself at the reception desk of the Royal Hotel in the guise of a travelling salesman.'

Shorton gave a bitter laugh. 'It was an easy task. I had already played Mr Jenkins in the past.'

Benjamin frowned. 'Jenkins? The hosiery salesman?'

'Yes,' said Slevin, curious. 'How did you know he was a hosiery salesman?'

'*Two Roses*, sergeant.'

'What?'

'If you were an aficionado of the theatre you would immediately recognise the character. He appears in the play by James Albery. It was a great success for Henry Irving at the Vaudeville Theatre back in '70. Irving was a great success as Digby Grant . . .' His voice trailed off, as if he realised that he had begun to ramble.

'I affected a rather ponderous persona for the man,' said Shorton. 'And with the right application of make-up and a suitable wardrobe, well, you know how effective they can be.'

'My compliments, Mr Shorton. Your disguise was, in many ways, perfect. It fooled me.'

Shorton frowned. 'Then how did you know it was a disguise?'

Slevin shook his head. 'I knew Mr Jenkins was not only bogus but was probably an actor from this company.'

'How?' Despite the situation, there was a note of irritation in Shorton's voice, rather as if he'd read an unfavourable review.

'We found traces of asbestos dust on the body of Richard Throstle.'

'So? That could have come from anywhere.'

'True. But then we found traces of the same dust on the body of a local miner.'

'A local miner?' Now Shorton was alarmed. It was one thing being arrested for crimes you had committed, but to be arrested for a murder you are guiltless of was quite another.

Slevin saw the alarm on his face. 'Oh, don't worry, Mr Shorton. Enoch Platt died quite by accident. But he had traces of the same asbestos dust on his clothing, and you – or rather Mr Jenkins – and he had been seen arguing quite violently on the steps of the Royal Hotel.'

Shorton blinked as the memory came back. 'Yes. He made a lunge for me and began screaming about how I was the Devil.'

Susan Coupe looked up. 'Was it the same man who accosted us the day we had been along the canal?'

'Yes, I think it was.'

Slevin took up the narrative. 'He was heard to mutter something incomprehensible about seeing the Devil, with two eyes and two heads. But of course, if he had already seen you, if he had stared into your eyes, which was one of his most disturbing habits, then he had seen your eyes. The irony is that poor Enoch, or Clapper as he is known generally, was merely checking your eyes – anyone's eyes – for traces of dust. Not asbestos dust, but coal dust. He was trapped down the mine for three days after an explosion, and when they found him he was cradling his brother's head in his arms. Brushing the dust away from his eyes. But what really sent him over the edge was the fact that he was cradling only the head – they never found the rest of him.'

There was a heavy silence on stage now as Slevin's words created their own horrific image.

'So Enoch saw your eyes. But I'm guessing that what he couldn't understand was how those eyes of yours, Mr Shorton, could be framed inside two different heads. Seeing those same eyes on a completely different face – the face of Mr Jenkins the hosiery salesman – was something his muddled brain could not take in. So you became the Devil. With two eyes and two heads. I knew, because Miss Coupe had told me when she complained about the dangers on the streets of the town, that you and Enoch Platt had already met. I simply made a reasonable deduction that you and Jenkins were therefore the same person.'

Susan Coupe gave a strangled gasp. 'Oh James! I . . .'

Slevin went on, his voice low, intense. 'You booked a room at the hotel but never stayed there. Your suitcase, which of course you had to have with you for the sake of appearances, was empty, and you merely allowed yourself to be seen in the hotel bar, and that's where you struck up an acquaintance with Richard Throstle. I presume you had an arrangement with your landlady to come and go as you please?'

'For an extra ten shillings, yes.' With a sigh, Shorton continued. 'It wasn't a difficult task. Throstle loved to talk about himself, although of course he never spoke of the darker side of his business. That would have been too risky, even though I presented myself as a willing companion and someone who was up for a challenge. But I think he liked my company, or rather, the company of Mr Jenkins.'

'Mrs Throstle said that on the night he was murdered her husband couldn't find his room key, that she heard him fumbling outside the door. She put it down to mere drunkenness, but perhaps he simply didn't have it. Perhaps you had already taken it from his coat pocket as you helped him on with his jacket.'

Shorton gave an appreciative nod. 'You are no fool, sergeant.'

'So when they go to bed, when Mrs Throstle locks the door with her own key and they settle down for the night, you wait.'

'Throstle told me his wife had taken a powerful compound. He told me, with a nod and a wink, that he had paid the pharmacist a little extra to ensure it contained enough chloroform to allow her a restful night.'

At this point, Constable Bowery came up and whispered something in his sergeant's ear. Slevin nodded, and almost immediately two constables, carrying a long wooden stretcher, walked over to the body of Herbert Koller and placed him on it. All eyes were on the shrouded body as it was borne past them.

Once it had disappeared through the wings, Slevin turned once more to Shorton. 'I won't of course dwell on the details of what you did in that room . . .'

Susan Coupe gave a bitter laugh. 'I was his director, sergeant. There's no need to protect my sensibilities. They were numbed a long time ago. What James did to that man he did under my direction. To the letter. Or rather, to the telegram. From his shrew of a wife. It was cast into the canal. Wrapped around a bloodied knife.'

Slevin gave a small nod. There was a part of him that acknowledged the justice of the act – justice in its strictest, most biblical sense.

'But why then, Mr Shorton, did you leave Mrs Throstle alive? There she was, asleep and defenceless, and you could have killed her there and then. Why did you leave her?'

Shorton gave a slow shrug. 'Lady Macbeth,' he said.

'Pardon?'

It was Susan Coupe who explained. 'Lady Macbeth goes to the chamber of King Duncan, whom she and her husband are planning to kill. She finds him in his kingly bed, asleep and defenceless. His guards are drugged. But she cannot do it. That most wicked of women cannot bring herself to plunge the dagger into that kingly throat. "Had he not resembled my father as he slept, I had done it."'

Shorton went on. 'Only with Duncan it was different. He was pure, innocent. To kill him was a vile and horrendous act. The woman who lay there was as guilty, in my view, as the one who perpetrated the foul defilement of a beautiful and innocent creature. No. It was simply a matter of courage. I lacked the courage to kill a woman. In that moment, I failed Susan.'

She reached up and clasped his hand. 'Nonsense. I had asked

more of you than anyone had any right to ask. It was I who later devised the way that foul fiend of a woman should die.' She turned to Jonathan Keele and gave him the saddest of smiles. 'I have Jonathan to thank for that. He spent an hour one day regaling us all about his time working for his son-in-law, who is a chemist. Remember how you said it was a poisoner's paradise, Jonathan? How quickly or how horrifically those poisons acted? "For a delayed death, use phosphorus, my dears. For an instant one, cyanide's the thing!"' Her voice had taken on the slow sonorous tones of the old actor. 'It was I who bought the rat poison and urged James to mix it into her medicine.'

Slevin looked at her afresh. He saw a human being, one of the most beautiful creatures he had ever set eyes on, who had become someone less than human. There was a darkness inside her that had extinguished the glow of life that could have thrived there if it hadn't been for that evil monster. He saw something else, too: she had become an actress because it gave her a stage on which to perform, where for a few short hours every night she could escape her demons and become whoever she wanted to be.

Shorton went on. 'I saw Georgina Throstle in the hotel dining room with her brother. That gave me the opportunity to deliver the lethal mixture. The foolish woman had left her door unlocked. When I set foot outside that hotel, I knew that I would never be returning. Even if you connected Jenkins with the murders, you would be looking for an invisible man.'

At this point, Benjamin walked slowly towards him. 'Can you explain why Herbert had to die? Is there a space in this dramatic monologue for some simple dénouement where Herbert is concerned?'

Slevin placed a hand on the actor-manager's shoulder and said, 'I think I can explain, Mr Morgan-Drew.'

Benjamin stopped and turned his attention to the detective.

'Mr Koller knew about the slides, the ones containing those vile pictures of Miss Coupe as a child.'

'But how could he possibly know of them?'

'He had seen them.'

Jonathan Keele stepped forward. 'Herbert was wild, Benjamin. You must know that. Whichever town or city we stopped in, Herbert would be out trying to seek the sort of immoral solace he desired. Those occasions he told you he needed to explore the town? He was walking down very dark pathways, my friend. In both a literal and a metaphorical sense.'

'But he had *me*!' Benjamin cried out.

'He told me he wanted money.' Susan Coupe spoke in little more than a whisper.

'What?'

'He followed me as I was on my way to meet James in the park. He said he needed a thousand pounds. For an investment. He had the gall to ask me to give him the means to invest in the very business that destroyed my childhood.' Now her voice had almost become hysterical. 'He had the means, he said, to destroy my reputation for ever. Certain influential people in London would make sure my past was made known to Irving and whoever else might become my sponsor.'

Slevin saw her eyes grow wide and fierce, and realised how close she was to a complete loss of sanity.

Benjamin gave a hollow laugh. 'The fool! I had such a surprise for him tonight. After the show. He would have become my partner in the business. I had such a surprise ...' He felt Jonathan Keele place an arm around him, and he gave way to the sobs that had simmered for so long.

'The man was evil. He deserved to die.' Shorton's voice cut through the air. 'So we planned the most public form of death. No actor likes to "die" on stage. He should have breathed his last, as it were, last night, but poor Toby Thomas stepped in to replace him and we had to remove the cigar we had planted in Herbert's costume and replace it with a harmless one. Herbert's cigar contained rat poison, incidentally. Soaked for hours, then dried.

Not a phosphorus base, mind. We needed something quick-acting so that he would be unable to point any accusing finger. Besides, phosphorus would have provided a link with Georgina Throstle's death. So I bought a rather more instant compound. Its cyanide base comes highly recommended. Amazing what one can buy in this town.

'Still, we had to act quickly yesterday afternoon. When I returned to the theatre to become Shorton once more, I was still in a state of confusion after my wrestling match with that clapping idiot, so Susan declared that the revolver was also missing, which allowed me to regain some sort of composure and get you out of our hair for a diversionary time, sergeant. No one was any the wiser. Tonight, though, well, you saw how well it went.'

The longer Shorton had spoken, the more Slevin realised how much the man had been affected by what he had done. He had no doubt that, before the idea of revenge was planted inside his head by his lover, he had been a man of normal sensibilities, a man who would baulk at any suggestion of wrongdoing the way a non-swimmer would shy away from the water's edge. But once he had been thrown in, once he had become a part of this gruesome undertaking, his feelings had gradually become numbed until the distinction between justice and revenge became completely blurred. He had allowed the rôle to take over.

'Why did you break into the Public Hall and daub the place with threats?'

Susan Coupe spoke, her voice low and tremulous. 'We needed to find the slides. Destroy them. That was my idea. But when James found it impossible to get into the safe, he came up with the idea of daubing the walls. If the police thought Throstle had been killed for a crazed religious purpose, it would divert attention from the real motive for his death. And of course lay blame on others when his witch of a wife met her end.'

Shorton held up his hands in an attitude of surrender. 'I suppose we will now be taken into custody?'

Slevin nodded.

Before he could move, Shorton had reached into his coat pocket and extracted a revolver, which he levelled at Slevin's head. Constable Bowery, who was standing in the wings, made a move towards him, but Shorton gave a warning yell. 'Stay where you are, constable!'

Jonathan Keele stepped forward. 'James. This is foolish. The gun is a prop. It's a futile gesture.'

Shorton smiled and raised the revolver. He pointed it at one of the painted skittles on the backdrop and fired. There was a loud report and the scenery swayed as the bullet tore through the skittle, leaving a gaping hole and the stench of cordite in the air.

'You damned fool!' Slevin shouted. 'Give me the bloody thing before someone is hurt.'

But Shorton, a look of manic confidence now spread across his face, moved quickly towards Susan Coupe. 'The presence of police made me nervous,' he said. 'Better to have some form of insurance, is it not?' He waved the gun before them. 'Come on, Susan!'

She gave Slevin a look before allowing Shorton to lead her slowly through the disrupted scenery that had represented the Wheatsheaf.

'Ironic, isn't it?' Shorton added. 'Will Denver runs away even though he is innocent. Whereas we . . .'

Jonathan Keele walked towards them, his right hand extended. 'If you don't know what to do with that,' he said, 'I'll take care of it for you.'

Slevin recognised it as one of the lines from the play. A line delivered by the detective, Samuel Baxter. Morgan-Drew moved to restrain the ageing actor.

'Jonathan! Please!'

Shorton laughed. 'Thank you, Jonathan, but I do know what to do with it, much obliged for your advice.'

He kept a wary eye on Keele as he and Susan backed away towards the far wings. But Keele kept moving forward.

'Oh Master Will!' he said, adopting now the rural accents of the faithful Jaikes. 'I can't tell you what she's had to go through! It's been a terrible hard fight for her, but she's borne up like an angel.'

Shorton blinked, as if he had misheard what the old actor had said. 'Jonathan? Are you mad? This is no play and this is no prop. Please do not make the mistake of thinking that we can all take our bows at the end and share a convivial drink together.'

Susan Coupe stood silent, like an obedient child, her head bowed low.

Slevin moved slowly to stand alongside Keele. 'Leave this to me, sir,' he whispered. 'He's killed three times. He may have a taste for it now.'

Jonathan Keele shook his head. 'I will be faithful to him to the end. It's what Jaikes would have done.'

Slevin thought at first he was talking about Shorton, for the character Jaikes was indeed the epitome of fidelity, never wavering in his loyalty to Wilfred Denver. But he saw the old man glance across at Morgan-Drew, who was watching with a barely concealed sense of horror.

'Jonathan! It's not what I want! Herbert is gone! He's gone the way everyone goes. Sacrificing yourself for some ideal of fidelity – it's futile.'

Shorton held the gun steady, aiming at Keele but keeping a wary eye on Slevin and Bowery. But the old actor inched forward once more, in small, measured steps that took him closer and closer to the fugitive lovers.

'Jonathan! That is close enough!' There was a wavering in Shorton's voice now. 'Please. You don't want to die!'

'He that cuts off twenty years of life cuts off so many years of fearing death.'

'The philosophy of the fatalist, old man! And a false philosophy at that. Cassius didn't mean those words. He was overwrought after killing Caesar, that's all.'

Slevin saw Susan Coupe reach up to touch Keele's face in a tender gesture of affection which distracted Shorton, who turned to her briefly. This was all Slevin needed.

'Bowery!' he screamed as he launched himself towards Shorton.

A startled look flashed across the actor's face as he frantically raised the gun and fired in the direction of the detective, who ducked. The bullet tore through his left ear, sending blood splashing wildly into the face of Jonathan Keele, whom Constable Bowery was even now dragging backwards by the stiff collar he was wearing. A woman's scream ripped through the theatre as the full weight of Slevin's body slammed into Shorton, sending him crashing through the stage set, the gun falling to the floor and sliding along the wooden boards. Shorton lay on his back, blood streaming from a gash on his forehead. His eyes flickered, and as he tried to raise his head from the mess of shattered scenery all around them, something drew him back and he gave a long, slow exhalation, turning his head to one side, where Slevin saw the thick wooden splinter from one of the shattered frames planted deep in the back of his neck. His eyes were screwed shut in an agony caused not merely by the pain of the injury.

Quickly, Slevin removed his coat, and with a show of making the man more comfortable, spread it over the terrible wound, so that it was now hidden from view.

Susan Coupe rushed towards her lover and dropped to her knees beside him. She touched his head wound carefully and looked around frantically for something to wipe away the blood. Finally she reached down to tear a strip from her own dress, the dress Nelly Denver wore in the play's opening scene, and began to clean the blood from his face.

Slevin stood up and reached a hand to his left ear. Only now was it beginning to sting.

Behind him, Bowery was helping Jonathan Keele to his feet,

the old man wheezing and fighting hard to catch his breath, his hands pressed hard against his stomach.

Suddenly he heard James Shorton begin to speak. His voice was hoarse and faint, and the words came out haltingly, with none of the bravado Slevin had heard earlier.

'Ah Nell! My bonnie, bonnie girl . . .'

Susan Coupe threw herself onto his heaving chest, clutching at him with a desperate longing. It was as if she were trying to claw her way into his body.

'I love you!' she said. 'I love you still.'

Morgan-Drew whispered in Slevin's unwounded ear, 'They are now Wilfred and Nelly Denver. These are lines from the play.'

Her voice was muffled, but there was no mistaking what she was saying.

'Never mind the past, dear. Come home and make a fresh start tomorrow!'

Shorton coughed, and blood dribbled from his mouth. His eyes began to turn in on themselves and he laid a hand on Susan's head. 'The sweetest and truest wife a man ever had . . . I can't stop, I'm going down, down as fast as I can go . . .'

His breathing grew even more laboured, and he seemed to make a Herculean effort to refocus his gaze on Susan Coupe for the last time. She raised her head and gazed down at him with her eyes filled with tears. He licked his crusted lips and spoke haltingly, and she brought her ear close to his mouth so that only she could hear what he was saying. Then his lips suddenly parted and remained thus, and his hand slid from his lover's head. James Shorton lay still and silent in death.

Susan Coupe did not throw herself on his lifeless body. Instead, she forced herself to her feet and turned to her audience.

'He was my Sir Galahad, you know. His last words will act as his epitaph – I will make sure of that.'

Then she took a deep breath and recited the passage from Tennyson that Shorton had uttered before every performance:

'How sweet are looks that ladies bend
On whom their favours fall!
For them I battle till the end,
To save from shame and thrall.'

She lowered her head and waited for the applause, but none came.

Epilogue

'Why did you put yourself in such danger, Jonathan?'

As the train pulled out of the station, the two actors sat back in their first-class compartment and looked out at the snow-covered scene. Farther down the train, in third class, the remaining members of the Morgan-Drew Touring Company were giving their own views on the drama that had unfolded before their eyes only a few days earlier. They had all agreed that the tour should continue, in the best traditions of the profession, and so now they were en route for Liverpool, where they would transform the stage of the aptly named Shakespeare Theatre into Ancient Rome.

Jonathan Keele allowed the rattle of the train to fill the silence before answering.

'I am dying, Benjamin. Soon I will be with my dearest Catherine again. I failed her so badly, you know.'

'Jonathan. We have been over this so many times. The doctors diagnosed melancholia of puberty. There was nothing you could have done while she was being cared for in that place.'

'I could have visited more often.'

'You were in America, as I recall.'

'Yes. When she took her life. I should have been here! If I had, then she would have confided in me.' His voice began to crack, and tears were beginning to glisten in his eyes. 'And I thought, now that I know my own end is near, why not take this opportunity to hasten the exit? I so dearly wanted Shorton to fire that gun.'

Benjamin shook his head and gazed through the window. Far off, he could see the stark winding-heads of the coalmines, black skeletal frames against the pure white of the snow that covered the fields and the endless rows of houses. He thought of Herbert, and how he had once more been completely taken in by what he thought was something precious and dear. Then he thought of the one Herbert had tried to blackmail.

'Poor Susan,' he said softly. 'I wonder what will happen to her?'

The old actor shook his head. 'I fear she will follow my dearest Catherine.'

'Surely not?'

'The girl isn't strong enough. She will face trial for conspiracy to murder, but given the evidence so ably gathered by Sergeant Slevin, a strong defence should ensure she will escape the clutches of the hangman.' He gave a long and heavy sigh. 'But she will doubtless face a prolonged period of incarceration. And she has already been incarcerated for so very long, has she not? Those places are diabolical.'

Both men remained silent for many minutes. Soon they would be in Liverpool, where they would recreate the might and the turmoil of Ancient Rome. But there was nothing grand, nothing spectacular, about the scene both of them brought creatively to mind.

The stage was bare, and the darkness was almost complete, save for the thick iron bars of a noisome, silent cell backlit by a flickering flame. A young woman was lying on the chill, damp floor, rearranging the hair on a child's doll and humming a lullaby to herself. She stopped as the shadows cast by the flames seemed to creep upon the doll until its tiny face was shrouded in black.

Then she looked out into the auditorium, and screamed.

Acknowledgements

I would like to thank Seán Costello for his sterling editorial work in helping to prepare the novel for publication.

I would also like to thank the University of Dundee, the City of Discovery Campaign and Birlinn Ltd for establishing the Dundee International Book Prize and providing encouragement for writers everywhere.

Dundee International Book Prize 2010

Act of Murder by Alan Wright is the winner of the Dundee International Book Prize 2010. The prize is the richest in the UK for new authors. For more details on the annual competition email literarydundee@gmail.com.

The Dundee International Book Prize is a joint venture between the City of Discovery Campaign, the University of Dundee and Polygon, the fiction imprint of Birlinn Ltd. It is supported by the Apex Hotel, Dundee.